DRAGON GAMES
BOOK TWO
of the

WEREDING CHRONICLES

Christian Boustead

DISCLAIMER

This work contains violence and nudity so be warned.
No person living or dead is described in this book and all events are of a fictional nature.

Published by Christian Boustead
Publishing partner: Paragon Publishing, Rothersthorpe
First published 2016
© Christian Boustead 2016
The rights of Christian Boustead to be identified as the author of this work have been asserted by him in accordance with the Copyright, Designs and Patents Act of 1988.

ISBN 978-1-78222-450-1
Book design, layout and production management by Into Print
www.intoprint.net
+44 (0)1604 832149

Printed and bound in UK and USA by Lightning Source

To Alan and Maria Barnett,
for their past and continual help.

ACKNOWLEDGEMENTS

I would like to thank the following people:

My brother Adam, who has had to put up with me and my writing for years; my parents John and Pauline; my other brother Daniel, and the rest of the family.

If I have forgotten anyone, then I apologise.

CONTENTS

PROLOGUE

"Grief oft blinds us to the truth."
The Book of the Wolf.

R obin stared at the gentle face that hovered before her.
"Robin avenge me," her father said, with his last breath.
"Father!" Robin screamed as his eyes closed and she felt
the drum that was his heart no longer beat against her breast. "No
father don't leave me!"

Robin's scream of grief woke her from the nightmare memory
that had racked her dreams for the last few nights. She looked bleary
around her at the dark hangings that framed her view of the grey
walls that surrounded her. For a long moment Robin could not
think where she was, then like a splash of cold water she remembered
that she was in the Lady Luna's tower. A thought that conjured the
Lady's square jawed face to Robin's mind and a smile flickered at her
lips as she lingered over the thought of the woman whose hair was
almost as fiery red as her own. Still thinking about the masculine
woman drew her mind back to her father's death and her grief. Even
as she recalled the events of her father's death it seemed to her that
this dark lady was linked with that dark day. It had been on the same
day that her father died that she had met the red haired lady. She
and her sister Rose had been out at dawn picking mushrooms, when
returning to the house they had heard the clash of swords not an
unusual sound at her house as her father and his guards often sparred
early. She and Rose had gone to greet their father, only to find to their
horror her father fighting with a figure clad in sable and his black
blade was stained with their father's blood. Even as they watched
the dark figure stabbed him in the stomach and when the figure that
was wearing a helm crafted to resemble a wolf's head withdrew the
blade he fell at their feet. As the girls had stood frozen to the spot
with shock, the wolf helmed figure turned to the stone arch that
stood on their land and began to cast some kind of spell. The figure's
snarling voice broke Rose's paralysis and with a scream of rage she

grabbed up their father's fallen sword and lunged after the wolf clad figure. Robin dropped to her father's side to check if he was still alive. Robin did not see what happened next, but when she glanced back up both Rose and the dark assassin had vanished into thin air. Robin did not understand what had happened to them or where they had gone, but her father's groan of pain made her look back to his pain twisted face. His grey eyes met hers and she saw recognition in them; he knew who she was, she was sure of it.

"Robin I am sorry my love I had so much to tell you."

"Don't talk father keep still I will fetch Scholar Vyman, he can heal you."

"No time," he gasped as a dagger of pain stabbed through his bowels. "Listen to me now Robin and warn your sister."

"Rose has disappeared," Robin said through a waterfall of tears.

"You must find her Robin you must save her from the dark..."

"Yes, yes we will save her together when you are healed."

"Robin I meant to tell you. . ."

What her father meant to tell her Robin never found out, for at that moment a great pain twisted his face and when his face cleared he had passed into the world of the dead leaving Robin to scream her rage, grief and denial into the grey sky. This was how the Lady Luna had found her moments later.

Robin had not been aware of the horse that had galloped up to her nor had been aware of the short leather clad figure that had vaulted out of the horse's saddle; she was only aware of another presence when strong hands gripped her shoulders and a deep voice shouted into her face.

"Let him go girl, let him go."

Robin had blinked tears away to see a blurred pair of green eyes staring into hers and she felt those strong hands pull her hands away from her father's bloody body and she watched not understanding as the small figure grabbed her by the shoulders and shook her.

"Get a grip on yourself girl," the voice commanded. "Tell me girl who did this?"

Robin opened her mouth to reply when she heard another voice, one she knew, speaking in familiar gruff tones.

"Take your hands off her before I put a hole in you." The speaker was the old and gruff master of arms Garm Greywing, her father's old friend and the captain of the family's small house guard.

When Robin glanced in his voice's direction it was to see him standing a foot away, his long sword drawn a grim look on his grey bearded face. The figure that gripped Robin gave him a withering glance and returned its attention to Robin.

"I old man am trying to find out who slayed your master and therefore made you useless," the deep voice said in a tone that was cold and chilled Robin even through her grief.

The old man at arms glanced at the body that lay on the other side of Robin and he cried out as he saw who and what it was. He nearly knocked Robin and the green eyed figure to one side, as he sprang to Robin's father's side and lifting him in his large arms stared down at his still face. Robin had never seen the old man cry, but tears fell on her father's still face now.

"Who did this girl?" snapped the dark clad figure who clutched her.

"Someone dressed up in a wolf helmet and wielding a black sword," Robin said, through chattering teeth.

"Kain," the figure spat and letting go of Robin turned away to face the stone arch. "Through here?"

"I don't know," Robin said, her voice all but breaking.

Seeming to notice that Robin was a quivering wreck, the short figure came back to her and this time placed a more comforting arm round Robin's waist.

"Are you alright?" the green eyed questioner asked and bit back a curse. "Sorry, that's a stupid question."

Robin looked at the figure taking in details, despite the numb feeling that had replaced her mind and heart. Robin saw that this figure was short (barely five feet tall), but it was slim and graceful. It was wrapped in black leathers and a short red cape. The green eyes that had already caught and held her attention were set in a strong jawed face that reminded Robin of her own the woman too had dark red hair like her own though the figure – was it a woman or a man? – had cropped its bright fiery red hair very close to the skull giving the broad jawed face a boyish appearance.

"Here drink this," the black clad figure said, as it pressed a small leather flask into Robin's hand.

Robin remembered her father's warnings against taking food or drink from strangers and his warnings about poisons only as the hot fiery liquor hit the back of her throat.

"Thank you," Robin wheezed as she blindly handed the flask back to the leather clad figure. "Who are you?"

"I am the Lady Airian Luna," the figured identified herself, as she turned her gaze away from Robin and towards the grieving statue like knight of her house. "You will need help to carry him up to the house grey beard; my bodyguard should be round here somewhere he can help."

The old knight did not seem to hear her so wrapped in his grief was he, so the Lady turned back to Robin to give her a shrug and sticking her long fingers in her mouth gave a long loud whistle. In response from the wooded end of the property there came the thuds of hooves and a huge black horse came pounding towards them. The horse pulled up before them and its giant rider leapt down to tower over them, its cold grey eyes fixed on the small Lady Luna. Robin feeling suddenly afraid started back, but Luna did not move and grinned in Robin's direction.

"Robin this is Wolf and he will not hurt you." Then to the giant she named Wolf, "Wolf this is the Lady Robin Canduss and she is a friend understand Wolf?"

The giant called Wolf did not speak, but grunting nodded its head though its grey eyes did not move from its small mistress.

"How do you know my name?"

"Because Robert, your father himself told them to me, it was he I came to see."

"I did not know he knew you! He has not spoken of you before!"

"Has he not?" the Lady said, offhandedly as she pointed at Wolf and then her horse.

Robin watched with relief, as the giant moved away from her to take his mistress' horse's reins and lead both horses off towards the trees.

"He is going to hobble the horses and then help carry your father's body up to the house," Luna explained, as she watched Robin's eyes. "But enough of clumsy giants, come girl you are needing rest and perhaps a draught."

As if the lady's words reminded Robin of her grief, she fainted dead away. Robin grimaced at that memory. All this had happened three days ago, or was it longer? Robin was not sure. All she was sure about was that today was her father's funeral and there was still no news of what had happened to Rose.

DRESSING IN DAGGERS

"Our belongings take on part of us, but with spell casters it is more and more!"
Takana to the Red Wizard, The Wereding Chronicles.

Robin was still thinking where Rose was, when a gentle knock came at her apartment's door.

"Yes," Robin said, sitting up and watching as the dark wooden door of her bedroom slowly even tentatively opened and a small and very familiar black head peeked round the door.

"Imp!" Robin said gladly, "where did you spring from?"

"Did I disturb you m'lady?" asked the head, as it slid round the door to reveal that it belonged to a tiny child of a woman dressed in black.

"I can't imagine my oldest friend ever disturbing me Imp," Robin said, as she looked fondly on her childhood friend and maid. "When did you arrive?"

Robin had been in a dazed stupor for at least a day after her father's death and had been brought by Luna's insistence to her tower so that she could recover.

"In surroundings less painful to you," as Luna had told her, when Robin had recovered her wits enough for the lady to tell her.

"I arrived last night my lady," Imp answered her, as she glided to the tall wardrobe and opening it began to look inside.

Robin regarded the tiny woman's back, and reflected on how the little woman had been looking after her as far back as she could remember. Imp or Imperitar Dorsal had been in service to her family as long as Robin had been in the world and was a member of a long line of Dorsals that had served her family. Robin realised not for the first time that she loved the dwarf like woman, who looked after her every need, seeming to know with a telepathic skill what Robin's wants and needs were before she did. The small woman turned from the closet holding a black dress, that Robin had never seen before.

"Oh Imp I can dress myself," Robin was quite perhaps too

independent and didn't like the woman fussing over her, though as now she usually gave up protesting and let the gentle if insistent fussing of the maid let her dress her or style her hair or whatever the servant wished to do.

"I know my lady, but I thought you would like me to show you what you have here to dress in," said the soft voice of the servant.

"Imp when have I worn a dress like that? I don't even own one like that?"

"I believe that the Lady Luna has provided it for you," the servant said, as she held up a similar if not so long dress.

"Don't you have any of my clothes from the house?"

The servant frowned at that and turned to where the clothes Robin had been wearing on that fated day were neatly folded on a seat. The servant wordlessly held up the leather britches, cotton shirt and vest that Robin had been wearing at the time.

"But my lady these are not black!"

Robin shuddered at the thought of wearing mourning, but she knew she would have to do it. She looked from the manly garb, that Imp held out to her and the dark dress draped over her arm and back again. As if the Lady Luna had read her mind, a knock came on the door and without waiting for a response the giant called Wolf walked in his huge hands holding a bundle of clothes that he wordlessly dropped on the foot of Robin's bed. Then without a word the giant turned and left as abruptly as he had come. Not that Robin expected him to say even a "good morning", for she had learned from Luna that her faithful manservant was dumb and she had even seen the stump that had been left by the torchers' pincers.

"That brute gives me the willies," Imp muttered under her breath, as she laid the clothes she had been holding to one side and approaching the bed began to lift an unfold the clothes the "Brute" had brought.

"He is intimidating isn't he? Ah now those are more to my liking," Robin exclaimed, as Imp held up for her to see similar clothes to her own only these leggings, shirt and jerkin were all black.

As Imp unfolded the clothes something fell to the floor with a clatter.

"It appears that the Lady Luna knows your liking of men's clothes." Imp said, as she laid the clothes in Robin's lap and bending retrieved the fallen object, which she held up for Robin's examination.

"It appears that she also knows about my need for a blade," Robin said, as she saw that Imp was holding up a dagger in a black sheath.

"So it would appear," the maid sighed, as she handed her mistress the dagger. "I will see if there is a belt in here for it."

As the maid turned back to the wardrobe, Robin drew the dagger forth to examine it. The dagger had a fine black leather handgrip and the long blade was wrought of dark grey steel with several strange runes or signs engraved into the flat of the blade. What really set the dagger apart however, was the fine ruby like stone set in the pummel.

A stone that glittered in the light of the predawn, a stone that held Robin's attention for long moments as she watched a fire at the heart of the stone flicker and dance like a living thing. Its flickering light seeming to draw Robin's mind deep into the stone's dark heart. Robin was only half aware of images that flickered at the edges of her consciousness, images of scantily clad women or the shadows of women that danced lewdly at the edges of the fire of the stone's heart. Robin was partly aware of these seductive shadow women, but her mind was too concentrated on the flame of the stone's heart, to consciously notice these cavorting wraiths. She might have been there a week later, if Imp had not broken her reverie.

"This one my lady?" she asked as she held up a simple black leather belt with a silver buckle.

"Fine," Robin mumbled, as she came back to herself.

She glanced down at the stone again and once more felt the stone's inner fires tug at her mind, in an attempt to capture her thoughts. Robin shook her head and shoving the blade back into its sheath through back the bed clothes and rising went to her dressing table to dress in front of a simple bronze mirror. In moments she was dressed in the black clothes and Imp began to run a comb through Robin's short if tangled hair.

"I do wish you would let it grow longer my lady. It is the fashion to wear it to the waist at the moment," the maid said, as she examined her work.

Robin, who wore her hair to her shoulders groaned, as she would if she could get away with it, would have cut it very short.

"Imp I'm not Ros. . ." Robin broke off, finishing her sister's name with a sob.

The maid understanding at once what Robin meant and what she could not bring herself to say.

"I'm sure your sister is safe my lady," she said, in a gentle whisper.

"But where is she Imp, what's happened to her?"

The maid of course had no answer, so she gave Robin a hug and then stood back from Robin and looked her over.

"You're just missing some jewellery," Imp said, turning to a jewellery box.

"No Imp, no jewellery, that's where I draw the line."

"But my lady!"

"How many times have we had this conversation Imp, I don't wear jewellery."

"Very well my Lady. Shall I get you your breakfast?"

Robin thought about food and her stomach rolled over.

"No thank you Imp, no breakfast I'm not hungry."

"Perhaps a cup of tea," the dwarf suggested.

"Yes, tea would be a good idea."

THE RED ROOK AND THE BLACK QUEEN

"Life is usually too chaotic to play chess with people's lives, but some people still play them like pawns."
Silver Skin to the Red Wizard from The Wereding Chronicles.

When Robin emerged from the short stone tower that Luna called home, it was to find its mistress dressed in almost identical black clothes and at her side was another woman that even Robin recognised. It was the Queen L. Bain. Robin bowed low to the tall woman, whose very white face and gold hair was known throughout the land.

"Your majesty," Robin said, in a suddenly rough voice. "I am honoured to meet you."

The queen laughed, her beautiful blue eyes flashing with amusement.

"The pleasure and honour are all mine Lady Canduss," the Queen said, in a light, high voice that tinkled with the bells of laughter. Then the laughter vanished and the queen took on a more regal and solemn manner. "Believe me, my Lady when I tell you that you have my deepest sympathy at this most difficult time."

Although the queen's words tugged at her emotions, Robin was to her relief able to keep them under control and she bowed again.

"Thank you my Queen, you don't know what that means to me."

"Are we waiting for anyone else?" Luna asked the queen.

"I don't think so."

"Then if our honourable captain of the guard is ready."

These words were directed at a figure that Robin had until now not noticed. He stood just behind the queen and a little to the left and was as tall as the queen, but much broader. He was dressed in full plate armour that was enamelled in dark green and his cloak was a forest green. His helmet was crested with a crouching leopard and even if his face was not familiar to Robin, she would know by this emblem who this must be.

"Lord Healm?" Robin asked hesitantly.

"At your service my Lady," replied the large man, as he half bowed. This giant was the King's nephew and Warder of the North was the captain of the King's bodyguard and was here to protect the queen.

"Well Tomas are you ready?"

"If you are my Queen," the lord replied though his face remained a mask and his tone was far from warm. Robin was not learned in court law, but she thought she could divine a formal coldness between the two as if they were only paying the formalities lip service. She must remember to ask Imp about it, once she had her alone.

"Then let us go to the temple."

Lord Healm turned to where a young page held the reins of a pair of magnificent black horses that waited for the queen and Lady Luna and he helped the tall queen and short lady into their saddles. Garm Greywing held the bridle of her own grey mare (Storm), and when the page took the rain he helped her into the saddle and after her Imp into a small horse's saddle.

"Thank You Garm," Robin said, looking down at the old guard in his grey male overlaid by the sir coat with its golden eagle standing on a rose that was her houses symbol. "You look very handsome."

"Thank you my lady, you too look most handsome."

"Thanks."

"Are we ready?" Luna asked.

"As we'll ever be." Robin said, in a suddenly choked voice as she realised exactly where they were going. She had of course known before where they were to go, but knowing it and going there were two different things.

The party did not seem to notice her sudden reluctance and they swiftly rode down the street towards Landon's main temple, where her father's body lay in state. As the party moved out Robin noticed that a double rank of royal guards flanked them falling in on either side and behind their long spears fluttering with her and the Queen's pennants. Robin also noticed as she glanced up into a cloudless sky, a dark spot of a hawk or some kind of bird far above and she wished she was that bird. Though as she returned her eyes back to the road before her, she wished that Rose was at her side.

"Rose where are you?"

But no one answered her whispered question and so before Robin knew it, she was standing before her father's open coffin and looking down at his now mask like face. He had been tended by the grey sisters and had been dressed in his full armour, a suit of plate male enamelled in red. With the golden eagle emblazed in gold on his chest and on the shield that lay at his feet. As Robin looked on this, she remembered her father saying how he only war the armour when he had too as it made him feel uncomfortable. Then despite her attempt at self-control, his face swam before her as the tears began to flow. She felt a gentle if firm grip take her elbow and Garm's voice murmured in her ear.

"This way my lady."

Robin let him guide her to an isle where she sat and listened to the Cleric muttering through the service to the triple fold god, but she took little of it in. She did however, take in the deep voice of the lord of the north saying that her father had been a tireless patron of the arts, a great scholar and protector of the people. The words made Robin realise that she had not known these things about her father, it made her wonder what else she did not know about her father. Then everyone was standing as Garm and the rest of her father's men at arms were bearing the coffin out of the temple to where a carriage waited to carry him to their home and his final resting place.

THE HOUSE OF THE DEAD

"Temples to the dead have been built into monuments, but these are houses to the dead they are not a place for the living."
Kye's personal journal.

They buried her father in their family mausoleum, a broad, but small building tucked away in the woods at the far end of the land. Robin watched as the priest said the last ritual over his body and Robin watched as two men at arms lifted the heavy coffin lid and began to place it over her father. Robin realised that she would not see him again and quickly spoke.

"No not yet," the guardsmen hesitated and looked to Garm who nodded. "I just want to look at him one more time."

She muttered as she stared down at his still face. As she stared at the still mask, she realised that this was the last time she would ever see him this side of the grave.

"Good by father, I love you," she said, as his face shimmered and then blurred beyond her sight. Then strong arms were round her waist and Luna's deep voice purred in her ear.

"Come on little one, let's get out of here, this place is for the dead not for us."

Robin only half understood Luna's words, for the next moment she found herself in bright light, the wind tossing her hair. Her eyes dazzled by a light that seemed painfully bright, after the dimness of the crypt. Robin took a long, deep breath of cold air and found it helped to centre her. Still, she nearly jumped out of her skin, when a long, thin hand was placed on her shoulder.

"Courage my dear," the Queen's voice, whispered in her ear.

Robin took another breath and was about to speak to the queen, when a flicker of motion caught her attention out of the corner of her eye. Turning her head, Robin saw a great hawk take off from a low hanging branch. Remembering the queen behind her, Robin turned her attention back to that woman.

"Will you come up to the house, your majesty?"

"I think not," the queen said, "I have urgent business at the court."

"Then I thank you, for taking time to visit us."

"I am pleased to have done so, now I will leave you in Luna's capable hands." The queen said, as she swept past Robin and to where Healm waited with the horses. Her waist long mane of black hair flying out behind her like a sable banner.

Robin looked down to the tiny woman at her side, surprised to find that the tiny woman still had an arm round her waist. What surprised Robin more, was that it felt good and right to be there, almost as if she were used to it. This should have pleased her, for she felt the beginnings of affection for the red haired Lady. Still, it also made her feel immensely sad, because, in the past Roses arm had embraced her like this and Robin despite the Lady's comforting arm could not help but feel a vast pit of despair opening before her.

"Rose I need you, where are you?"

"I know, I know," soothed Luna, her hand stroking Robin's lower back, its touch stirring feelings in Robin that both excited and scared her. So she was pleased when Garm approached and Luna glairing backed away from Robin, as if she did not want the old knight to see her embrace.

"My Lady," said the old knight gravely, "With your permission we will precede to the house, where Imp and her ladies have prepared a repast for you."

Robin did not answer at once, looking after Luna, who turning away stalked towards her horse, when she did respond she was distant.

"Fine Garm fine."

"My Lady," Garm offered his arm and Robin let him draw her away, but her eyes seemed to look for someone else, though whether she was looking for Rose or Luna she no longer knew.

THE WARDER OF THE NORTH QUESTIONS

"Men have an overwhelming desire to claim the land for themselves,
not realising that the land owns them."
Bright Eyes from The Wereding Chronicles by the Red Wizard.

High above the house of Canduss the great hawk screamed at the sun and wheeled away to fly to the city of Landon. Where it swooped and flew round its high towers until it came to a round tower that seemed to stand alone and from a high point above the stone building the hawk looked with its golden eyes down on the top of the tower. Where on a wide platform between tall spear like battlements a figure lay on its back, its own eyes looking blankly skywards. As the hawk looked down at the figure, it heard the barely remembered voice that commanded it.

"Return Kit, remember who you are and return."

Hearing the name Kit the hawk remembered who and what it was and with a final scream of defiance, it stooped to the battlements and the figure that lay there. As the bird landed with a scrabble of claws, it lifted its great wings over the figure and screamed, but even as the stone threw the cry back at the bird, the cry changed from the high scream of a bird to the deeper cry of a human's voice and the feathers of the wings seemed to ripple and then fold back to reveal a paler form beneath. When the figure got to its feet, it turned its tall broad shouldered form to find not a bird standing before it, but a short tawny haired girl all but naked save for a cloak of brown feathers.

"Kit?" asked the tall woman, who had been lying on her back. "Have you come back to us?"

"Bright Eyes?" the girl croaked, in a voice that was hoarse from disuse.

"Yes it is I Kit, you are back."

"Back," groaned the girl that was Kit, though her memories returned slowly, she knew that she was no longer the hawk, but Kit the skin swapper.

"Here, drink this," said a new voice, a deep booming voice that belonged to a giant of a man, whose long black and white hair glittered in the light.

Kit turned to the new comer and accepted a steaming cup and exchanged a lingering look with his glowing green eyes.

"Kit do you know us?" asked the deep voice of the woman referred to as Bright Eyes as she accepted a second cup from the green eyed man.

"Thanks Tigress."

"You were with me Bright Eyes you must know what I am," the girl replied in her hoarse voice, her yellow eyes those of the hawk she had been only moments before.

"Yes and the mind I was with was that of the hawk, even now the joy of flight flows through your veins," shot back Bright Eyes.

"Ladies, Ladies," purred Tigress, as he tried to calm the women. "Kit what is your surname?"

"Cloudcloak."

"There Bright Eyes are you satisfied?"

"Yes," the tall woman said, as she sipped from the steaming cup, her yellow eyes taking in Kit's shivering form and turning to Tigress asked him to help her. "Tigress perhaps you could fetch Kit's robe."

Tigress opened his cloak, to reveal that within its folds was a folded robe which he passed to Kit so that she could wrap herself in its brown folds.

"Better?"

"Better," croaked Kit and after another long look at Tigress (that took in his black and white striped mane, his glowing cats eyes and the thick sideburns and cat like whiskers that sprouted from his square jawed face), she leapt into his arms and wrapped her arms round his neck and buried her face against his broad chest.

Bright Eyes watched this charming picture for a long moment, giving the couple as much time as she could then when she reckoned that enough time had passed, she loudly cleared her throat. Kit and Tigress sprang apart and the short girl turned a yellow eye on the taller woman.

"Kit as you know I can only perceive impressions through the link, can you remember what you saw?"

"Enough to tell you that the girl was comforted by the Red Rook and the Black Queen was there too."

"Then Luna is still up to her old tricks," growled Tigress.

"So it would appear," Kit said, as she looked up at the clouds, as though she were still pining for the wind beneath her wings.

"This is not good news, Kye and Silver Skin must be told," murmured Bright Eyes.

"Why is this girl and her sister so important?"

"I don't know Tigress, I only know that Kain killed their father and the other sister followed him through a portal to the Birches. Where your Grandfather Kit and your princess Tigress, saved her from a poisoned dagger. It was because, of this that Kye asked for information regarding the girl."

"Well you can tell him that she is in the company of She wolves," Kit said, as she fingered the rawhide thong that held the stone medallion that hung about her neck.

"I think we should become more involved, in this matter," Bright Eyes said, crinkling her brow.

"Is that wise Eyes?" Tigress asked, though his Eyes were on Kit. "After all it's likely that the girl is already lost, if Luna has her under her spell."

"She may not be totally under the witches spell," murmured Bright Eyes, under her breath.

Tigress opened his mouth to say something, but he never got the chance for somewhere within the depths of the tower there rang a bright bell.

"Someone is at the gates," Bright Eyes said, her yellow eyes suddenly going distant as if she could look within and see the intruder.

Kit strode to the high battlements and craning out over the stone battlements to see if she could spot the visitor.

"Be careful Kit," Tigress warned. "You can't fly now."

"It's Healm," Bright Eyes said, from where she stood with her eyes shut, as if she were speaking to the man in question. She proceeded to hold a conversation with the unseen visitor. "How can I help the Warder of the North?"

At the gates of the high wall that surrounded the towers grounds, the tall mountain of a man that was Healm shivered under his plate and leather, as Bright Eyes' disembodied voice spoke to him.

"Ambassador Silverbrow," Healm said, uncomfortably as he

looked about him for the source of the voice. "I would like to speak with you."

"Do you come in peace?"

"I do," the knight said, though his hand moved unconsciously to the pummel of the short sword at his side.

"Will you leave your sword at the gate?"

"If you wish it," replied the knight, though he was clearly reluctant to do so.

"I do wish it brave knight, I would have no blade enter my home."

Several stories above the gates, Bright Eyes smiled to herself, at the irony. Most people were not allowed to carry a blade longer than a dagger within the limits of the city, but as the captain of the King's Guards Healm was allowed to bear a short sword when not on duty. still he who was more privileged than most, was loathed to give up this weapon.

"Little does he know that the blade would be of no use here," Tigress said, slyly as he touched the gold medallion that hung about his own neck.

At the gates Healm unbuckled his sword belt and laid it across the saddle of his horse that was bound by the reins to a ring in the wall. As he did this, the gates opened for him. Still even though the gates had opened he could for a moment not move, for the gates had not so much opened as disappeared entirely, leaving only a grey mist.

"Well are you going to enter or not," asked Bright Eyes' disembodied voice.

Gathering his courage Healm stepped through the mist. The knight half expecting the mist to solidify around him, trapping him in the heavy wood. But he passed through with no worse than a slight chill that made him shiver. Once he had stepped through he found himself in a tree lined path that lead to the wide archway at the feet of the tower.

"We will meet you in the entry," Bright Eyes' voice said, echoing around him as if it came from everywhere at once.

At the top of the tower Bright Eyes turned to her companions.

"The Shield of the North approaches," she said, grandly and glancing in Tigress's direction added, "Tigress you might want to put your game face on."

Understanding Bright Eyes' cryptic signal, Tigress gripped his gold medallion on the end of its silver chain and drawing on the spark of magic embedded in its crystalline heart, he summoned from the mystic item a glimmering of magical force and whispering the words that flowed into his mind he felt a slight tingling flow over his face.

"How do I look?"

Bright Eyes now saw not the cat like features that she knew and loved, for Tigress's green eyes had lost their vertical pupils, his whiskers had become a dark beard and his black and white striped hair was now blond. So that he now looked like a normal, if handsome blond man. If she concentrated she could see through the illusion to detect his real face beneath the illusionary mask.

"Hideous," she said, laughing at his expression both on and beneath the mask.

"I can see through it, if I try," Kit said, as she stroked his arm "But the illusion should fool the lordling."

"If the man can see through it, will be the real test," Tigress said.

"I wish it were not necessary," Bright Eyes said, as she led them to a trapdoor in the battlements and descended a ladder to the floor below.

"We do not know this man," Kit pointed out.

"His reputation paints him a good man," Tigress said, as he watched his lover descend below him.

"Reputations must be proved."

"That is why I am eager to meet him," Bright Eyes said, as she rushed down a spiral stares. "So hurry, he is already waiting for us."

Bright Eyes found Healm waiting for her in a small hall way. He was stood to one side, considering a tall display cabinet that stood against one wall. Displayed inside the case were two six foot staves of wood. One was made of what looked like a light wood, but the other might have been carved from ebony, so black was it. Its darkness making the silver symbols and runes stand out. Both staffs were shod in iron, but one was capped by a large stone and the black staff was capped by an iron head moulded to resemble some kind of twisting rune.

"Are they magical?" Healm asked, when he sensed a presence behind him.

"My Lord magic is illegal in your realm," Bright Eyes said softly, as she considered the staves.

"In the south land's magic is forbidden," Healm mused aloud. "But I have been led to believe that this tower and its lands are something of an embassy and so our laws do not hold here within these walls."

"How can I help you my lord? I doubt that you came here to debate such points of law!"

Healm glanced about him and dropped his voice to little above a whisper.

"Ambassador Can we go somewhere more private?"

Intrigued by Healm's wish for privacy, Bright Eyes considered his request and then shrugged her very broad shoulders.

"We might be more comfortable in the lounge. Please lord step this way."

Bright Eyes turned to the short flight of stairs that led up from this small entrance to a larger hall lined with many tapestries. One of them depicting a giant crowned with a stag's horns, had been drawn aside to reveal a low doorway that Bright Eyes ducked through.

"There are three steps down my lord," she said, as she disappeared.

Healm ducked through the low door and descended three steps into a long low room lit by a log fire that a slender woman was kneeling before, her slender figure outlined by the dancing flames. Healm was forced to duck even when he had descended the steps, for the room had low beams from which many herbs were drying. As Healm drew a breath, he inhaled familiar smells of mint and sage that took him back to his childhood and the low cottage that he and his brother had been raised in. His reminisces were interrupted by a deep voice that spoke from a sideboard.

"Can I offer you a cup of mulled wine lord?"

Healm glanced in the voices direction, to see a large blond man tending to a decanter and cups.

"Yes thank you. . ."

"Forgive me lord," Bright Eyes said, from a low couch. "Where are my manners, Lord Healm, may I introduce Tigress StaffSword and this is Kit Cloudcloak."

The girl that Bright Eyes identified as Kit Cloudcloak bowed at the waste and without a word moved to sit on the couch beside Bright Eyes, the tall blond man handed Healm a cup and then sat on the floor at Kit's feet. Healm sat on the couch opposite them and considered the three Weredings across from him. Bright Eyes was almost as tall and wide as Healm himself, her broad form swathed in a brown robe and her black hair fell to her shoulders. Her long narrow face gave hints to her Werewolf heritage, its long jaw and flat nose giving her a lupine appearance. Though the biggest hint of her shape shifter nature were the eyes that gave her her name. She considered him with a pair of feral yellow eyes that seemed to glow with an inner fire, even in the low light of this lounge. The girl that sat at her side was if anything the ambassador's opposite, though she had about her a look that made Healm think that they must be kin. She was small and slight of stature, though her own yellow eyes held a strength and wild spark that made Healm think of the hawks he had hunted with as a boy. Though her mane, with its reddish brown hair reminded him of a lion. His attention moved on to the tall blond man that like a huge cat sat at her feet. This Tigress looked the most human of the three fairy people, though there was something about his calm regular features that seemed wrong to Healm. As he stared at the blond man he thought that his face flickered an instant, as though he were seeing a mask slip to reveal the real face behind. Then the face was as it had been and Healm dismissed it as a flicker of fire light. Bright Eyes cleared her throat and Healm's gaze snapped to her face.

"Much as I enjoy sharing a cup of spiced wine with you Lord, I do not think that this is what brings you to our tower?"

Healm considered what to say and whether it was wise to speak before them. Could he trust these people. The ambassador he knew personally, as he had to deal with her before concerning his office, but he had never met these other two before. He had heard the name of StaffSword before, the lady Aleena StaffSword was known throughout the border lands as the White Which, this blond man must be a relative. Though that made Healm doubt this blond face even more, as the White Witch was a beautiful if terrible mixture of woman and cat.

"I too have not come here for just your company," Healm said, hesitantly. "I have come to ask you if you have heard from your people of any increase in Darkling activity."

Healm had expected the naming of the Evil Weredings would draw a response from the three watchers and he was not disappointed.

Tigress gave a growl deep in his throat that raised the hairs on the back of Healm's neck, for it was the snarl of a jungle cat. Kit hissed like a startled cat and Bright Eyes reached for the silver disk that hung about her neck. The Darklings were a part of the fey folk's culture and history that they wished did not exist and in his experience some of them did not even acknowledge the Orcs' and goblins' existence.

"The Darklings, why do you ask my lord?"

"Because, Lady Bright Eyes we have been seeing them more and more regularly on the wall," Healm replied, watching her reaction and wishing that her eyes were not so feral. It made it harder for him to look into them and even harder to read any reaction in them.

"Orcs?" Tigress shot at Healm.

"No, Goblins and a troll once, but we have lost two patrols in the Bad Lands and Hill Town has reported that a Hag might have tried their defences."

"A Hag?" The girl called Kit, spoke in a hoarse whisper, but her yellow eyes flickered with interest at the news of a hag.

"So the reports say, we have not heard from the lone tower for several weeks."

"Why is that?"

"The two patrols we lost were attempting to reach them, but they never came back and I decided that it was unwise to send any more patrols before I had better information."

"So you came here to see if we had that information," Bright Eyes said, making it a statement not a question.

"But lord do you not have any communication with the Kings?"

Healm shrugged reluctantly, as he replied.

"The Queen and her council would have me never speak with the Kings, but yes I have sent two ravens, but have had no reply."

This reply seemed to nonplus the three Weredings. A long silence stretched and then Bright Eyes spoke into it.

"I am not aware of any Darkling activity, but I could try contacting the gatekeeper if you wish my lord?"

Healm gave an involuntary shudder at the mention of the Gatekeeper. The White Wolf as he was known (Healm had never found out if this was just a nickname or if it was another title given to his opposite number), was not a man that Healm could think of and not shiver, for the White Wolf was even more animalistic than

Bright Eyes. As Healm recalled the tall white haired man that he had dealt with twice in his life, he remembered the man's piercing green eyes that seemed to cut through your flesh and read the soul beneath.

"I would appreciate any help you could give me in this matter lady Bright Eyes," Healm hesitated, as he drew near the point of his reluctance. "There is one more favour I would ask of you lady and of your companions."

Not for the first time did Bright Eyes speak as if she had read his mind.

"You do not wish me to speak of this meeting to anyone outside these walls?"

Healm nodded for he was no longer able to speak past the lump in his throat.

"Then you are not acting in the King's name?"

"I am acting as I see my duty requires," Healm said, stiffly as if the Werewolf's question-statement had hurt his pride, then he said more softly. "But you are right I am here under my own initiative, no other in the court knows of this meeting."

"I, we will do as you wish, however, I feel I should worn you that not much stays a secret in this city."

"I will tell the King and the court when I have too," Healm said, with a bitter smile. "But I would rather have something to tell them."

"Which is why you come to us."

"Yes, I thank you Lady Silverbrow and your companions for your help and discretion. You have my thanks and if there is any way in which I can repay you."

Kit and Bright Eyes quickly exchanged a glance and when Bright Eyes met Healm's own, her broad mouth was a large grin.

"As it happens my lord, there is something that you could help us with."

Bright Eyes watched surprise and then regret flash across Healm's broad honest face. Bright Eyes wondered how this man had been able to survive so long at court, he could not hide his thoughts to save his life. He was wondering what he was letting himself in for. Still he said nothing and waited silently for Bright Eyes to tell him the price of his information.

"What my lord can you tell us about the Lady Robin Canduss?"

In the woods near the Canduss estate Luna stalked through the woods, her green eyes glowing with a fierce light. When she came to a nearby clearing, she stalked into it and snarling with rage she drew her dagger and drove it into the nearest tree.

"Curse the Greywings," she snarled, as she did so.

Seeming to sense something behind her, Luna ripped the dagger out and spinning round put her back to the tree and stared out at the open clearing behind her.

"Who's there?"

Receiving no response she hissed a word and her dagger was suddenly sheathed in blue flames that lit up the growing shadows. Still nothing came for her, but Luna was still convinced that something was there and she began to chant in a low voice. As she did, a blue light began to form around her left fist and forearm. By the time a shadow emerged from the trees, Luna's left arm was sheathed in a gauntlet of crackling energy, that made it appear as if she had tamed a lightning bolt to decorate her arm.

"Stop right there or I will turn this on you," Luna said, as she raised the glowing fist towards the tall shadow.

"I have only come to talk," came the low hissing reply.

Bright Eyes actually attended Healm as he left the tower and watched him as he climbed upon his great grey horse.

"A fine animal," Bright Eyes said, as she watched him from the misty gates.

"He is," Healm said, as he looked down at her from the beasts back, a broad smile splitting his usually grim face.

"His name?"

"Bane."

"And is he?"

"I thought him so when I bought him," Healm said, as he slapped the horse on the side of its neck.

The horse neighed and spinning galloped along the road carrying Healm back to the city.

"Fear Healm even when baring gifts," Tigress joked from behind Bright Eyes.

"Certainly he brought a mixed cup of news," Bright Eyes replied, as she watched the knight fade into the distance.

When Bright Eyes turned from the gate, it was to find that Tigress had dropped the blond man's mask and had returned to his feline features.

"I thought he would never leave," Tigress sighed. "I had to cast the spell twice and I'm not sure that I could keep it up for much longer."

"I noticed," Kit said, from beside him.

"Did he?"

"I am not sure," Kit said, her eyes taking on a distant look. "I think he suspected that he was seeing a mask, but I don't think he saw through it."

"At the moment that does not matter," Bright Eyes said, as she turned the gates back to wood. "What does matter is that the Kings have not replied to his raven."

"Could that be your grandfather just being quiet?"

"The White Wolf would respond to such a raven," Bright Eyes said, as she stalked past the couple.

"Then what is the next step? A Raven?"

"No, I will try to speak to him myself."

"That means she is about to lock herself in her study for hours," Tigress whispered to Kit.

"What do you want us to do?" Kit asked, as she followed Bright Eyes to the tower door.

Bright Eyes stopped and turning back to face the smaller woman, she grinned broadly.

"I have no reason to know this, but I fear that we may be due a visit from the dark brotherhood, I suggest that you and Tigress attend to your researches."

"You wish us to redouble the wards?" Tigress asked, as he knocked back the last of his wine.

"I think it a good idea."

Bright Eyes entered the tower and striding to the first story entered her study, where she removed from its cabernet a large stone bowl or basin its edge carved with many runes. She filled the bowl with water from a stone jug and after casting in a handful of herbs, began to chant over the bowl. After a certain point of time she cast into the water a piece of white hair or fur. At this point the water went cloudy and slowly a face took form in the mirror of the water. Bright Eyes watched as in the water there appeared not her reflection, but a face that boar something of her looks. The face that stared up at her, was long and lean with her long jaw and high cheekbones. However, its eyes were not her yellow, but a dark depthless green and where her hair was a dark black this face had a mane of snow white hair.

"Granddaughter is that you?" the voice that came from the water was a soft whisper that still held power, as if it was the whisper of thunder heard on the edge of hearing.

"Grandfather it is I, Bright Eyes."

"What have you done to your hair?"

"It is dye Grandfather."

"Ah yes I am forgetting you have the Landon post."

"Grandfather I do and it was here in the Tower of the Glove that I received Healm of the wall."

"What there in Landon? What is he doing there and not at his post?"

"That is not what we discussed my lord."

"Then what did he want?"

"He was asking if we knew of Darkling increases!"

The White Wolf's shape shimmered in the water as if the water had been disturbed, but nothing had moved the water and from the bowl there came the growling of an animal.

"Well Grandfather what is your answer?"

The water was still again and the White Wolf's dark face once again stared out of the mirror, but his eyes danced with a fierce flame.

"Why does he ask?"

"Because, he has lost two patrols. But why do you ask my lord Tristen?"

"Because, I have myself lost a patrol and the second patrol came back with half their men claiming that they were attacked by an Orc band over a hundred strong."

"How did they survive?"

"They would not have, but my Lady of the White Robe was summoned to them and it was her magic that turned the Orcs back."

"Was she harmed?"

"Thank the Goddess no."

"Thank the Goddess indeed. Have you had any more attacks?"

"No, but I have closed the gates."

"What do you make of this my lord?"

"This band may be all there is, but my blood says not."

"Then what do you think?"

"That the rats are building up to some attack on the Kings."

"Have you the strength to withstand them?"

"Without knowing their strength I cannot know, but I will hold against even the Crimson Dragon himself if he comes."

"I do hope he does not my lord. But if you are in need can you not send to the Shield?"

"I can Eyes, but I have not heard from them for long days. But I think I will not need to the village of Port Cullis has grown large in these last years I am not short of bodies even if they are Wolfbloods and not true Werewolves."

"I am glad to hear it grandfather. But if you need me please send to me."

"I will granddaughter and please tell the Warder of the North that I come to his aid if he needs it."

"I will grandfather. May the God and the Goddess watch over you!"

"And may they watch over you too," Tristen Silverbrow growled as his grim visage faded from the water.

Bright Eyes stared at the now still waters, her eyes seeming to see something other than the mirror.

"There is something about this I do not like."

She carried the basin to a work table covered in parchment, herbs and vials and bottles of every size and shape. Bright Eyes emptied the bowls contents into a large metal vial, before returning it to its cabinet.

When she returned to the towers tree lined square, it was to find Tigress and Kit hard at work as they bolstered the towers magical defences. When Bright Eyes stepped from the tower, it was to see Kit drawing with a forked stick on the flag stones. When Bright Eyes looked beyond Kit it was to see Tigress stood by the boundary wall his medallion glowing with throbbing power as he held it before him with one hand and traced an intricate design on the wall with a piece of charcoal. As Bright Eyes watched, Tigress stepped back from his handy work and raising the pendant high spoke the last word of his spell and the dark symbol flashed bright with an intense red light and then the glowing symbol faded away as its light seemed to leach into the stones themselves. As though the mortared stones were thirstily drinking up the magic. When Tigress opened his hand, the charcoal he had been drawing with fell as dust to the earth, the spell drawing on its substance to power its magic.

Turning away from the entrance to the grounds and the tower, she followed the flagged path that encircled the tower until she came to the back of the tower where a small kitchen garden spread out its herbs.

The tower that was the Fairy embassy was home to only a handful of people, one of these inmates was the short muscular youth, who at the moment was chopping fire wood. Bright Eyes stopped and watched the powerful muscles under this boy's shirtless body flex and not for the first time wondered why she had not taken him for a lover.

"Cole, I need you," she said, after watching his bare back knot and flex.

Cole laid his axe aside and turning met her Yellow eyes, with an unusual pair of his own. His right eye was a coal black, which might be where he got his name, but the left was the feral yellow of a wolf. Cole was one of the Wolfbloods a descendant of Werewolves and humans. Cole was not a Werewolf, his blood was too watered down for that, but he still boar the physical marks of his Wereding blood. The yellow eye was not the only trace of his magical blood, for across his bare shoulders he wore a thin strip of black fur. Cole served the Tower of the Glove as Gardner, carpenter and general handy man and his sister Clover was their cook and maid. Now the short youth stood with patient stoicism, as he waited for his new orders.

"Put your shirt on," Eyes told him reluctantly, as his short leather jerkin hid his muscular body. "I need you to take a message to Healm The Warder of the North. Do you know where he lives?"

"Yes my lady," replied Cole, in his whisper of a voice.

"Then wash and put on your long cloak and then come up to my study where I will give you the message."

"Yes my lady."

Bright eyes was turning away when she had a thought towards the towers defence.

"Cole have we any toadstools in the grounds?"

"I believe that there are some under the old oak my lady."

"Well do me one more thing before you clean up, gather me some of them and bring them to my study would you?"

"As you wish."

When Cole entered the study it was to find Bright Eyes bent over a large tome her eyes studying the complicated recipe written in its pages.

"The toadstools my lady," Cole said as he lay a small basket beside the book.

"Well done Cole. Now take this scroll to the Warder and make sure that you place it in his hands alone do you understand?"

"Of course my lady."

"Good, now go and may the lady lend you wings."

"And more besides," the youth said, with a rakish smile.

Bright Eyes did not answer, but watched as the youth spun on his heal and strode from the room.

"I may grant that wish one night Cole," she whispered to the empty air.

THE PEN AND THE SWORD

"The pen may not be mightier than the sword, but tell a wizard hurling lightning at you that."
Halmer Healm to Cole the Wereding Chronicles by the Red Wizard.

When Tomas Healm returned to his residence it was to find an unexpected visitor. Sat at the small dining table in the Spartan tower, was a small wiry figure bent over a huge tome.

"Halmer!" Tomas exclaimed, in surprise as he beheld the small wiry man reading a faded and spidery handwriting.

"Tomas," the man named Halmer leapt to his feet and rushed at the larger man.

Tomas wrapped the younger man in a bear hug and then held him at arm's length.

"Halmer what are you doing here?"

"What's wrong, aren't you please to see me big brother?" Halmer asked, in a dry humourless voice.

"Of course I'm pleased to see you, but I thought you were beyond the wall digging in some ruins."

"I was, but I finished days ago and got in only hours ago."

"And did you find anything?" Tomas asked, a look of stern reluctance crossing his face.

Tomas was hoping that his brother would say no, because, Tomas was not entirely happy with his brother's researches into the past, particularly as Tomas knew that Halmer wanted to discover magical secrets, researches that were all but forbidden. So his heart sank, when his brother's wind burnt face, split into a broad grin.

"Little enough, but I did find this," Halmer said, animatedly as he taw open his shirt, to reveal a string from which there hung a ring. "Here look at this Tomas."

Halmer held out the ring on his palm and Tomas took it and held it up before him. The ring was undeniably old, it was made of silver that was tarnished almost black, but the Safire that sat among several engraved symbols flashed in the light. As Tomas Healm looked on the ring, his mind recalled Tigress' hand, as the Wereding passed him his mulled wine.

"I have seen a ring like this before," he said softly, as he handed the ring back to his smaller brother.

"You have?" Halmer exclaimed, in surprise for his brother was the last person he had expected to recognise his find. "Where have you seen this ring?"

"On the hand of a Wereding," Tomas said, in a low voice.

"A Wereding, yes that makes sense," Halmer said, excitedly. "Which Wereding Tomas? Where did you see him?"

Tomas glanced about, unwilling to discuss this anywhere where an unsuspected ear may hear them.

"Not here brother, come let us debate this in my bedroom."

Tomas led his brother to his small cell of a bedroom and he sat on the narrow cot, while Halmer sat on a wooden seat at the side of the bed.

"What's with the secrecy Tomas?"

"The Wereding who was wearing the ring, was at the Tower of the Glove."

"Their embassy, what of it? You must have to go there from time to time, you are after all the Warder of the North."

"I have been there maybe twice over the years and every time I must inform the King or the Queen."

"I didn't know that things were that bad," Halmer said, as he fiddled with the dark band.

"The throne has always been afraid of the Weredings," Tomas whispered. "But the Black queen is almost paranoid when it comes to anything concerning them."

"So when you went to the tower, this time you went without telling the Queen?"

"Correct," Tomas growled.

"So that is why we are being so friendly! But the Wereding, Tomas who was he?"

"A SwordStaff, Tigress I think he was called."

"A relative of the White Witch?"

"I think so, though if he is he looks nothing like her."

But Halmer appeared not to be listening.

"Tigress...and he was wearing a ring like this?"

"Like! I would not swear it was the same Halmer, but looks like it at a glance."

"Then perhaps he will tell me about this ring."

Halmer's words confirmed Tomas' fears.

"Halmer, please be careful, if the Queen becomes aware of you dabbling it will make things even more difficult for us."

"For you, you mean," blurted Halmer. "What can she do to me?"

"For a start, she could denounce you to the Crimson Circle and claim you are working magic."

"Let her, I'm not doing anything illegal."

"You are studying magic and its workings." Tomas pointed out, as he checked that the door was shut with his eyes.

"To study magic is not illegal," Halmer shot back.

"Halmer, are you willing to debate that point with the dark brothers?"

"Let them come," Halmer said bravely, but Tomas who could read his brother like a book, knew that Halmer was putting on a front. The way his fiddling with the ring increasing, showing just how worried he actually was.

Tomas might have said more, but at that very moment a knock came on the chamber door.

"Who is it?" Tomas asked, his hand moving to the hilt of his short sword.

"I am sorry to bother you my lord," came a familiar voice of Tomas servant.

"Yes Robert what is it?" aside to a pale Halmer. "It is Robert my servant."

"My lord, there is a man here saying that he has a message to give you personally."

"That might be the Silverbrows response," Tomas muttered to himself. "Very well Robert, I will be with you in a minute."

Tomas turned to Halmer and saw him slipping the ring back inside his shirt.

"Stay here brother and listen, I may need your opinion."

Halmer did not reply, but nodded as Tomas rose from the bed and striding to the door he left the sleeping sell and entered his dining room to find Robert standing by the side of a short but muscular man. Who was swathed in a great brown cloak, its hood frown back to reveal the man's dark black hair and the black eye that now regarded Tomas closely. This youth who Tomas had never seen before, regarded him with only one eye as the left was covered by a black leather eyepatch.

"You have a message for me?"

"Yes my lord," said the messenger, in a husky whisper. "I was bid by my mistress, to place it in your hand alone."

Tomas nodded, in approval of the secrecy and held out his hand. Into which the youth placed a sealed scroll. Tomas took it to where a candle burnt and studied the scroll. Seeing that it was closed with Bright Eyes' seal of a half female, half wolf mask that was her personal seal. Tomas broke the seal and unrolling the scroll, at first saw nothing, for the scroll was blank.

"This is blank," he growled, looking up at the youth for explanations.

But it was Robert who supplied the answer.

"My lord the scroll!"

When Tomas looked back at the scroll, it was to see that small precise writing was slowly appearing on the scroll, as if an invisible hand and quill were writing the message even as Tomas watched.

"Lord Tomas, I and my Grandfather Tristen Silverbrow send our regards and confirm that Darkling numbers have increased. My grandfather, sends his reassurance that if you need his help he will give it. You have but to ask. If you are concerned about this message falling into the wrong hands, I tell you that a spell lies on this parchment that means that only you can read this scroll. With hope that you are well Bright Eyes Silverbrow."

"Wait here a moment," Tomas said, as he turned and re-entered his bedroom and showed the scroll to Halmer. "Can you read it?"

Halmer took the scroll and looking at it shook his head.

"I can read it, but it makes no sense, the letters are jumbled and some of them look like no letter I've ever seen."

"I will explain later," Tomas said, and returned to the dining room where the messenger was still standing silently beside Robert. "If you wait a moment I will give you a response."

As Tomas sat at the table and scribbled a note, he was still aware of the messenger's eye upon him. After sealing the letter with his signet ring, Tomas looked up to find the messenger's eye no longer fixed upon him, but fixed on the ajar bedroom door.

"Take this and place it in ambassador Silverbrow's hand."

"I will my lord, but I will have to tell her that our conversation was observed by a third party."

Tomas growled and Halmer's voice hissed from behind the door.

"Come out, Halmer," Tomas growled, as he slapped the scroll into the messenger's hand.

Halmer emerged from the bedroom and strode up to stand beside Tomas chair.

"This is my brother Halmer," Tomas said, to the messenger, who bowed at Halmer.

"I am pleased to meet you my lord," whispered the messenger. "I am Cole."

"You are a Wereding?" Halmer asked, as he stared at the man his eyes seeming to search for any animal signs.

"Halmer!" Tomas snapped, "Have some manners will you."

"It is fine my lord," Cole said, as he slid the scroll into an inner pocket of his cloak. "I am and I am not."

"Cryptic."

"I am what your people call a Wolfblood. I have Werewolf blood in my veins, but not enough to make the change."

"Then do you know anything about magic?"

Tomas opened his mouth to object, but he stopped himself when he saw that Robert had left the room and could not overhear them. He trusted his servant not to betray his conversations, but the less the man knew the less Tomas would worry for his safety.

"I have seen magic cast, but I have non myself."

"Do you recognise this?"

As Halmer asked, he held up the ring on its cord. Cole did not leave his side of the table, but he looked closely at the dark ring and its dark blue stone.

"It looks like a ring my Lord Tigress wears," Cole said, after a long hesitation.

"Are you sure?"

"To be honest my lord I am not," Cole said, as he turned to go. "You might be better consulting Tigress, he would know better than I."

40

"I will come with you now then," Halmer began to say an eager light in his eye.

"No Halmer," Tomas snapped, his hand shooting out and gripping his smaller brother's arm. "If you go with this man now people might notice and we are trying to keep this as low a profile as possible. If you must speak to this Tigress you will have to go later."

"When no one can see me you mean," Halmer snarled.

"That might be best my lord Halmer," Cole added from the door. "It would be best if I warned my lord Tigress of your interest."

"Very well, then would you please ask him to expect me at nightfall?"

Cole did not reply, but his cloak rustled as he disappeared through the door.

"That's a strange one," Tomas muttered.

"Oh I don't know, I think I like him."

ROBIN'S REVELATIONS

"To realise that you have found your lover, is a revelation that can make your world heaven!"
Eloo to the Red Wizard, The Wereding Chronicles.

R obin found that Imp and the handful of servants that made up her family's household, had put on a good spread for the handful of guests that had followed the procession from the temple to the estate. These guests congregated in the grant dining room that her father had held large family or was that clan banquets, though now Robin thought about it, she could not remember who had attended those feasts. She looked around at the many strangers that now filled this large room. At her left hand stood Garm an overflowing tankard in one hand and a trencher of stewed pork in the other. On her other side there stood her nearest relation, Ant Isabell a tiny woman who must be in her seventies. But as Robin looked about her at the dark clothes and in a few cases bright jewels she realised that she was looking for someone who wasn't there. Was that person Rose or Luna, Robin couldn't make up her mind. What was she thinking? It was Rose she wanted to see wasn't it? Robin shook her head, unable to shake free of the fog that seemed to fill her head. As she did she did not realise that she was clutching her dagger's hilt.

She was just about to ask Garm if he had seen Luna, when a flash of bright red appeared at the corner of her vision and looking in that direction she saw that Luna had just slipped into the room and was looking about her. Robin was surprised to feel her heart quicken with excitement, at the appearance of the red haired woman. Robin felt a sudden need to be with this woman, who she hardly knew. Why did she feel this way? Could she be falling in love? No that couldn't be, she couldn't be falling in love with a woman could she? It was true that she had never found men particularly attractive, but did that mean that she loved women? She was distracted from this strange thought by Imp offering her a platter of crab pie. Robin refused

42

the food and excusing herself from Garm and her Ant, she moved through the room her destination the red haired woman at the other end of the chamber.

Luna saw her coming and Robin's heart leapt, when Luna smiled at her.

"I'm pleased to see you haven't left yet," Robin said, when she reached the short lady.

"I wouldn't leave without saying goodbye," The short, slender woman said, in her deep almost masculine voice. "But I would like to speak with you Robin."

"Please speak," Robin said, frilled that the woman wanted to talk to her.

Luna glanced about her, as if checking who was within hearing distance.

"I would prefer to talk to you in private," Luna said, in a low whisper, as she dropped her voice. "Is there somewhere we can go that is more private?"

Robin felt a frill of pleasure, at the thought of being alone with this woman, who seemed to be surrounded by a perfume that intoxicated Robin.

"We could go to my father's study," Robin said, after a moment's pause, and she did not realise that the mention of her father did not raise a pang of grief for she was too entranced by Luna to notice this.

"That would be fine," Luna whispered, and taking hold of Robin's wrist guided her from the room.

Robin felt an almost electric frill pass through her, at the smaller woman's touch and the perfume that surrounded her seemed to increase. It was because, of this charming sent that it took Robin a moment to realise that it was Luna who was guiding Robin and not the other way around.

"How many times have you been to our house?"

"Many times," Luna said, as she pulled open the door to her father's study and glancing inside entered pulling Robin in behind her.

"Then why is it that I can't remember you?"

"Because, I always came in secret," Luna said, as she looked around the small room with its floor to ceiling book filled shelves. "I think I have seen you and your sister a handful of times."

"But why?"

"As to that it must wait Robin, there are more important matters for us to debate, such as your sister."

"Rose! What about her? Do you know where she is?"

Luna held up a slender hand, to stop the flow of questions.

"Please Robin wait, I haven't much time."

Robin was suddenly filled with a feeling of loss, that was almost a physical pain.

"You're leaving? Where?"

"I have to investigate a rumour," Luna said, her eyes closely watching Robin's face. "A rumour that your sister is in the North."

Robin's heart went still and a shiver went up her spine at that idea.

"The North, you mean the Weredings' lands?"

"I believe so," Luna said, her voice and face grim. "If I am right, your sister followed one of the worst Weredings that lives, through a portal that led into Mercia and the Wereding woods."

Robin felt her eyes misting, as tears gathered at their edges.

"Rose," she breathed, as fear filled her heart.

Luna, who had been watching her from across the room, was suddenly by her side and to Robin's delight her arms slipped round the taller girl's waist and a soft kiss brushed Robin's throat. A kiss that seemed to fuel a fire that suddenly flared up in Robin, a fire of lust? A fire that might eclipse her fears for Rose, if Luna had not spoken.

"Don't worry about your sister Robin, as I say it is only a rumour that I have heard. It may not be true, but I have to check it out for your sakes."

"But why would you go to so much trouble, on my and Roses account?"

Luna smiled back up at the taller woman, her smile crooked and mysterious as if only she knew the answer to some secret joke.

"Because, I promised your father a long time ago that I would watch over you and that is only the first reason," Luna said, her look locking with Robin's as if she would convey that there were other reasons that she would not put into words.

"Thank you," Robin stammered, as she felt herself blushing, as she felt the lust for this woman and was embarrassed by it.

Luna grinned at Robin, her smile suddenly mischievous and she might have said more, if the study door had not creaked open at that moment and Imp's dark head had not peeked around it.

"My lady your Ant is asking for you."

"Alright Imp I'm coming," Robin said, almost snapping as she felt that the servant had interrupted something important here.

When she turned back to Luna the girl had disappeared into thin air, leaving Robin wondering how the girl had vanished for there was only one door out of the library. Still, how the woman had gone was not as galling as the realisation that she had gone. This realisation made Robin feel bereft of a new, but precious friend and perhaps more than a friend. Still, Luna's absence might also allow Robin the distance to sort out her feelings. Her feelings, which at the moment felt to Robin like a whirlwind of lust, confusion, fear and need to see Rose.

"Return soon and bring Rose with you," Robin breathed and turning returned to the wake.

PLUCKING THE ROSE

"Roses are beautiful, but you must never forget that they too have thorns!"
Kye to Lightning, The Wereding Chronicles.

In the Tower of the Glove, Bright Eyes was bending low over her scrying bowl. Her yellow eyes only inches from the water, as she watched the dark waters swirl and form into a face almost identical to her own.

"Bright Eyes is that you?" asked her sister.

"Yes Silver Skin, can you not see me?"

Silver Skin was an almost twin of Bright Eyes, but her mane was an almost complete sheet of silver hair save for the dark braid that was slung across her right shoulder.

"There seems to be some interference," Silver Skin said, her voice and face shimmering and flickering before the Druidess eyes.

"I have news of the Canduss girl."

"Good Kye will be pleased."

"Not when he hears what I have to say."

"Then speak dear sister."

"At the father's wake the Black Queen was present and the girl was comforted by Luna."

"That will not please Kye," Silver Skin said, as she looked back at her sister with their similar yellow eyes. "Then is Luna stalking the girl?"

"We believe so."

"That is not good."

"Do you want us to take any action sister?"

"I don't know about that Eyes! I will have to consult with Kye and perhaps Great Mother before we act."

"Can the girl Rose give us no idea why Kain is after them?"

"She can answer nothing at the moment, she is in a magical coma recovering from the poison on Kain's blade. Though no doubt Kye and Eloo will ask her once she recovers."

"Then I will have to wait won't I."

"You may have to be patient my sister, the girl could be out for days yet."

"I will be patient Silver, but the Crimson Circle may not."

"What of the dark brotherhood?"

"I have no proof Silver, but I suspect that we may have to close this embassy soon."

"By the Goddess I hope not!"

"As do I, but we are prepared for the worst. Please let me know once you hear anything from Kye."

"You will be the first to know Bright."

"Then till the moon rises."

"The moon rises," Silver Skin replied, as her blurred image faded from the mirror.

"Silver Skin?" asked Tigress from the studies door.

"Yes," Bright Eyes said, not turning to face him, but staring at the still but blank mirror. "But I could not see her clearly, as though something was blocking us."

"The moon is only just beginning to wax," Kit's hoarse voice, croaked from behind him.

"You could have a point Kit," Bright Eyes said, softly.

"But you don't think so," Tigress was making a statement rather than asking a question.

"I think that the net may be closing about us," Bright Eyes said, after a long pause as she turned towards her two companions. "I think that we should summon the nations in the city to gather and that we should mount a watch from now on."

Tigress and Kit exchanged looks and Bright Eyes saw that they were communicating with that almost telepathic communication that existed between lovers.

"Eyes what makes you fear an attack, have you seen something we have not?"

"No Tigress, Kye is the seer of the family, but I still have my danger sense and it is telling me that I am being hunted even if I have run to ground."

In another tower, Luna hunched over her own scrying mirror. Her dark green eyes focused on a shrouded figure hanging in a hammock.

"So Kain was at least right about Rose being infected by his poisoned blade, but is she dying or recovering?"

Even as Luna watched, a tall figure appeared and leaned over the red haired girl and laid a hand on her forehead.

"Kye!" Luna hissed, with the venom of a spitting cat.

As if Kye heard his own name, he looked up at Luna, his feral yellow eyes meting Luna's and she reeled back from that penetrating gaze. As she did, the image in the mirror shattered as if an invisible stone had been cast into the water.

"Curse you Kye for a meddling Werewolf," Luna spat at the rippling water. "Still I have what I wanted, Rose is wounded and in the hands of Kye's people. If I pitch right I can achieve my goal. Robin will be mine."

PLAYING WITH MAGIC

"Magic is not a toy, it is not to be played with."
Bright Eyes to Halmer from Bright Eyes' journal.

Halmer waited in the hallway of the Tower of the Glove and like his brother before him was, drawn to the two staves on display. He stared at them and paid particular attention to the runes picked out in silver on the black staff. Before he knew what he was doing, he had turned the small key in the cases door and had opened the case and was reaching inside to take the staff, but as his hand reached for the staff it met an invisible barrier. As smooth and shiny as glass, but he couldn't see it.

"You can't remove them, unless you know the correct word," came a deep booming voice from behind Halmer.

The little man jumped and turning found a tall, broad, blond man towering over him.

"I didn't mean to take them, I just wanted to look more closely at the Runes," Halmer explained. "Tigress, I presume!"

Tigress nodded and after a searching look, he reached past the little man and with a whispered word removed the staff from the case. He then held it in front of Halmer.

"Is that better?"

Halmer stared at the staff, which to his eye seemed to be made of darkness made solid, as if the stave was a darkness made solid that drew light into itself. It made him think that Tigress had plucked a piece of the nights sky from the heavens and crafted it into a stave. A thought that was strengthened by the bright runes that stood out like stars against the night sky of the staff.

Halmer reached out with a finger and traced one of the runes. Then he drew from its place under his shirt, the ring, he had recovered and holding it up beside the staff compared the runes on the staff with one carved into the ring.

"As I thought, they match," Halmer said, excitedly.

"Yes they match," Tigress admitted, as he replaced the staff in the case. "But do you know what they mean, is the question."

Halmer's fallen face, gave Tigress his answer. The big man laughed and clapped Halmer on the shoulder, a blow that nearly knocked the smaller man off his feet.

"Don't look so sad little man, I will give you the answer to the question, once you answer a few of mine."

"What questions?"

"Like where you got the ring in the first place?"

"I found it in some ruins in the no-man's-land between our north wall and yours."

"The lands south of the Kings?" Tigress asked, as he led Halmer up the stairs and to the small lounge that they had entertained Tomas Healm in.

"Yes, there are many ruins there from the time of the great burn. I have found several artefacts there in the past."

"But those are dangerous lands," Tigress said, as he poured Halmer some mulled wine.

"I have never had any trouble."

"Then you are very lucky."

"Perhaps, but you told me you would tell me what the rune meant?"

Tigress nodded and handed Halmer the wine. As he did Halmer caught his broad hand and looked closely at the ring on his middle finger.

"It is the same as the one I found," he said, as he released the hand and sipped the wine.

"No, not the same, but it is a brother to mine in that is of the same nature of ring."

"What do you mean?"

"They are both rings of air," Tigress said, as he blew on the ring and as he did, the large blue stone began to glow with a bright blue light.

"What is that?"

"My ring is charged and primed for air magic, the magic of the mind. I have just given it a little more energy."

Halmer pulled the ring out from his shirt and holding it before his face, he blew upon the stone and his face lit up as it was lit by a soft blue glow from the heart of the stone.

"Does that mean that this ring now has magic within it?"

"Possibly, let's see," Tigress said, as he closed his eyes and drew a medallion from beneath his own shirt and Halmer watched with wide eyes, as the crystal within the medallion glowed brightly as Tigress began to chant. His ring blowing brightly too, as the hand upon which it sat weaved an intricate pattern through the air.

As Halmer watched, he thought he saw Tigress's face shimmer as if he were seeing it through a heat haze, but he was not sure of this. What he was sure of was that Tigress' eyes changing from their dark green to a glowing blue that were the same shade as the light glowing from the ring and the medallion. Tigress' glowing eyes swept over Halmer and came to rest upon the ring that Halmer was holding up before him. The glow lasted for a moment and then they all blinked out though the glow still seemed to remain in his eyes.

"What magic was that?" Halmer asked, in a breathless voice, for it was the first magic he had ever seen and it had as he had always hoped left him feeling changed and delighted.

"A tiring one," Tigress sighed, as he drank deeply of his wine. "Let this be your first lesson in magic my lord. Magic is not a toy, it is dangerous to the user as much as an enemy."

"Is all magic so draining?"

"Some magic is more so than others," Tigress admitted, as he put the wine cup to one side. "But all magic's draw upon the casters own store of energies. That is why it is easier to draw upon reserves of stored magic."

"The ring and medallion?"

"You catch on fast young Halmer."

"The magic you cast it allowed you to detect magic?"

"Correct."

"So is the ring magical?"

"It is and it has a spark of magic energies stored within it, but its reserves are all but drained, you must refill it if you wish it to serve you."

"And I do that by breathing on it?"

"That Is one way," Tigress agreed, "There are other ways."

"And if I do refill the stone, what can I do with it?"

"Many things," Tigress said, as he gave Halmer a long searching look. "You can if you learn the magic, protect yourself from lightning, cast lightning fly and even hide your appearance."

These words made Halmer make a leap of logic and guess that what he had seen was not a shifting of light or an imagination, but a slipping of a mask.

"As you are now masked?"

Tigress looked at Halmer long and hard and for a long time Halmer thought that the Wereding would attack him or order him to leave, but after a long stare Tigress flung back his head and roared with laughter.

"Well you are a clever one aren't you," he finally managed to splutter. "I think you will go far."

Halmer watched as Tigress spoke a word and wiped his face with the back of his hand. When his hand had travelled from brow to chin, the blond man was gone and a different face was in its place. Halmer sat open mouthed, as he stared at the black and white stripes of Tigress' mane. The long twitching cat's whiskers and most startling to the young man, the Wereding's glowing green eyes.

"What's wrong my lord, does my true face offend you?" Tigress asked, though there was no anger in his voice. Halmer realised that even the Wereding's voice had changed, deepening and becoming more like the growl of a big jungle cat. "I can put the mask back if you like?"

"No," Halmer squeaked, finally finding his voice. "No, this face is fine, if it is your true one."

"It is," Tigress purred, as he leaned forwards so that Halmer could get a good look at him.

"Do you always wear a mask when you meet guests?"

"If I am meeting them for the first time," Tigress admitted. "I am not happy with the deceit, but I have found that it is easier if people do not see this face until they have got to know me."

"I see, then you wore this mask for Tomas?"

"Yes, your brother does not know this and I would be grateful if you did not undeceive him yet. Just as I would be grateful if everything we had said and even the fact that we have met a secret between us."

"As you wish, but Tomas knows, is that a problem?"

"Your brother knows that we have met, he does not yet know what we said and unless you tell him he will never know."

"He is my brother I trust him."

"If I read your brother aright, he will not question you too closely for he does not wish to know what you do here. Still if he insists on knowing tell him that you have given your word not to reveal our secrets. He will not ask any more after that."

"I do give my word, not to share what you tell me."

Tigress smiled broadly, but a dangerous glint entered his green eyes.

"I knew that you would so swear, but I am afraid that I must insist that you make a binding oath on this."

"More magic?"

"A binding spell that will bind your tongue," Tigress said, as he watched Halmer closely. "If you do not agree, I am afraid that we will not be able to meet again and I can teach you no more magic. Do you agree?"

"I do agree, I think it unnecessary, but I agree to take whatever vow you wish."

"Very well move to the fire."

Halmer rose and approached the fireplace, where a fire of pine wood was still giving off its fragrant scent even as the fire died in the grate. Tigress dropped a new log on the embers and with a snap and crack of flames, the fire flared up filling the room with dancing flames that cast strange shadows on Tigress' square face and strange lights flickered back from his glowing eyes. Tigress tossed leaves onto the fire and a smoke curled forth wrapping around the two men like a binding mist.

"Give me your hand," Tigress said, in a voice that sounded like it was coming from the mouth of a huge cat.

Halmer held out his hand and the two men clasped hands, not at the forearms like brothers but palm to palm as if they were to shake hands. As they did, Tigress spoke a word and Halmer felt an electric shock pass from the larger man's hand. The shock however, was not too painful and Halmer did not let go.

"Whatever happens do not let go of my hand until I tell you to," Advised Tigress, his voice seeming to come to Halmer from a great distance out of the fog like smoke and it was surrounded by the echoes of animalistic snarling.

Halmer wanted to ask Tigress why he mustn't let go and what might happen, but he did not need to for he understood on an unconscious level that if he let go he would forfeit the oath and that he would be tested. An idea that was confirmed in the next breath, for he was no longer holding the hand of a large cat man, but the forepaw of a great tiger that looked down at him with wild eyes its great jaws painted scarlet with the blood of its last kill. Its huge voice roaring like a thunder clap in the rooms small space. The Tiger roared and lashed its tail and Halmer wanted to leap back and run from the room, but he also knew that the limb he clutched was still Tigress' hand he could sense it in his mind and so he was relieved when the mask of a cat seemed to fold back like a cloaks cowl to reveal Tigress' smiling face. Tigress lifted his ringed hand and spoke a long stream of words in the ancient language that Halmer had read but never heard spoken. Once the litany was complete, Tigress spoke to him in his own tongue.

"Halmer Healm repeat what you have learnt."

Halmer opened his mouth to speak, but could not speak.

"Speak," commanded Tigress in a thunderous voice.

Halmer tried to speak, but could only shake his head. Seeming pleased with this result, Tigress spoke more words and then addressed Halmer in his own tongue.

"Halmer Healm, do you pledge to repeat nothing of what I teach you to anyone, unless I give you permission?"

"I so pledge," Halmer heard himself say.

"Then be warned, you are bound by this oath. If you break this vow, you will forget all my lessons do you understand and agree to this pledge."

"I agree." Halmer heard himself say, in a voice that sounded to his own ears as if the voice that spoke was far away.

Only once Halmer had agreed did Tigress release his grip of Halmer's hand.

"Come my friend let us drink to your success," Tigress said, as he wafted away the coils of smoke that hung about them and striding to the sideboard poured them more wine.

Halmer stared at the back of his hand, to see that a dark rune had appeared there and turning over his hand saw a similar rune branded on the palm.

"Here drink," Tigress said, holding out the cup to him.

"Tigress, what is this?" Halmer asked, holding out his branded hand to the Wereding.

"That is the physical representation of the magic bond between us," Tigress said carelessly, as he sipped his wine.

"But won't people notice this?"

"No because, the brand will fade quickly and then only we two will be able to see it. Now drink."

"To hell with the drink I want to learn, what can you teach me?"

"Well a little patience, wouldn't go a miss," Tigress said, gently mocking his young student. "You have enough for now, drink and go home, you have the ring I'll give you a scroll of some simple spells and you will be able to practice between now and our next session. Though, if you are going to practice magic I suggest that you find somewhere isolated to practice. As you no doubt know it is a hanging offence to be found practicing magic, so I recommend caution."

HOUSE KEEPING

"You can put a thing off as much as you want, but putting it off doesn't get it done."
Eloo to the Red Wizard The Wereding Chronicles.

Robin was woken by Imp, with a cup of tea and as she adjusted to the light coming through her window and looked around her she realised that she was in her own bed in her own room at the Canduss house. As she realised this, the last few days came back to her and she had to fight to keep her emotions under control. She was distracted from this wave of grief, by Imp's words.

"My Lady, Garm and Scholar Vyman wish to break their fast with you."

"Garm and Scholar Vyman?" Robin asked, not quite understanding what Imp was telling her.

The master of the household guard and the Scholar, had been wont to meet with her father early in the morning, but she had rarely eaten with them at this hour.

"Why Imp?"

"My Lady?"

"Why do they want to meet me?"

"I'm afraid I don't know my Lady."

"Then guess," Robin ordered.

"Then if I was to guess," the tiny woman said, hesitantly. "I would guess, that they wish to go over the estates with you."

That answer, filled Robin with a mixture of fear and trepidation. She had little to do with the running of the estates and did not have the first idea, how to manage their large household.

"But I know nothing about running this house," she all but cried.

"But my Lady that is what Garm and the Scholar are for. I am sure that you will be fine," soothed the tiny maid.

Robin closed her eyes and took a long deep breath, when she opened her eyes she felt much calmer.

"What do you wish to dress in my lady?"

"The clothes I wore yesterday, will do fine."

"As you wish my lady," Imp said, primly and Robin could tell that the maid was not pleased.

But Robin did at this moment not care, she liked the dark clothes that Luna had provided her. As she dressed, she picked up the large dagger and once more considered the large ruby that decorated the pummel of the hilt. As she stared into the heart of the gem, she thought she saw sparks of light dancing in glittering patterns and once more she felt her attention being drawn into the heart of the stone. She might have been held entranced like this for hours, if Imp had not broken her spell bound trance.

"My Lady, Garm and the Scholar are waiting for you," the servant suggested gently.

Robin grunted and strapping it to her belt, she followed the tiny woman to the dining room. Where the large table that had been used the day before, had been moved back against the wall and Robin found the large old worrier and the tall but thin figure of the Scholar sat around a small table, set for breakfast. When Robin sat she found that despite the table being round, she was still sat opposite the two men.

"My Lady, I hope you slept well?" Piped the high voice of the young man that sat swathed in white robes, to Robin's right.

Robin who had slept badly, her dreams filled with fleeting images of demons with Luna's and Rose's faces, nodded and thanked the Scholar for enquiring.

"Milk my lady?" Garm asked, lifting an earthenware jug. "Or if it please you, I can ask for some wine to be brought."

"No Garm, milk is fine," Robin answered him, as she lifted her cup to meet the lip of the jug.

Robin gratefully sipped the chilled milk and regarded the two men over the cups rim. The two men seemed hesitant, as if they did not quite know how to handle this woman. Which surprised Robin, after all she had known Garm for years and Vyman though he had only been with them for the last year or so, was a man that she had grown to like.

"Porridge my Lady," Imp asked, as she placed the bowl on the table before Robin.

"Thank you Imp," Robin said, as the servant spooned out the

thick liquid into her bole.

"Porridge is so nicer with honey, don't you think my lady?" The Scholar asked, as he sipped daintily at his spoon.

"Especially when you know that the honey and oats come from your own land," the grey worrier said, as he shovelled great spoonfuls into his mouth.

This comment seemed to agitate the Scholar, even more than usual.

"Scholar Vyman Garm not that I don't appreciate small talk, but I doubt you summoned me to talk about porridge and honey."

Her words made Garm snort and lay down his spoon.

"Like your father, to the point," the big man said, as he wiped some spilt porridge from his beard.

"So will you come to it please," Robin said, looking down at the bowl was surprised to find it empty.

"Eggs, bacon my lady?"

Robin nodded to Imp, but her eyes were now fixed on Garm.

"My Lady, the point is that you have an estate before you," Garm said, as he used a dagger to cut his bacon.

"Estate, what estate?" Robin asked, cutting at her bacon, though she was more interested in the large man's words than what was on her plate.

"Perhaps we should discuss this after we have eaten," interjected Vyman.

"Very well," Robin agreed, though she would rather know now, but she remembered her courtesies and turned her attention to her plate.

Once they had finished the bacon, eggs and mushrooms and were turning to the toast and honey, that Robin could hold her tongue no longer.

"So will one of you tell me, what all this is about?"

"My Lady," Vyman said, over his cup of tea. "Your father left his wishes with us; you are to inherit this house and its estates."

"What estates? I know we have the small would at the north end of the land, but you make it sound as if I have a farm. . ."

"Well actually you own about three farms," Garm cut in.

"Three farms, but I thought we were a small house!"

Garm and Vyman exchanged a look and the large man shrugged,

clearly reluctant to answer this and leaving the nervous man to answer this point.

"Well as to that," Vyman said, after a long pause. "No the Canduss house is no longer one of the great houses, but you still have enough land and holdings to live comfortably, your father made sure of that."

"And what of Rose, you speak as if I alone inherit this Estate!"

"Rose, well of course you are a joint inheritor with your sister, but a she has disappeared. . ."

"And have you no news of her? Are you doing anything to find her?" Robin suddenly stopped, realising that her voice was steadily rising, as her emotions slowly rose into a rising tide of fear and anger. To try and control herself, Robin got up and paced to the rooms door and back to her chair.

Vyman possibly wisely held his tongue until, Robin had resumed her seat before answering her questions.

"I have asked the General council to watch and listen, for your sister, but no one has heard or seen your sister. Garm has written to his relatives asking too for news, but no unfortunately my lady we have no news of your sister."

"What about Luna's rumour, of her being in the Wereding lands?"

The two men exchanged looks, as if they were trying to guess how Robin might react to their next words.

"Well what is it?"

"My lady we have put this rumour to the Wereding ambassador, but we have heard no reply."

"No news, or no reply?"

"The Tower of the Glove remains silent," Vyman clarified.

For a long time, Robin was silent and still as she digested this information.

"Perhaps I should speak to the ambassador myself," she murmured.

The two men looked very nervous at this suggestion.

"My lady we were discussing your estates," Vyman put in trying to distract Robin and guide her back to a subject that he clearly felt more comfortable with.

"Scholar Vyman, am I right in thinking that you and Garm are the managers of this estate?"

"You are quite correct my lady," confirmed the big man at arms.

"Then unless you have any objections, I will leave it in your capable hands and will get on with finding my sister!"

The two men squirmed, under Robin's suddenly steely gaze. Her voice, suddenly as hard and unyielding as the dagger that was suddenly in her hand.

"As you wish my lady," Vyman said, meekly as he eyed the dagger. "But if you are set on contacting the Weredings perhaps it might be better to wait for Luna's return. . ."

"I can't wait that long!" Robin all but screamed, her frustration and fear building to dangerous levels.

But the Scholar put his hand up to stop her protest.

"I was going to say, that in the mean time you could consult Scholar Galmor."

That took Robin aback, Galmor had been the Scholar before Vyman, but the old man had retired and Vyman had taken over his duties.

"I thought that he had returned to the College," Robin said, her voice lower and seemingly more in control.

"He retired yes, but he was given a small cottage on your father's estates in gratitude for his many years of service," Garm said, gruffly.

"But why would he be best to ask about the Weredings?"

Vyman turned away from them, as if he were looking to someone who was not present, or was trying to make up his mind as to what to tell them. When he turned back to them, he was wearing a grim expression.

"My lady I cannot answer that question, you must ask him that question yourself, but please take my word that he will be able to help you with this matter."

Robin considered that and nodded, in assent and for the first time seemed to notice the dagger in her hand. What was she doing with it? She went to replace it in its sheaf, but instead she placed it on the table in front of her where she could inspect the fiery jewel in its hilt.

"My lady," Garm asked, as he watched her staring at the dark stone. "Is there anything you wish of us?"

Robin finally tor her eyes from the stone, to meet Garm's eyes.

"No thank you Garm, but please tell me if you hear anything."

"As you wish my lady," said the big man, who stood and marched out of the room.

Vyman too rose, but seemed to hesitate as if he would say more, but when Robin seemed not to be aware of him he to left Robin staring at the ruby.

Robin's eyes were fixed on the firefly flecks of light that seemed to dance intricate patterns within the jewel's heart, but her mind's eye conjured a very different set of images. Robin did not know if it was Vyman mentioning her name or if she really did have her on the mind, but she was obsessed with the image of Luna who paraded before Robin practically naked, flimsy cloaks and scarves placed tantalisingly over the small woman's charms. Robin felt a deep heat starting inside her and she had to make a great effort to come back to herself and clear her mind of the erotic images that had possessed her imagination. Without thinking about it she swept the knife from the table and as the connection with the dark heart broke, she found herself with one hand thrust between her legs and she shuddered with horror and embarrassment at the thought of Imp or one of the other servants discovering her like this. She was frightened to find herself like this and she decided that she had to take her mind off this and do something. She did not however, regret the images as she bent and retrieved the dagger, for they were she realised were exactly how she wanted to see Luna. See her and what's more get her hands on her body. A thought that stirred up more of the dark lustful thoughts and without a second look at the blade, she shoved it into it scabbard and rushed from the dining room, to see if she could find out where the old Scholar lived and discover if he had any answers for her.

Robin found Scholar Vyman in her father's study, where the thin man was studying an ancient map in a book that must have been two inches thick, the parchment yellow with age.

"My lady, how can I help you?"

"You neglected to tell me, where your predecessor now lives Vyman."

The spare man blushed and bowed his head.

"I am sorry my lady, he lives in a cottage on the other side of your long wood."

"Among the tithe village?"

"Yes my lady."

"I thought that the game keeper lived there?"

"Parker does live there, along with his daughters and several other members of your household, but Scholar Galmor lives in a cottage apart from the other houses where he still carries out certain work. His is the first cottage you come too from this side of the woods and it is further within the boundries of the wood itself. It is a large cottage, you can't miss it my lady."

"Thank you Vyman. What is this?" Robin asked, her attention momentarily drawn to the map laid out before her.

"One of your father's collection," Vyman said, as he pointed to the fading lines of the map that outlined the land she was familiar with, but within the lines of the kingdom everything was different, all the rivers had different names and followed different beds. Even the towns were different and hills and mountains were in different places.

"This map is all wrong."

"It is different my lady, but not wrong. This is a map of Britaina before the great burning."

"Is it?" Robin's interest suddenly shifting, from the map and back to her pursuit of the old man who had been her father's Scholar. "Thank you Scholar Vyman, I will seek your predecessor."

Vyman watched, as Robin turned and swept out of the room. The tall thin man shook his head, he could sense that something had changed in Robin, but he could not put his finger on it and he was not yet sure if it was change for the better or not. He would have to wait and watch, but for now he turned his attention back to the map.

Robin strode through the oaks and ashes, of her father's long wood. The long narrow strip of woods that was her family's hunting preserve. Her long strides, carried her through woods that she had played among as a young girl. She knew the narrow tracks that thread the woods like the back of her hand. So she let her legs remember the way for her, while her mind tried to search through the many questions that were buzzing around her mind. Where was her sister, was she alright or in trouble and had she killed the strange black clad assassin? Robin came from under the trees boughs to find a small clearing, brilliantly and beautifully lit by sun light. For a moment Robin was dazzled and she stopped to look about her. She was in a clearing that she knew, but she had been miles away and so had not expected to find it so quickly. Robin despite her need to be with the Scholar paused for a moment, to take in the delight of the sun's warmth. For a long moment she just stood there, listening to the sounds of the wood. Near at hand came the cough of a pheasant, while deeper into the woods came the beckoning tap of a woodpecker. Familiar sounds, calming sounds that centred her and made her feel at home. Then once she felt at peace with the world, the world changed. The sun moved behind a cloud and Robin felt the warmth disappear, making her open her eyes and she glanced about her, as if reaching for a source for the shadow.

As she slowly looked around her, she felt eyes upon her. She instinctively drew her dagger and dropped into a crouch, as she scanned about for a threat. She relaxed, as she found her watcher. From a nearby branch, a great hawk watched her with its predator's eyes. Robin stared back expecting the bird to fly away, but for a long moment it just perched there staring back. Then it opened its great hook of a beak and filled the clearing with a cry of rage and then it leapt into the air and was spiralling its way into the higher airs.

"Wings now they would be a real gift," Robin muttered, as she watched the hawk become a dot against the blue canvas.

Robin looked down at the dagger in her hand and the red stone in its hilt seemed to blaze up, as if a fire had been lit inside it. Robin looked around her and suddenly felt the presence of Luna and as if the woman was in the clearing with her, Robin could suddenly smell the alluring sent that had surrounded her the last time she had seen Luna. Robin though she could not say how she knew, new that Luna had been in this clearing and not too long ago.

"Luna?" Robin heard herself whisper, and as if her voice was a shout, it shattered the silence that had fallen over the clearing and the sun was suddenly cut off by a cloud and the stone's fire was quenched. With the dimming of that fire, went the illusion of Luna's presence.

Robin shook her head and sheathing the dagger, reminded herself that she was not sightseeing. She had a purpose and that was to find the old man that had been her father's advisor.

Robin found the cottage exactly where Vyman said it would be, a large wattle and doab cottage in a broad clearing just within the woods borders. The dark building, surrounded by well-tended herb and vegetable plots and as she approached Robin noticed a thin curl of smoke snake its way up from a chimney. As she approached the property, a great raven came flapping round the corner and landed on the gravel path at Robin's feet. Robin looked down at it and the large bird cocked its head and looked back at her, with one of its dark beady eyes.

"Friend?" croaked the raven, surprising Robin with the question. She had heard that ravens could speak, but had never actually heard one.

"Yes I am a friend," Robin whispered, back to the bird. "Where is the scholar do you know?"

"Hello," came a dry, papery voice from inside the cottage and as Robin picked her way round the raven, the small wooden door creaked open and a familiar though long unseen face squinted out at her.

"Scholar Galmor, it has been a long time," Robin said, to the man that she had not seen in at least twelve months.

"My Lady Robin," wheezed the old man, as he recognised Robin's voice, his all but blind eyes moving behind heavy lids. "I am pleased to see you! Please come, the kettle has just boiled."

Robin smiled, as she remembered the old man's love of strange flavoured teas.

"Scholar I would have come before, but I did not know that you were here. I thought you had returned to the Scholar's Tower."

"I have retired it is true," wheezed the old man, as he led her into the dim light of the cottage, where his weak eyes could see better. "But by the consent of the council and the grace of your father, I was given this cottage so that I could be close to my grandchildren."

"I didn't even know you had grandchildren," Robin admitted, as she took a low seat on the other side of the small brick fireplace.

"Yes my Lady, Cole and Clover work in the city, but they visit me when they can. But pleased as I am to talk about my family, I think that you did not come to humour an old man. How can I help you?" Galmor asked, as he took a kettle from its hook over the fireplace.

As Robin looked at the small, withered apple of a man in his faded white robes, she wondered why she had come. Surely this ancient man who had grown old in her family's service, could not have the answers she sought on the other hand she did not know where else to turn.

"You have heard about my father?" Robin asked, her voice only slightly quavering.

The old man's face fell and the colourless eyes that squinted at her glistened.

"Yes," he sighed, his voice quavering. "A great loss."

"I did not see you at the funeral," Robin said, voicing a thought that had only just come to her.

"I would have liked to come my lady, but I am all but blind these days unless someone guides me I hardly leave this cottage," explained the old man, in his papery voice. "I went to the mausoleum after the funeral and paid my respects there."

"Then why didn't you come to the wake?"

"I did not wish to impose my lady."

"You would have been no bother and we would have been glad to see you."

"Thank you my lady, but it would have been too painful for me to return to a house that I no longer know."

"I see," Robin said, though in actual fact she did not see, but she did not know what else to say. "If you have heard what happened, then perhaps you know why I am here?"

The old man cocked his head, in a manner that reminded Robin of the raven on his path outside.

"I am sorry my lady, but I do not understand what is it that you think I can help you with?"

"Where has Rose gone? Who was the assassin? And a hundred other questions I have for you Galmor," Robin said, breaking off as she realised that she was spitting her questions at the old man, her frustration leaking through into her voice.

The old man rocked back in his chair, as if he had been knocked back by the slap of her questions. Though his eyes looked upwards, as if he were considering what Robin had said.

"If you forgive me my lady," he said hesitantly, "I have only heard rumours from the rest of your household, but if they tell it aright, you were there and witnessed these events."

"I was," Robin said, the image of her father's face swimming up behind her eyes.

"It would help me, if you told me what you saw."

Robin shuddered, as she realised that she would have to recall all the events of that terrible day. She closed her eyes and began to speak, as she did her voice sounded hard and distant even to her own ears. Eventually she finished and opening her eyes, found the old man was no longer in his seat. He had moved as she spoke and looking around, she saw that he was hunting among his books and scrolls some of which were in a book case others were scattered loos on a table.

"Where is it?" the old man muttered and then pulling down a thick tome, and grunting with satisfaction, he staggered over to her and dropped the great book on a low table between them. He pulled the book open to a much thumbed page and pointed to it with a brown fingernail. "Did your father's assassin look like this?"

The old man was pointing at a once brightly coloured illumination of a figure standing above a slain bear, a long, black sword held high above its wolf helmed head. Though the ink of the painting had faded, the image had captured the darkness of the blade and the metallic helm that had snarled at her father, as its black blade had taken his life.

"That him!" Robin said, after a long time, her voice a hoarse whisper its strength stolen by the astonishment that had stolen her voice. "Who is he?"

"He, she or it, is called Kain," Galmor said, as he stared at the picture before him. "Who he is, is something of a mystery, but what we do know is that he is an assassin for the Weredings. . ."

"Then the Weredings are responsible for my father's murder!" Robin snarled, her hand curling round the hilt of her dagger, as if she meant to draw the blade and cut her father's killers down.

The old man hearing her words, held up a hand to still her.

"My lady I did not mean that!"

"Then what did you mean?"

"What I meant, was that we are told by Scholars that a figure called Kain and baring these tokens of the black blade and the wolf helm is known to be an assassin for the Weredings, but many know this. Since no one has ever seen this Kain's face. One man could imitate him as much as another and besides we know so little about the Weredings that to blame the whole of that nation for the actions of one member is a grave mistake."

"But then who is to blame for his death?" Robin snarled, as she drew the dagger from her belt and strode around the room stabbing its point at the old man to ethicise her points. "I will have blood for

66

my father, Scholar and if the Weredings are responsible, then I will have their blood."

The old man watched her with concern, this aggressive anger was new for Robin. She had been such an intense wilful child it was true. One who would have preferred to be riding or fencing than learning maths or herb law. But this near fury was something new.

"My lady please listen to me," the old man begged in his whisper of a voice.

Robin seemed to hear him and to his relief seemed to gain a measure of self-control. For she sheathed the dagger and returning to the fireside seat, sat on its edge and stared at the old man with an intensity that seemed to burn into him.

"Well?"

"I have studied the Weredings and their twisted politics and I suspect I may be able to help you discover your father's killer, but I will need time to get to the bottom of this matter. Please Robin, do not do anything rash before we know the truth about your father's death."

"How long do you need?"

"A month maybe two."

"A month!"

"My lady I can hardly leave this house without aid," Galmor explained, to an increasingly agitated Robin. "I must wait for word to reach me."

"In the meantime, you expect me to sit on my hands and do nothing?"

"My lady I ask for a month to ask questions, if after that time we do not have the answers then you can do what you like, but please do not let your heart rule your actions, that is the last thing your father would have wanted."

Robin glared at the little man, for a long moment and then she spoke in a steely voice.

"Very well Scholar Galmor you have a month, but if Luna comes back with other news then I cannot speak for my actions."

Robin did not stay to watch the Scholars reaction, but swept from the room and strode back to her house. Galmor stared after Robin a tear glistening in his pale eye.

"Oh Robin what is Luna doing to you?"

As if in answer to his question a light tap came at the cottages door and when the old man looked up it was to see Kit's feather clad form standing before him.

"What does she know?" Kit hissed, her yellow eyes glittering in the rooms dim light.

A DAGGER IN THE DARK

"Sometimes it doesn't matter how many wards and defences you build,
Death still comes calling."
Cole, from Bright Eyes' journal.

Bright Eyes wondered what had woken her; had it been some movement of Cole beside her? She glanced across at where the stocky youth lay beside her, one of his muscular arms draped across her waist. No, she decided it had not been Cole, for she had discovered that once they had finished their love making, he fell into an almost unconscious sleep. A sleep that even now was unbroken, as she gently moved his arm from her and laid it on the bed, as she slid out from under the cotton sheet that covered her bed. Bright Eyes stood and looked about her small cell of a bedroom, searching for the source of the sound that she had heard in her sleep. Suddenly the hairs on her body stood to attention and a low animal growl crawled out her throat, as she realised that the wolf inside her sensed that it was being hunted.

Turning to the chair where her clothes lay, she searched for the narrow belt and the dagger that hung from it. Her hand closed on the hard dagger and even as she did so, she felt more than heard a movement behind her. Swinging round she brought the still sheathed dagger up before her, the leather sheathed blade connecting with something and even as Bright Eyes realised that she had blocked a blade, a tall dark form materialised before her. Before her, a glittering blade seeming to float out of the dark at her. Bright Eyes' wolf eyes could see in all but the deepest darkness and could normally see everything in her room despite the lack of light, but before her was a figure shrouded in a darkness so deep that she could only make out a clot of darkness before her. From which the dagger seemed to leap at her. She drew her own blade and with one hand blocked the blow and with the other she reached for her silver medallion. Even as she did, a hand reached out of the mirk and grasped her wrist. The fingers that held her in an iron grip, were colder than ice.

Bright Eyes gasped in pain, as the grip drew warmth and strength out of her. The blade the shadow was wielding, glinted as it raised it to strike. Even as it made to strike, Bright Eyes' fingers grasped the edge of her silver disk and she barked out a word of power. As she spoke the word, a bright burst of silver light shot from the enchanted medallion and as warmth flowed through her body. The burst of light stabbed into the darkness and as if burning off the shadow, stabbed into the eyes of the dark figure, at the clot's heart. He cried out and releasing her wrist staggered back, his strike falling, but short. Bright Eyes snarled several words and the burst became brighter. The room was filled with the smell of burning flesh, as the shadow figure screamed with pain, as the bright light became a steady beam of silver fire. The light revealed to Bright Eyes the face of her attacker, for the clot of shadow that reeved him had disappeared to reveal a short man in a dark robe. Though his identity would have been difficult to make out, for his face was now a burnt mask of pain. The hooded figure turned away from the burning light that had died to a dim glow, gleaming from her disk.

Bright Eyes, however, was not going to let him get away and even as he stumbled towards the door of her room, she lunged at his back. Her dagger cutting cloth, but the ring of steel told her that her attacker was wearing mail beneath his robe and it had protected him from her blade. However, he got no further, as Cole dove off the bed and flung himself on top of the cloaked figure dragging him to the ground. Bright Eyes heard the two men panting, as they struggled on the ground; she held her medallion high and spoke a word that made the moon disk glow brightly again so that the room was brightly lit. Before her she saw Cole and the hooded attacker grappling with one another, both trying to strangle the other. Bright Eyes' heart was suddenly grasped by a hand of fear, as she watched her new lover fighting for his life. Her paralysis of fear and the attacker's nose was broken, as Cole snapped his head into his combatant's burnt face. The blow driving a scream of agony from the already hurt man. The attacker's grip loosened as he lost concentration and possibly consciousness as Cole intensified his death grip on the man's throat.

Bright Eyes suddenly knew what she had to do. Gripping her pendant, Bright Eyes drew upon her connection to her goddess to draw down power which she translated into a spell by chanting the words she had committed to memory days ago. As she did she reached out with her other hand and laid it upon Cole's back. Her fingers feeling the fur beneath them, as she passed the spell to Cole. As this was done, Cole suddenly found that his strength had suddenly increased incredibly and the figure beneath him squirmed in its death struggles, as Cole felt the man's Adams apple crunch beneath his vice like hands. Suddenly the man's tongue was protruding from its mouth and with a final weak kick the man was still beneath Cole's suddenly drained body.

"Cole are you alright?" Bright Eyes asked, as she gripped his shoulder.

"I could do with a drink!" he croaked hoarsely.

Bright Eyes sobbed with laughter, as she pulled Cole to his feet and locked him in a fierce embrace. That was how Tigress found them, when he burst in a naked blade in hand, a halo of fire flaring around the other.

"Eyes are you alright?" He gasped, as he saw the burnt and blackened body on the ground.

"Thanks to the Goddess and Cole yes."

"Cole are you alright?" Came a whisper, from behind Tigress as Clover appeared peeking under Tigress's arm.

Clover Cole's sister was a dwarf standing only three feet in her slippers. She slid past the tall man to see better, though she stopped in her tracks, when she realised that both her brother and Bright Eyes were naked. Though Cole had at a young age accepted the Wereding way of walking about unclad, Clover had remained modest and was embarrassed at the sight of their nakedness.

"I am fine," Cole croaked.

"But in need of drink," Bright Eyes added.

"I will fetch it," Clover said, averting her eyes and looking at the ground as she spoke.

"Tigress any idea who or what he is?" Bright Eyes asked as she led Cole to the bed and making him sit back down, for she knew he was drained by the after-effects of the magic.

Tigress was searching the attacker's body. He grunted as he found something and standing held it out for the tall Wereding woman to inspect.

"We at least know who sent this assassin," Tigress said, as he pointed at the item Bright Eyes now held.

"The Crimson Circle," Bright Eyes snarled, as she looked down at a dark red metal ring like pendant on the end of a neck chain.

"There is no sign of any other attackers," Kit's voice croaked from outside the cell.

"Then he was a lone assassin," Tigress said, as he kicked the body.

"But how did he get in I felt none of the alarm wards we set go off," Bright Eyes said, as she watched Tigress without really seeing him.

"Mulled wine," whispered Clover, from without the cell.

"Give it to me," Kit said and a second later she handed several glasses to Tigress who handed them round.

"Don't come in Kit," Tigress said, as he looked round him at the tiny cell. "It's too small for more bodies."

"He did not set off the wards because, he did not come in through the gate or over the walls."

"Then how did he get in?"

"He flew in," Kit said, as she stuck her head round the door.

"The tower," Bright Eyes guessed.

"We forgot to ward that." Tigress snarled, striking his forehead with his now flameless hand.

"But how did he fly in?"

"He is not a skin swapper," Tigress said, as he looked at the corpse again. "He is wearing a cloth cloak not a feather one."

"Magic?"

"I am not so sure," Kit said. "There is a slight scratch on the stone and a smell like heated metal and sulphur up there."

"Fire Drake?"

"Perhaps," Bright Eyes said, frowning, "But if that is the case then we and the rest of our people are in very great danger if a Fire Drake is working with the Crimson Circle."

DREAMING WHILE WAKING

"Many dreams may visit you, while you walk under the sun."
The Druid handbook.

Robin slept badly that night and woke wet from a dream of Luna and some kind of huge bath. Robin was surprised to find that she was clutching the dagger. Though it was still in its sheathe and Robin could not work out why she had grabbed it up from where it hung on a belt from the post at the foot of her bed.

"What is happening to me?" Robin asked herself, as she laid the dagger down and striding to her window looked out at the thick mist that had veiled the world from her.

Robin was left feeling that the world had been taken away and that she was cut off from it.

"Rose where are you?"

No answer came of course and with a deep sigh Robin turned from the window and tried to find the answer to her own question. Returning to her bed she sat and staring into mid-air as she tried to work out what had happened to her sister.

Whatever she tried to think about her thoughts always led her back to the Weredings and the fact that she knew absolutely nothing about them. Well that was not entirely true, she had heard her nurse tell her all sort of horror stories about the half man half beasts that were the Weredings and how they would come and take her away if she was naughty, but she had only ever half believed them. But when she reflected on those nursery stories, she realised that they told her nothing about the actual people, why was that? Why had Vyman or Galmor for that matter not teach her about such a strange people? She decided then and there to find out why?

Rising from her bed she strode from her room and finding at the end of the corridor a narrow staircase she climbed it and entered into the house's only tower where the Scholar owned a meagre cell. Robin knocked on the door, but got no response. She knocked again, but still receiving no response she slowly pushed the door open to find an empty room and a neatly made bed. It seemed that the scholar was already up and about, though the dawn had only just broken.

"Now where will he be at this time of day?" Robin muttered to herself, as she looked around the Spartan room. "Of course the library!"

Robin did in deed find Vyman in her father's study, bending over an old tome ink and parchment beside it, as he noted something down.

"Vyman," Robin said as she entered.

The thin man looked up from his parchment and gasped in horror and surprise.

"Lady Robin!" the thin man flustered and sputtered in surprise.

"What?" Robin asked, as she realised that she was only waring her bed robe.

A thin silk thing that clung to her sweat drenched body and which made her look all but naked to the thin man. At that moment Imp who had no doubt shadowed Robin, appeared in the door with a thicker robe made of wool.

"Here my lady your robe," the little woman said without further comment as to Robin's dress. "Will you break fast here my lady?"

Robin did not know what to say, she was herself astonished by the fact that she had not washed or dressed before coming to the scholar. So she nodded and sitting opposite the Scholar took a few steadying breaths. The scholar who had returned the book he had been studying, sat opposite and after a moment's pause he asked the obvious question.

"Well my Lady what is so urgent this morning?"

"I have been thinking about the Weredings, but I know nothing about them. Scholar why didn't you or Galmor never teach me and Rose about them?"

The thin man looked uncomfortable and for a long moment he did not answer her. This pause lasted long enough for Imp to bring them tea, black bread, cheese and a thinly cut smoked ham.

"My lady I cannot speak for Scholar Galmor, but there are two reasons why I never touched on that subject. The first is that I know so little about that people that I could not teach you if I wished."

"And the second?" Robin asked, as she sipped at her cup of tea without really tasting it.

"The second reason is that the day I took my position here your father ordered me to teach you nothing concerning either the Weredings or the lands in the north."

Robin almost dropped her cup as she heard this, and for a long time she stared open mouthed at the Scholar.

"My Lady, Robin, are you alright?"

"Did my father say why?" Robin asked, when she could find her voice again.

"No he did not say, and I did not dare to ask him," admitted the thin teacher.

"If you could make a guess, why would you say?"

If anything, the Scholar looked even more embarrassed and nervous than when he had seen Robin all but naked.

"My Lady I am a Scholar, I am taught not to guess."

Robin did not know whether to scream or laugh, so she took a deep breath and said what she was thinking, "Vyman, use your logic to give me a possible answer if you cannot make a guess."

The thin man responded to her request and closing his eyes, seemed to try and use what he called logic to deduce her father's motives.

"Your father has one of the greatest libraries on Weredings in the country and yet he forbad me to teach you."

Robin was surprised to hear this muttered by the thin man and she was drawn to the high book lined walls, but Vyman was still speaking and she paid him close attention.

"This might mean that he either did not want you to know about his studies, or that he had discovered something that he thought might harm you and your sister?"

"Well which is it?" Robin demanded, as the thin man opened his eyes and took a long gulp of his tea.

"I am afraid that I can't answer that question."

"Would Galmor know?"

The tall spare man frowned and then shrugged.

"Maybe!"

"That settles it," Robin snarled, as she leapt to her feet and strode for the door.

"My Lady, where are you going?"

"To find Galmor and find out what's going on!"

"My Lady wait," Vyman cried after her.

Robin would have ignored the adviser, but the urgency in his voice stopped her in her tracks.

"What?" she called, over her shoulder.

"I should come with you to explain my reasoning, besides you need to dress, a dressing gown is not best to go visiting."

Robin sighed in frustration, for she wanted her questions answered now, but she was not so stubborn that she could not see the Scholars reasoning as wise.

"Very well I will dress and then we go and see Galmor together."

Robin returning to her room, found that Imp had laid out for her tunic and britches in grey wool and leather. Robin dress quickly and as she grabbed up the dagger, she had a fleeting image of Luna's face and she was possessed by a need to see the small woman. She was interrupted, from these thoughts by Vyman's knock on her door. Robin strapped the dagger to her belt and opening the door, followed the tall thin man as he led her from the stone manner house. This time they did not go through the woods, for the scholar chose to take the thin track that skirted the long wood and led them round it to the tithe cottages that served as the servant's homes. As they moved through the thin band of wood houses they came across the squat sunburnt form of her family's game keeper Parker, who had taught Robin how to fish and hunt.

"My Lady," he greeted them, taking his long clay pipe from his mouth to speak to them. "Can I elp yeh?"

"No thanks Parker!" Robin said, as she grinned at the broad wrinkled man "I and Vyman are on hour way to see Galmor."

"Ah, I ave bin meaning to visit em meself," grunted the bandy legged man. "Give a sec. and I'll get me bow and I be with yeh."

Vyman did not look too happy about this, but he kept his peace and once the bandy man returned with his short bow, they continued to the large house just beyond the small village, but as they approached Parker stopped and sniffing the air growled something under his breath.

"Whats wrong?"

"Em ne sure," growled the old man, "but someting ain't rite ere."

"What do you mean?" Vyman asked, as he nervously looked about him.

"Ne smoke," replied the old woodsman and he pointed with his bow to the chimney, which was as he said smokeless.

"Perhaps he has no wood to burn?"

"Ney, I gave em a new tree yestedar."

"When?" Vyman asked, struggling with Parkers broad accent.

"Yesterday," Robin who had grown up with Parker's strange way of talking translated. "You may be right, the last time I was here there was fire and Galmor made me tea."

"Let m go fist Robin," the woodsman said, as he strung his bow and fitted an arrow to the string.

Robin nodded and drawing the dagger aloud his short form to lead, as they circled the large cottage. As they rounded the corner they found a bloody message lying on the path for them.

"By thee gods!" Parker snarled, as he went down on his haunches and probed at the body.

"What is it?"

"Galmor's raven," Robin said, as a cold feeling began to creep into her heart. "Quick the Scholar maybe in trouble."

The old man grunted and led the way into the dim cottage and snarled a curse, once his eyes had adjusted to the dark light. Robin stepped in behind him and hissed out a curse of her own, for the cottage could not have been more different than the last time she had visited it if a whirlwind had hit it. To Robin it looked like a whirlwind had blown through the room, breaking furniture and scattering the books and scrolls. But for a long time she did not notice the damage, for in the middle of the room lay Scholar Galmor. His fading white robe stained dark with his blood and a pool of his blood drying beneath his dead body. For a long time Robin could not speak, but when she could only speak the thoughts that had popped into her head when she saw he was dead.

"Now I won't get my answers."

"Get er out Vyman," Parker snapped, as he circled the body and bent over it.

"My Lady perhaps we should..."

"No," Robin snapped, "I am not leaving until I know who killed him."

"What's tis?" the old man asked, as he bent low over the body.

"You've found something?"

"He's get somthing en is and mes thinking."

"Here let me," Vyman said, as he joined the gamesman at his side.

Robin moved to the other side of the body, to see more closer what they were doing.

"Watch the blood my lady," Vyman said detached.

Robin wondered as she looked down at the old man's face why she was not being sick or fainting, she had seen death before, but she thought that she should feel more for a man than a stag. At the moment she only felt numb, though she did feel a dim measure of grief at the passing of the old man who had taught her since she could speak. She watched dispassionately, as Vyman gently tweezed the thing that was clutched in the dead man's hand.

"What is it?"

"It's parchment," Vyman said, as he held up the crumpled piece of parchment, so that he could better see it.

"What does it say?"

The thin man frowned, as he peered at the parchment.

"Vyman?"

"It is one word," Vyman said, his frown deepening.

"Is it in Galmor's hand?"

"Yes."

"Is it the name of his murderer?"

"I don't know about that," Vyman said, his face screwing up in concentration.

"Well, what does it say?" Robin asked, her voice rising as frustration crept into it.

"Weredings," Vyman said, as he held the parchment out to her.

Robin taw it from his hand and holding it up stared at the spidery writing that scrawled across the fragment of parchment. It took her a moment to understand what she was looking at, but after a moment of staring she too saw that on the parchment scrawled in Galmor's familiar hand was the one word: *Weredings*. For a long moment, she stared at the note and then she crumpled it in her fist, as she screamed wordlessly at the rafters.

She might have blacked out for a moment, for when she came back to herself, it was to find that she was kneeling on the bloody floorboards, Vyman standing over her, a flask in his hand.

"My Lady please drink this," the man said, his face covered with concern.

"I don't want drafts," Robin snarled and the man stepped back surprised by the venom in her voice. "I want the Weredings to pay for their crimes."

"But my lady, you can't blame an entire people..."

"Just watch me," spat Robin, as she lurched to her feet and turning ran from the cottage. She ran through the woods, her goal the house and her father's small, but well stocked armoury. She now knew that the Weredings had murdered her father and once Galmor had started asking questions they had killed him to stop him from telling Robin. At that moment, as she ran through the woods her long mane of hair flying out behind her like the tail of some vengeful comet, she was consumed with one desire. To feel a sword in her hand and to plunge that sword into the heart of the black clad assassin and every other Wereding that lived.

When she reached the house, she would storm into the armoury and grabbing her sword would claim a hoarse from the stables and riding to the Tower of the Glove would strike down the Weredings' ambassador and every other Wereding she could find. Such was her rage, that her sight was filled with the images of bestial men falling before her blade. But when she finally stopped running and shook her head to clear her sight she found that she was not in the armoury, but her bed room. Why was she here she wanted the armoury, but she had come blindly to her bed room, why? A sound from the bed drew Robin's attention to it, to see a figure reclining there. Robin blinked, not believing her eyes.

"I'm dreaming," Robin whispered, for the sight before her had robbed her of her breath.

There reclining on her bed was the lithe form of Luna, her muscular body completely naked. A wicked grin on her lips, as she looked up at Robin from under her long lashes.

"If this is a dream, then it is going to be a very wet one," Luna said, seductively as she languidly spread her arms and legs one hand beckoning to Robin. An invite that the young woman could neither believe, nor deny.

THE LION KING AND THE LEOPARD PRINCE

"Men adopt animals as their Sigel's, not realising just how they come to resemble their own symbols."
The White Wolf to the Red Wizard, The Wereding Chronicles.

Tomas stood at the feet of power and looking up beheld the King of his world. His Uncle King Haymer, was an old man, but for years he had ruled the kingdom from this throne. With my help, Tomas thought, as he looked at the Lion of Leamore, as his uncle was known. The old man had been a great warrior in his day, tall and powerful like Tomas himself, but he was old now. As Tomas looked on the shrunken and wrinkled man that lay rather than sat before him, he wondered if he was looking at his future self. Was this what he would become? A flutter of white at the corner of his eye, made him shift his gaze slightly and he saw a tall white form stood at the king's side. Tomas wanted to say the Black Queen, but he had learnt before that she or one of her lackeys could read his lips. Her lackeys, that was most of the court. The ruling council were all but hers. Tomas looked about him at the black clad Crimson Master one side and Gold Hand on the other. Tomas felt like a deer among a pack of wolves. He looked around him and noticed that the Red Rook was not present. That was not a complete surprise, as Luna was not always present at the meetings, but her absence made him feel nervous. Like many men of action, he preferred to have his enemies before him in reach of his blade. His blade, as the King's bodyguard he was one of the few men allowed to bear a sword here within the castle, but although he could have struck down these wolves about him, he was not sure that it would matter if he drew his sword on them. The Crimson Master was a spell caster of the darkest kind. The Golden Hand, as the treasurer was known, was probably warded by some kind of bought magic, even though it was illegal to possess such magic. As for the one Tomas wanted to kill more than any, the Black Queen was (it was rumoured), a magic user too. Though she had her dark guardian to protect her person and although the thin woman did not openly wear a sword, Tomas was certain that she had a blade on her person. Tomas' attention was diverted back to his King, as the old man spoke in a papery whisper.

"Well Paul, what have you to tell me about Lord Canduss's death?"

The King's question, was addressed to the short, powerful man that stood before them. His sandy hair glinting, in the dim light of the throne room. This was Tallon Paul, the man who had the honour of policing the capital, For he was captain of the city watch and the king had ordered him to investigate the death of the former courtier. For although Canduss had been a close friend and councillor of the king, he had long been absent from court and had all but retired from public life, but the king still thought of him as a friend and wanted to know who was behind the man's death.

"My King," rasped the short man, whose voice was always raspy and little above a whisper, a result of someone almost taken his head off and had left his throat a scarred mess. "I have questioned both the Lady Robin Canduss and the Lady Luna..."

"Luna saw this attack?" Interrupted Scarison, the Crimson Master in his deep booming voice.

"No my Lord," Paul said stiffly, for he liked Scarison no more than Tomas did. "She came across the Lady Canduss just after her father had died."

"And what did they tell you?" The Queen Lilly L. Bain's voice, was as soft as silk, but it sheathed a will of iron.

"They told me that the Wereding Kain might have been the Lord Canduss's killer."

"The Weredings!" the Crimson Master snarled, his outrage expected, for it was known to all that he either hated or feared the Fay. "How long will we allow these half men to live amongst us? They are monsters..."

"What does the Tower of the Glove say to this?" the King's whisper, cutting through the giant's boom.

"My Lord, I have not spoken to the Weredings," Paul rasped, as he kept his eyes on his king.

"And why not?" the Queen demanded.

"Because, my Queen I have no proof that it is the Weredings," Paul replied quietly, though his eyes never left the King, for like

Tomas he too seemed not to like the Queen and although he and Tomas had never been friends, Tomas began to feel a liking for the short keg of a man.

"But you just said it was a Wereding that killed Canduss!" said Golden Hand in his sly voice.

"What I said Lord Tallier," Paul said, dryly as if he would rather step on the smarmy man, "Is that the evidence of the Lady Canduss is that someone appearing to be Kain killed her father, but anyone can wear a wolf helmet and wheeled a black sword. I thought it better to bring the facts to the court, rather than present half formed and unsubstantiated accusations to the Ambassador of the Weredings and therefore worsen our relations."

A heavy silence fell over the long hall of the throne room, after Paul's long reply. Tomas glanced around him, and realised that Paul's response had not gone down well. The silence when it was eventually broken, was broken by the King.

"So Paul, you do not think that this was the Weredings?"

"I neither know if it is the Weredings or not, my King there is just not enough evidence to say."

"If It was a Wereding, why would they want the Lord Canduss dead?" The question was put by a new voice, and it came from the back of the great hall, Tomas recognised the gravelly voice and looking past Paul saw the large white clad form of Scholar Ragnar the court Scholar.

"Scholar Ragnar?" Paul acknowledged the old if robust healer and teacher.

"I ask again, what would the Weredings gain by Robert's death?" the large man asked as he moved past Paul to take his place at the table set just below the throne, where Tomas and the rest of the King's council sat.

Tomas regarded the large broad shouldered man in his white robes, it had not escaped him that the Scholar had used Canduss's first name, as if they had been close friends. Tomas was not aware that they had been close, but as he reflected the Canduss and Ragnar were men who had grown old with their King and the strange and almost secret affair of the Canduss exile had all happened before Tomas' time.

"The answer to that question is outside my offices," Paul rasped.

"Does that mean that you can't think?" snapped the large Scholar.

"Ragnar," whispered the King, as his fading roomy eyes saw Paul flinch beneath the old healer's harsh tone.

"What I think is that I was charged with finding out the identity of the killer not his motives," Paul said, frostily.

"And you don't think that the two are related?"

"Paul," coaxed the King, "do you have an idea why the Weredings might want Robert dead?"

Paul looked down at his boots and when he spoke he was clearly not happy.

"I have an idea my King," then he raised his head and met his King's eye, a thing he did not often do so Tomas knew that he wanted what he was about to say be noted. "But it is only an idea, I have no proof for it and I would not like my Liege to think that it is true."

"Very well we have noted you're reluctance," snarled Ragnar.

"I believe, believe note Scholar, that the Weredings or rather factions of their race may have wanted Lord Canduss killed to provoke a war between our two nations."

Tomas looked around at his fellow councillors and although the Crimson Master and Gold Hand kept up their masks, Tomas thought he saw a flicker in their eyes. A flicker of what? Fear, hate? Now he understood why Paul had been so reluctant to bring his thoughts into the light, they had added fuel to the fire. The Crimson Master and his faction, had been pushing for war with the Weredings for years and such a suggestion would only add to his arguments. This awkward silence was finally broken by the Queen's honeyed tones, which dripped sweet poison into the silence.

"What are your next steps?"

"As I said, I brought my report to the King and his council I would like now to go to the Tower of the Glove and ask the Wereding ambassador what she may know of these matters."

"After thinking that they might want war with us, you expect her to tell you the truth?" Gold Hands asked, his ever ready grin appearing on his sly face.

"I too, am interested in your thinking Lord Provost," Ragnar said, his dark handsome face marred by a frown.

"My thinking, is that as I have said the killer may be a rogue killer and have nothing to do with the rest of the Weredings and the ambassador may know of it."

"Or she might know of an invasion and cut your throat," suggested Gold Hands slyly.

If he had wanted to make Paul blanch at this idea, he was disappointed for the short man drew himself up to his full height of Five one and said proudly.

"I am not afraid of death my Lord."

"Then what do you fear man?" Ragnar asked, seemingly genuinely interested to know.

"Dishonour and failure of my duty," Paul rasped simply.

"Well said Paul," the King whispered. "You may with our blessing approach the Wereding ambassador, but be careful! We do not want to lose such a loyal servant."

"My King," Paul said saluting his King and turning on his heal strode from the room.

"What an idiot," Gold Hand muttered, under his breath.

"Perhaps," Ragnar answered the treasurer's whisper, as if it had been said openly. "But you cannot question his loyalty."

"The man has no imagination," complained Gold Hands.

"He does not need imagination to be loyal," Tomas said, softly.

"Never mind the Provost," boomed the Crimson Master. "The matter we should be concerned with, is whether we are under attack?"

"Attack?" Ragnar asked, his bushy, grey eyebrows rising in surprise. "Attack from whom?"

"The cursed Weredings of course you idiot," snarled the large sable robed man. "The Weredings could be about to launch an attack on us, even as we sit here doing nothing."

Ragnar did not like being called an idiot, it was clear by the look on his face, but any argument between the two physically imposing men was prevented by the quiet whisper of their King.

"My Lord Healm you are the Warder of the North, have you seen any proof of an invasion?"

Tomas would have preferred not to be drawn into this argument, but the King had addressed him formally and had even used his family name as well as his title, rather than calling Tomas by his first name as was his custom. It was clear, that the King wanted Tomas to show that Paul was not the only loyal man at his court.

"My Lord King and Council," Tomas spoke haltingly, for he was reluctant to start a war with a people that he hardly knew. "It is true that I have seen an increase in Wereding activity beyond your walls..."

"There you have it from the Warders own lips," Interrupted Scarason. "They are about to attack..."

"Forgive me Master," Ragnar cut him off. "That was not what the Lord Healm Said."

"What do you mean Tomas?" the Queen asked sweetly, as if she was on his side.

Tomas who suspected that the Queen was manoeuvring him into an impossible position, new that he was in the trap and on the spot. So all he could do was say what he thought and hope that no one realised that he was in contact with the Weredings.

"What I mean my Queen, is that I have lost a couple of patrols and there have been sightings of Darklings in the dead lands, but I am not sure that this means that the Weredings are about to attack us."

"Darklings, what are Darklings?" Gold Hands asked, as if it mattered.

"The Darklings are the evil kin of the Weredings," Ragnar explained, in a teacher's voice. "The Darklings are Orcs and Trolls and all that is evil among the Wereding people."

"They are all evil," the Crimson Master snarled.

"That is not true my Lord," Ragnar said loudly, his face beginning to redden with anger.

"My Lords," broke in the King, his voice ringing with exasperation. "I will have piece in my halls. Tomas you have lost men?"

"Yes my King."

"Why then have we not heard of this?" the Queen asked softly and dangerously. "Why my Lord Tomas have you not reported this to us before?"

Tomas was suddenly grasped by the idea that the Queen knew of his involvement with the Weredings. It was the way that she was almost crowing over this matter and the cat that got the cream look on her face. Well damn her, she would have to prove it.

"I have not reported it because, I did not know what it meant! I have been trying to find out what is going on, on my own. I hope that I have not displeased my Lord King?" Tomas said, as he bowed towards the King.

"The wall is your responsibility! It is your duty and judgement to do whatever you think necessary to guard it," the old man said, his voice noncommittal but Tomas thought that he was not being rebuked.

"What information about the Weredings can you discover here in Landan my Lord? The Wall is in the North," the Queen said slyly.

Tomas knew that if he did not come up with a quick answer, she would have him dangling on a hook.

"I have heard little here in the city it is true my Lady, but I am not just the Warder in the North. I am also the King's Shield. My duties mean I must be here as well as in the north."

"Then perhaps you are too stretched," Lily said, her voice no longer soft, for a edge of ice had slipped in and Tomas believe that he had escaped her trap, but that he might have to pay for it later.

"My Queen may have a point," the King said and Tomas was suddenly concerned that he might be being punished already.

"You would send me from you my lord! I would hope that I had not disappointed my Liege, so much that he would dismiss me."

"Tomas, you have not disappointed me and I do not send you away as a punishment, but Lily does have a point. If there is trouble brewing in the north, perhaps that is where you should be. Please perform your duty as my Shield in the North and return to the wall and do all that you can to discover what is happening out there."

"As you command my King," Tomas said, bowing and turning he moved to leave.

"Tomas," Ragnar called out stopping him.

Tomas turned back to the Scholar, wondering what the old man would ask and feeling as if he was being punished all the same and that the Queen had succeeded in ridding herself of him.

"What do you think is happening up there in the north?"

"I do not have enough facts to know."

"But you can think," Ragnar said pointedly. "What do you think or guess."

"If you want my suspicions Ragnar, I would say that the Darklings are spawning again and that they will attack us and the Weredings both as they did in the old wars."

"Speculation," cut in the Crimson Master. "As you said Tomas, you have no proof."

"No my Lord, I go to find it," Tomas said, grimly as he struggled to contain his anger with the dark man.

"Then go," snarled the dark man, as he seethed under Tomas' dangerous stare.

Tomas turned and he could feel several pairs of eyes, burning into his back.

A TEST OF FIRE

"Fire burns, but it also cleanses and enlightens. Fire can show us the truth."

Lightning to Rose from The Wereding Chronicles by the Red Wizard.

Robin opened her eyes, to find that she had not dreamed the last hour; Luna's tousled red head was still lying on her bared breast.

"Then it wasn't a dream," she muttered, as she felt her new lover suckling at her breast.

Luna muttered something and nibbled at her breast. Robin reached out and tangling her fingers in Luna's red main, tugged. Making Luna moan in protest, a vibration that sent tingles through Robin's flesh.

"I want to look at you," Robin whispered, her voice hoarse from screaming.

Luna groaned in protest, but reluctantly let go of Robin's nipple and lifting her head looked up at Robin. Her green eyes sparkling with mischief, her face glistening with sweat and other liquids.

"So was it good for you?" Luna asked, in a husky whisper that sent tingles through Robin.

"Where have you been all my life," Robin whispered back.

This question drove the grin from Luna's face and a look of grimness moved across her face.

"What is it? Have I said something wrong?"

"Yes and no," Luna said, as she slid off Robin's body and climbing off Robin's bed padded to where a jug of water stood. "But you have reminded me why I came here."

"You mean you didn't come to to..."

"Yes, I did come for that! I have wanted to love you ever since I met you, but I have also come with news about your sister."

Suddenly the afterglow of love making was gone and a blade of ice was twisting in her stomach.

"Rose? You know something?"

"Perhaps you should dress and we can talk about this over food or a strong drink," Luna said, after drinking some of the water.

"Please Luna, tell me now," Robin pleaded.

"At least put on a robe," Luna said, as she picked up her cast off tunic.

Robin wanted to refuse until she heard what Luna had to tell her, but she pulled on her bed robe to cover her nakedness.

"What have you heard?"

"Robin," Luna said, taking one of Robin's clenched hands and smoothing it out, so that she could entwine her fingers with Robin's. "I want you to be brave because, what I have to tell you is not good news."

"She can't be dead, please don't tell me she's dead," Robin moaned, tears beginning to well up in her eyes.

"No she's not dead as far as I know," Luna said, as she kissed away the tears that were running down Robin's cheeks. "But I fear that she has fallen into the worst kind of company."

"But she is alive?"

"Yes when I saw her she was alive, but she may have been corrupted by dark magic."

"What do you mean?" Robin asked, her nightmares of Roses face on draconic bodies returning to her mind's eye.

"Robin I am afraid to tell you that she is in the company of two of the worst kind of Weredings there are."

"Weredings!"

"Yes the Werewolf Kye and the Elf Eloo," Luna snarled, her face twisting in a look of hate, her voice full of venom.

"Werewolf?" Robin asked, all her nurses tales of men eating monsters coming back to her memory.

"Yes, the Weredings protect themselves and their lands with the cursed Silver Shield which is made up of clans of Werewolves and Kye and his brothers and sisters are some of the worst and most powerful and Eloo is a witch besides."

"What will they do to her?" Robin asked in a strengthless whisper. "They won't kill her..."

Luna's strong fingers tightened on Robin's.

"No I don't think so, you needn't worry on that score, but she might as well be dead."

"What do you mean?"

"Robin I need you to be brave now, if Rose is in their hands, she is as good as dead to you. They will use magic on her to twist her mind and perceptions, she will come to see the world from their point of view. She will come to hate all that you hold dear and even worse she may come to forget you exist or worse she may try to kill you."

"No, it isn't true Rose would never..."

"Robin I have seen these two do it before, they are very good at what they do. Your sister doesn't have a chance."

At hearing this a great wave of despair swept over Robin. Then the despair turned to rage and a hot fire seemed to kindle within Robin's heart.

"No, no!" Robin screamed, as she forgot where she was as the boiling wave of anger swept over her.

Luna was shocked, as Robin taw her hand from hers and she watched disbelieving as Robin leapt to her feet and ran from the room.

"Robin wait," she called, but the girl was gone.

Robin did not hear Luna's cry, she was senseless to everything and everyone. Her blind dash carried her through the house and out onto the grounds. In fact she found herself by the stone doorway, where her father had died. The sight of the tall stones was like a splash of cold water to her rage. The anger was gone and only the despair remained, as the stones shimmered and dissolved under a veil of tears. So when the darkness fell about her, Robin wondered if her eyes were so teary they were failing her, but then she heard a harsh voice hissing words in a language that she had never heard before, but which made her blood run cold. For they seemed to be said in a voice as sharp and cruel as a blizzard and indeed a blizzard seemed to be all around her. As an icy wind seemed to blow from the pole itself and she felt her tears freezing on her cheeks. She knew that if she did not do something soon, she would be a statue of ice frozen in place. But she might as well be a statue, for she could not move or even cry out in fear or pain. Then from somewhere deep inside her, a voice seemed to speak and Robin heard her own voice whispering words she did not understand, but which she felt ring with power. Even as she whispered those words of power, she felt the cold shrink from her veins and when she repeated the words in a stronger voice, the icy wind dropped away losing strength and when she spoke it a third time in a very loud voice, the veil of utter darkness too folded in on itself until the world as she knew it was about her. Robin looked about her for the speaker of the cold voice and saw standing only a few feet away, the familiar and hated form of the black armoured figure with its wolf crafted helm.

WINGED WORDS

"Words of wisdom, may come to us on the wings of death."
An ancient saying of the Druids.

Tigress stood upon the high platform at the top of the Tower of the Gloves battlements. His green eyes staring into the blue sky, soon he spotted the dot he was looking for.

"Kit here," he cried, his gloved fist held up before him.

Onto his arm, stooped the great hawk that was the skin swapper Kit. Her yellow eye regarded him, with a wild fury that seemed to ask why he called her. Tigress extended his hand and stroked her feathers gently. Even though she flicked her wings and screamed at him.

"Kit," Tigress said softly. "It's me Tigress, you know me don't you? Please Kit change back, come back to me."

The hawk cocked its head and fluttering her wings, jumped from Tigress' fist and half flew, half dropped to the floor. Where she stretched her wings wide and stretching her neck out screamed and screamed. As she did, her voice slowly changed from the wild cries of a hawk, to the hoarse cries of the woman that she slowly shifted into. She looked about her blearily, as if she did not know where she was and Tigress knew this to be partly true, the transition from animal to woman was disorientating for Kit and sometimes it would be several hours before she would come back to him. Tigress though, had learnt ways of quickening this process.

"Kit here drink," Tigress said, giving her mulled wine.

She took it and drank it down, then he wrapped her in her robe and finally wrapped her in his arms.

"Kit do you know me?"

For a long time she did not respond, her yellow eyes still wild and animal, but after a long time recognition seemed to flicker in those hawk eyes.

"Tigress," she breathed.

"Yes Kit it's me," Tigress said, in relief, for although he knew that he could not stop Kit from changing and flying as the hawk, but every time she changed he feared that she would not know him and would remain the hawk.

"I am back?" Kit whispered, her voice tinged with regret.

"At the tower yes," Tigress said, hoping that he had not lost Kit, as he feared every time he watched her change and fly from him.

"You went to Galmor's to tell him what we knew of the Canduss girl," Tigress said gently, as he tried to remind Kit's sluggish mind what her human purpose had been.

"Galmor," Kit screeched and she pulled back from Tigress' embrace, the move surprising him.

"Kit what's wrong?" Tigress asked, half fearing that he had lost part of Kit.

"Galmor is dead," rasped Kit, her yellow eyes flaring with rage.

This news caught Tigress completely by surprise and combined with his fear of losing Kit, made him lose control of his own humanity. Deep from within his throat, their rolled forth a deep animalistic growl. This was such an unusual event that Kit stepped back several feet, her hands rising before her in curved claws. But with a shake of his head, Tigress managed to recover his wits and he smiled at Kit and extended a hand towards her.

"I am sorry Kit, I did not mean to give into the beast. The news of Galmor's death came as a shock and I lost control."

"I understand," Kit croaked. "It is a shock to me too."

"What did you see?"

"I flew over the clearing intending to land and change so that I could speak with him, but when I got there the Canduss girl ran from the hut and two men one a Scholar left moments later carrying Galmor's body."

"Are you sure it was Galmor?"

"I recognised him and once they left I changed and entered the hut, there was blood everywhere and the smell of death hung like a fog over everything."

"You don't think it was the Canduss girl that killed him?"

"I don't think so, she had some blood on her, but not enough to account for his death."

"Then who?"

"I used magic and detected a presence. A presence that I suspect was Kain's."

"That black hearted fiend should have been drowned at birth," spat Tigress.

"Perhaps, but first someone must tell Cole and Clover."

"I will do that, you need to rest."

"Perhaps, but it should be me who tells them. It was I saw it."

"Very well, but please Kit, after that rest."

"I will, but what do we do next. Do we approach the Canduss girl ourselves, rather than through Galmor as we had planned?"

"I don't know the answer Kit," Tigress said, as he stared possessively a the slim girl. "Luna has got her claws in the girl, it may be too late. I will ask Bright Eyes, she is the ambassador. Perhaps she can do something, but if Luna has poisoned the girl against us already it will be of no use."

"Perhaps," Bright Eyes' voice broke in, as she emerged onto the battlements. "But it must be tried. Though Galmor might be able to smooth the way.."

"Galmor can smooth nothing," Kit cut her off.

Bright Eyes' yellow orbs bored into Kit as she asked with her eyes for Kit to explain herself.

"Galmor is dead," Kit snarled.

"Dead," Bright Eyes hissed in disbelief. "How did he die?"

"He was murdered, possibly by Kain," Tigress explained on his lover's behalf.

"That is grievous news," Bright Eyes sighed, her shoulders slumping as if under a great weight. "He was a good friend to the Wereding people and his grandchildren are close to me too."

Tigress and Kit deemed it wise, not to mention that Cole was so close to her that he had become her lover.

"I was going to tell them now," Kit said.

"I will come with you," Bright Eyes said, her look of grief suddenly gone. "They may need my support."

"And what about the Canduss girl," Tigress asked, looking from Kit to Bright Eyes.

"Gildor has decided to join us at the tower, I will send him or one of his suns with a scroll to the Canduss girl," Bright Eyes decided.

"A scroll will that be enough?"

"At this point Tigress, I fear that whatever we do will only pour oil on the fire, but we must try for the girl's sake if not our own."

Having decided on a course of action, Bright Eyes and Kit left the high place to go and break the bad news to the Galmor grandchildren, leaving Tigress to look out from his high eerie at the sprawling city below.

"A scroll won't be enough," Tigress growled to himself. "Perhaps I should take a paw myself."

THE ROBIN AND THE WOLF

"The magic can be like a fire, it can flare up and burn the chimney."
Luna from Robin's account of the Wereding Wars.

Seeing the tall black clad figure before her, its head clad in the wolf helm, Robin screamed and flung herself at it, or she would have, but her feet would not move. Glancing down, Robin saw that the thigh high grass had seemingly come to life and had entwined around her lower legs and locked her in place. Robin pulled against the springy grass, but even as she felt the grass tearing the wolf clad figure was snarling more words of power. As Robin watched, the air round him seemed to freeze and his hands clawed a the air in mystic passes, a whip like lash uncoiled from his arm and coiled like a living snake before him. Robin tugged at the grass in growing frustration, but as she did the whip arched like a striking snake and snapped out to encircle her in its cold length. For whatever the thing was made of (and from its deeper than darkness, blackness Robin could believe that it was a thing of shadow), it was colder than steel on a freezing night. Robin could feel it leaching her body's warmth from her and if she didn't do something soon she would pass out, but the lash had encircled her completely and was pinning her arms to her sides trapping her. Once again Robin felt her rage and hatred boil inside her. From that place deep inside her, that she had not known of before today, there weld up a ball of power that forced its way up her throat and out her mouth in a spat incantation of strange words that suddenly filled Robin with warmth as if she was standing in the full rays of the sun. She felt the cold lash fall away and when she looked down at herself, it was to find to her amazement that her body was now reeved in a halo of dancing red flames that warmed her but which did not burn her. Though they seemed to burn away the whip and the entangling grass.

"Curse you Canduss and your dragon blood," snarled the wolf headed figure, its voice cold and stabbing like daggers in the mind. Its very words seeming to stab at Robin and cause her pain.

Robin looked around for a weapon to use against this mailed figure, but she had rushed out without even her dagger. She spotted a large stone and lunging for it lobbed it at the figure's head. The rock bounced harmlessly off the armoured helm, but it did at least interrupt his next round of incantations.

"Enough of this playing, now you die," snarled the figure in his painful voice.

With these words the figure drew from a back sheath the long ebony sword that had killed her father.

Robin knew she was going to die, so drawing herself to full height looked the figure in its glinting eyes and tried to show no fear, as she embraced her death with all the dignity she could gather. But the death blow did not come, from nowhere there charged a huge form and the wolf helmed figure was sent flying by Luna's man Wolf who had charged from the side to send the figure that might be Kain flying. The huge mute that was Wolf drew a dagger from his belt and was about to attack the wolf man, when it spat forth another spell and Wolf too was frozen in place.

Robin was suddenly very frightened, for if someone as large and powerful as Wolf could be stopped by this cursed monster then they were in very big trouble. Then from beside Robin there purred a voice that throbbed with power and a wall of fire sprang up between Wolf and the black mailed attacker. Robin half recognised that purr and looking down, was surprised to see Luna at her side, her hands weaving through the air before her as her deep voice chanted the words of what was obviously a spell. A spell that seemed to unfreeze Wolf, for he recoiled from the fire and moved back towards his mistress.

"Wolf the fire will only last a moment more, when it fails be prepared Kain will probably launch an attack." Luna was correct, even as Luna stopped speaking the wall of dancing flames winked out, as if a great wind had snuffed it out. The black figure snarled at Luna and he moved towards Wolf, his black blade held before it.

Even as it moved forwards, cries rang out behind them and an arrow fell at the wolf man's feet. Robin glanced over her shoulder, to see Garm and a handful of his men pounding towards them. A hiss from before her made Robin look back to the wolf man, to see him cast black powder at them. Robin jumped back as the powder landed at her feet, but was still engulfed in a black cloud of inky darkness that clouded her sight, but seemed to do little else. At her side Robin heard Luna whisper a word and a breeze sprang up and blew the cloud from around them, to reveal Wolf stomping about like a frustrated animal, but of the black clad attacker there was no sign.

"Where is he?" Robin asked, casting about her, but she could find no sign of him.

"He probably went back through the door," Luna said, as she looked to Wolf. Who in response to her glance, pointed to the standing stones.

"More cursed magic," Robin snarled and then stopped, as she realised that she herself had cast some cursed magic.

By the amused look on Luna's face, Robin guessed that she knew the irony of this statement. After all Robin had herself seen the small woman cast the forbidden magic. Robin opened her mouth to ask Luna, but the tiny woman put a finger to her lips silencing Robin, as Garm and his men came up with them.

"Are you alright my lady," wheezed Garm.

"Yes Garm I am fine, thanks to Luna and her man."

"You have my thanks Lady," Garm said, coldly to Luna.

Luna ignored Garm and turning to Robin, she gave her a long glance and beckoning to Wolf spoke to Robin in a low voice.

"We need to talk."

Robin nodded and followed the small woman back to the house, where Imp was waiting with a heavy robe for Robin and cups of hot wine.

"Thank you Imp," Robin murmured, as she swallowed down the mulled wine.

Luna gave Robin a pointed look, which Robin did not understand, forcing Luna to put it into words.

"Lady Canduss I would speak to you, alone," she added pointedly.

"Thank you Imp I can manage here," Robin said to the maid, who with a formal curtsy left the room in a swirl of skirts.

"Thank you for saving my life," Robin said, as she filled Luna's glass.

"For that you are welcome, though you weren't doing too bad yourself."

"He had me dead, when he drew his sword."

"Perhaps, but he should have defeated you long before that, but enough of that for the moment tell me Robin how long have you been a spell caster?"

The question rocked Robin back on her heals and she went pail.

"What do you mean? I have never cast magic in my life!"

"Robin I saw you I heard you, you cast magic against Kain."

"And the wall of flames was just my imagination?" Robin shot back defensively, though she was afraid for she knew magic was illegal.

"Only you saw it," Luna shot back, though her lips did curl at a smile. "Robin I am a spell caster it is true, but I have been for many years and the officials know about me, but I have not heard of you. So I ask again how long have you been a spell caster?"

"I have never cast magic before today."

"I thought as much," Luna sighed and sat back, her green eyes looking up at the study ceiling.

"Will you tell the officials?" Robin asked, in a small voice.

"Yes I will."

"What will they do to me?"

Robin's voice broke, as she asked this and when Luna glanced at her, it was to see tears leaking down her face.

"Robin what's wrong?"

"Magic is illegal," Robin sniffed.

Luna laughed and walking round to where Robin sat, took both of the young woman's hands in her own.

"Robin you are too good, yes magic is illegal to those who do not have the approval of the Crimson Circle, but I do and soon so shall you."

"You mean I won't be punished?"

"Not if I have anything to do with it," growled the little woman. "Besides so far only you and I know about this we might be able to keep it that way."

"But I may not be able to hide it," Robin murmured, "The magic came out of me, I didn't call it."

"Yes that is what I thought," Luna said, as she poured more wine and gave it to Robin. "Robin let me ask you if there are any spell casters in your family history."

"None that I know about," Robin said, as she sipped the wine finding strength in it.

"I wonder," Luna said, staring off into the middle distance. "I wonder, the magic rose up to defend you."

"It was as though someone else was speaking the words," Robin murmured.

"I wonder."

"Luna is there something wrong with me?"

"Wrong, what do you mean kitten?"

"Am I possessed?"

"Possessed, no I don't think so Robin, but it is strange," Luna said, looking sideways at Robin. "I think it is something else."

"What else?"

"I don't know Robin. I am learned in magic, but it is such a broad and strange subject that I can't know everything, but the Crimson Master may know more."

"Crimson Master who is that?"

"He is the head of the Crimson Circle, the order who polices magic in the realm and he was the one who taught me magic."

"He might know what this is?"

"He might Robin, the question is will this happen again and if it will what affects will it have on you?"

"Effects? What do you mean?"

"Powerful magic is almost a living thing, those who use it are never left untouched; they are never the same afterwards."

Robin stared at Luna for a long time. Then standing went to the fireplace and standing before it, shed her robe and flimsy bed robe and stood before Luna naked and back lit by the blaze of the fire.

"Do I look different?"

Luna stared at her with open lust and envy in her eyes.

"You look magnificent," she breathed and it was true, for stood there silhouetted against the fire Robin stood tall and proud and her red hair seemed to glow brighter than the coals. Her skin was flawless and glowed with its own light.

"Please Robin, put your clothes back on, or I will have to take you here and now."

"I want that, too," Robin said, a look of lust kindling in her own eyes.

"No not now, Robin I am tired. Spell casting draws on me too."

"But I need you," Robin complained, as she stood there her arms at her side, her legs akimbo, her nipples hardening.

"I want to Robin, but I have stayed overlong as it is. I must be with the Queen."

Robin turned away sighing with bitter disappointment and bending, she gathered up her robes and was about to put them back on, when Luna spoke.

"Wait!" Thinking that Luna had changed her mind Robin began to turn back to her, but Luna's hand pressed against the small of her back holding her in place. She shivered, as the small woman's long finger slid across her skin, making her shiver with pleasure.

"That's nice," she breathed huskily.

But when Luna spoke her voice was not charged with lust, but with concern.

"Robin how long have you had this red mark on your back?"

"What mark?" Robin asked, suddenly confused and alarmed. "I don't have any mark on my back."

"I didn't think so, but I thought I might have missed it earlier, but you have it now."

"What mark?"

Robin felt Luna's fingertip glide across her silky skin, until the feeling seemed to lessen as though Robin was still feeling Luna's touch, but through a harder material.

"Here," Luna tapped a point over her left shoulder blade.

"What is it, what is it like?"

"A small coin like patch of raised red skin, it's like scale," Luna said, as she stroked Robin's back. A feeling that only slightly distracted her.

"A mirror, I need a mirror," Robin whispered hoarsely.

"I don't have one," Luna said.

"Ring the bell, Imp will have one."

Luna moved to where the bell ropes hung and tugged on it. A moment later Imp appeared at the door, gasping when she saw Robin standing naked before the fire.

"A mirror," Luna snapped and Imp who remembering herself, vanished returning moments later with a small hand mirror which she passed to Luna, though her eyes never left Robin, who stood staring into the fire.

Luna held the mirror up behind Robin and the girl feeling her tap her on the back looked over her shoulder to stare at the reflection of her back. She gasped when she saw the bright red spot of dark, hardened skin that seemed to flash glossily in the fire light.

"What is it?" Robin all but screamed.

"I'm not sure," Luna said, frowning up at the tall woman. "It could be a side effect of the magic."

"What does this mean?"

"I don't know Robin, but I swear that I will find out."

"Luna what is happening to me?"

"Robin I must go," Luna said, "But I will write to Scarason and ask him about this please Robin don't leave the house until I return Kain may try to attack you again and I'm not sure you could resist him again."

"Please Luna don't leave me." Robin whispered, as she glanced to where Imp waited.

"I must go, the queen wants my council." Luna glared at Imp "I promise Robin I will return to you before nightfall."

"Promise," Robin whispered.

"We will sleep together tonight I promise you."

Reassured by that promise Robin smiled slightly and turning her gaze away stared at the fire and after hearing the study door close she turned to find Imp standing there her robes over her arm.

"My lady you must dress."

"Imp have you ever noticed this mark on my back?"

The small lady in waiting, slowly approached and stared at Robin's back and gasped at what she saw.

"No my Lady you have not had such a mark before, I would know."

"I feared so,"

"My Lady what is it?"

"I wish I knew Imp! I wish I knew!"

"Shall I fetch the Scholar?"

"You can, but I am not sure it will help."

Imp turned at the door and looking back at her mistress, returned and handed her the robes.

"My Lady you should still dress or you might catch your death."

Robin laughed at that.

"My dear Imp ever dutiful, it may be too late for that."

HEALM'S WARNING

"News oft comes from unexpected sources."
Eloo to the Red Wizard, The Wereding Chronicles.

Deep within the great wood, known as the King's Forest, there stood the remains of a crumbling tower that might at one time towered above the trees, but which was now only one story tall. Its upper stories ragged and crumbling stones. It was in this open stone ring that Halmer had come to practice and experiment with the magic ring and the scroll that Tigress had given him. He had judged this abandoned tower isolated enough to practice magic, guessing that no one would see the flashes of light that might occur when he unleashed the magic. Halmer had hung the ring up, where it was exposed to the wind and had blown on it every chance he had gotten and as a result when he unwrapped the ring from a leather cloth, the stone glowed like a blue coal. When Halmer slipped it onto his hand, he felt it vibrating with unleashed energy. In fact it was vibrating with so much power, that for a moment he wondered if he dared use it. Then the need to feel that power unleashed got to him and holding the ring high he spoke the few words he had learned from the scroll. At first Halmer thought that nothing had happened, but then he realised that where there had been no wind before, now there was a gentle breeze.

"Yes," he yelled, as the breeze flicked at his cloak and the light in his ring flickered and seemed to glow even brighter as it bathed in the magical breeze that Halmer had conjured up. Halmer spoke the words again in a louder voice and the breeze blew stronger and his cloak snapped in a strong wind. Then the light of the ring dimmed and Halmer felt suddenly drained and he realised that he had gone too far. Fortunately Tigress had thought to give him the counter spell and as he muttered the words the breeze disappeared entirely. Leaving Halmer drained of strength and feeling the beginnings of a pounding headache.

"It seems that I am trying to run before I can walk, still I have to begin somewhere."

Halmer's musings where interrupted by the wicker of his horse, or was it another horse. Halmer rushed from the room and down the cracked and crumbling stone steps to the entrance of the tower, to see a horseman approaching his secret hiding place. At first he thought that he had been discovered in spell casting, but after blinking a couple of times the looming figure in crimson robes transformed into the real form of a short, skinny girl. A short, skinny girl that Halmer knew.

"Sky," Halmer cried in surprise. "I told you I wanted to be left alone."

The skinny girl swung out of the saddle and after catching her breath, began to gesture madly with long thin hands.

"Slow down Sky, you know I can't read you when you stutter," Halmer protested, as he tried to read the mute girls sign language.

The girl stopped, took another calming breath, started again, but made slower motions with her hands.

"You come with a summons from Tomas?"

The girl nodded quickly, once Halmer had understood her.

"Where is he?"

As Halmer watched, the girl pointed at his heart and then pointed into the sky.

"He is at our home at the tower?"

The girl nodded her assent.

"Any ideas what he wants me for?"

The girl shook her ginger head.

"Alright Sky, I understand. Can you ride back with me?"

The girl called Sky, nodded and remounting her horse turned it to face back the way they had come.

"Wait a moment and I will fetch Wave."

The girl could not answer, but when Halmer led his milky white mare from where he had tethered her, it was to find Sky waiting for him.

"Come then Sky lets go and see what big brother wants."

Halmer found Tomas, in the courtyard of the short tower that the Healm's had possessed for generations and which they held as a garrison for the King's guard. Tomas was mounted on his great, grey Bane and was surrounded by many of his familiar retinue. In fact to Halmer's surprise, almost their entire small household was mounted, as if ready to leave the city.

"You're leaving?"

Tomas' grim visage cracked into a thin smile, as he replied.

"I have been ordered back to the Wall," Tomas' manner which was grim did not deceive Halmer, he could tell that Tomas was not pleased. This too was a surprise; Tomas usually preferred the north and his beloved wall for he was never comfortable at the court with its web of politics. Halmer would have liked to ask Tomas more about it, but he knew better than to ask Tomas such a dangerous question in the open, even before their household.

"I have left you a letter," Tomas said pointedly, as if he was trying to give Halmer a clue. "As I did not know where you were and thought I would miss you."

Halmer suddenly caught on to what Tomas was trying to tell him, Tomas never left him letters when he was leaving the city, even if he did not know where Halmer was. He would have left a note with Sky, if he missed Halmer. No there was some message that Tomas wished Halmer to read and it no doubt explained what had happened to drive Tomas back to the north.

"I understand," Halmer said, and to his surprise a tear came to his eye. "Will you be gone long?"

Seeing his brother's eye Glisson, Tomas smiled more broadly and he laid a hand on Halmer's shoulder.

"I do not know Halmer, I do not know, but if I guess aright you will see me soon." Then his mask of grim determination, fell back across his features and he was all business again. "I have left Robert to follow on after us with the rest of the guard, but you have Sky and the tower is yours for as long as you need it. Until we meet brother, I pray you good heart and good health. Pray the wall stands."

This comment about the wall, was a family saying and it brought a slight grin to Halmer to hear it.

"Pray the wall stands," he said back, saluting Tomas as his brother wheeled Bane and rode him out of the courtyard's gate and into the dimming light of the glooming.

Halmer blinked back tears and before he knew it the courtyard was empty and the echo of hooves on stone were fading into silence.

"Well Sky it looks like it's just you and me now," Sky did of course not answer, but she grunted and pointed to the tower.

"Yes the tower," Halmer nodded in response. "Let's go and see what Tomas has left us."

What Tomas had left them, was a scroll sealed with his crouching leopard. When Halmer broke the seal, he red with growing fear the letter that his brother had left for him.

"Halmer, I have been ordered back to the wall, in case the Darklings have mustered for war. What I must tell you now if only my impression, but it must not go further than you and I pray you burn this letter once you have read it. The Queen has it in for me and has contrived to get rid of me from the court. I must follow this order and return, but you of course need not so oblige. However, little brother I warn you that the Crimson Brotherhood will grow in strength and any who are close to the Weredings or who practise magic beyond their leave will be in danger of death. So I pray be careful little brother, till we meet again. If you must leave the city in a hurry go to where we were born and I will meet you there. Pray the wall stands Tom."

Once he had read the letter several times, Halmer crossed to where a fire had been made up, but not lit and taking flint and steel Halmer lit the fire. Once it was roaring he cast the letter into the flames and watched as it curled and became ashes.

"Well Sky we're in the bear trap now."

Sky did not respond to this, but going to the table (where the letter had been left), poured a cup of the wine from the decanter there and offered it to Halmer. Who smiled at the girl, who despite not having the ability of speech, seemed to communicate well enough.

"Yes Sky you too can have a wine, I think a toast is in order."

Halmer stopped for a long moment and considered the skinny girl, over the glass. He thought back to the occasion that the girl became his shadow. It had been one of the few times that he had been beyond the Kings. He was in the small port of Port Cullis, just beyond the rampart of the Kings and just inside the Weredings' land. Among the small huts of the traders and river men, he had found Sky begging outside the visitors hall reserved to traders and other travellers. Halmer had decided not to pay the girl in coin, but instead had given her his water skin to drink. She had drank long and deep from it and had given it back to him. He had not seen her after that and although he had stayed in the port for another day or so, had not seen any sign of the beggar girl. However, once he had left the Twins and travelled out into the desert and swampy lands that lay like a grave yard between the north and the south, he had found her trailing him on foot. He had tried to persuade her to return to the twins or Port Cullis, but she had not responded other than to shake her head. He had left her looking after him as he trotted away, but that night she appeared at his camp fire and paid for his water by putting a rabbit on the spit. Halmer who did not believe that anything as wholesome as a rabbit lived in the wastes, asked her where she had gotten it, but once again she only made gestures and he had finally realised that she was a mute. After that she had ridden with him on his horse and had helped him with his exploration of the ruins, ever since then she had served him. Tomas had tried at first to convince him to get rid of her, but Halmer refused to do so. He had grown used to her and she was as good a servant as Halmer had ever had.

"Well old girl, it looks like it's you and me against the world once again."

Sky in response, refilled Halmer's glass and gestured to the plate of bred and meet that was set before him.

"Quite right Sky," Halmer said, smiling widely. "We mustn't forget to live in the present, food first solving problems second. A full belly and a drink in the hand is the best way to live and even not a bad way to die."

With this Halmer emptied his glass.

LUNA'S NEWS

"The truth is often hard to find, especially when reeved in lies."
Bright Eyes to Robin from The Wereding Chronicles.

For a long time Robin stood staring into the fire, trying to work out what was happening to her and her world. Eventually, she shrugged into the robes and deciding that she needed tea rang the bell for Imp. The tea and the Scholar arrived at the same time. Imp baring a tray with tea and several fruit cakes. While Vyman had a bag of instruments and a collection of salves and potions.

"Imperiter tells me that my Lady is ill."

"That's the thing Vyman," Robin said, her voice wavering with uncertainty. "I don't know what it is."

"Let me see," the Scholar coaxed gently.

Robin let the robe drop to her waist, seeming more shy before the man that had tended her for the last few months, than when she had stood before Luna. The Scholar looked at her back and sucked in his breath between teeth, when he saw the raised scale of skin.

"Do you know what it is?" Robin asked, in an almost breaking voice.

The Scholar did not reply, but touched her with something.

"Does that pain you?"

"No," Robin said, for although she could feel the pressure that he was applying, she felt no pain. "What is it?"

"To be honest my lady, I do not know," Vyman admitted, after a long silence. "I have never seen anything like it; I will have to consult my books."

"Never mind your books," Robin snapped, her anger razing its fiery head. "What is it?"

"I'm sorry my Lady, but I really don't know," the scholars face showed his confusion. "I have, as I say, not seen it's like before."

"Is, is it a disease?"

"I am not sure my Lady, you seem none the worse for it and yet the spot is not your skin."

"So, what do I do about it?"

"At this point, I am hesitant to suggest anything," the Scholar said, though he glanced at the small coffer that contained his jars and bottles of salves and potions.

"You want to try something?" Robin asked, reading his mind.

"I was wondering, if a salve might help."

"Will it?"

"I would like to try, my Lady."

"Very well Vyman, start painting."

Vyman painted a strong smelling paste onto her back and wrapped a bandage round her shoulder to cover the salve and the skin. Then he left to return to his laboratory and his books, to see if he could find a corresponding illness and cure. Robin paced round the room, waiting for Luna to return to her. Garm looked in on her, to make sure she was ok and she only half listened to his apologies. Once Garm left her, she watched the fire die. Eventually, Robin decided to read to pass the time and she looked at the many books that filled the room. She noticed that one of the large leather bound volumes was standing slightly proud of its neighbours, as if someone had taken it out and not properly put it back. She drew it forth and putting it on the table opened it. The book fell open to a beautifully and brightly coloured illumination of a strange centaur like creature. It was a beautiful and practically naked woman above the waste, but below she had the body of a dragon, complete with bats wings.

"Behold Campe," Robin red. "The queen of Drakaina guardian of the gods and a Wereding myth."

Robin turned the page to see if there was anything more about this woman. The next page showed a woman who was either wearing skintight snakesskin or her skin was covered in a latticework of scales. As Robin looked at the half mask of green scales that covered her face, she had a kind of vision. She saw a similar mask before her mind's eye, but the face beneath the mask was her own and the mask of scales was red. The world began to swim and Robin would have fainted, but strong hands had suddenly gripped her wrist and waist. Robin blinked back tears and saw to her great relief Luna's face swam before her.

"Sit down before you fall down girl," she whispered and forced Robin into a chair. "Drink this."

Luna thrust a small flask into Robin's hand.

"Luna what's happening to me? What am I changing into?"

"Drink," Luna insisted, as she glanced at the book and its picture on the desk.

Robin sipped from the flask and almost choked on the thick and powerful liquor that dribbled from the bottle.

"Sorry I should have warned you," Luna almost chuckled, as she patted Robin on the back. "It's strong I warrant, but you need it at the moment. As for what you are changing into Robin, I do not know, but I believe I may know a way of preventing it from spreading and turning into something Like Lamia if that is what you fear?"

"You know a cure?"

"NO, not a cure exactly, more of a medication."

"I don't understand!"

"Robin I have consulted the Crimson Master and he believes that your condition is linked to the use of magic."

"Because, I used magic I've sprouted this, this..."

"We believe so."

"So if I don't use magic, it won't spread?"

"I'm afraid Robin, you've gotten it backwards."

"What?"

"We believe that magic is in your blood, it will build up and explode out of you, if you don't siphon it off."

"I don't understand, what are you telling me?"

"Robin somehow you have gotten a great source of magic in your blood and if you don't use magic to draw the poison off, it will kill you."

Robin gulped, as she began to realise what Luna was saying.

"You mean I have to learn and cast magic?"

Robin dreaded Luna's answer, for her father and her nurse had all warned her that using magic was evil and would twist and change a person that used it.

"Yes, that is what I am saying," Luna said, as she took the flask back. "If you learn and cast magic, you can prevent the poison from building up in your blood and skin and changing it like it has already."

"But what about the Crimson Circle?" robin whispered.

"I have cleared it with the Grand Master," Luna said, softly as she rubbed Robin's arm. "He has agreed that if you join their ranks, you will be cleared to practice magic. For the mean time you must wear this."

Luna took from a belt pouch, a ring made of a dark metal and taking Robin's hand slid it onto her finger. As the cold metal slid onto her finger, Robin felt a jolt of energy flair up her arm and the room seemed to swim around her.

"Robin are you alright?"

"I think so," Robin said, shaking her head and focusing on Luna's voice and her short form before her. "What is this about Luna, I don't really wear jewellery."

Luna grinned widely at that.

"The ring tells those in the know that you are awaiting initiation into the Crimson Circle and that you can practice magic under supervision."

"Your supervision?"

"Perhaps," Luna said, grinning back as she understood what kind of supervision Robin meant. "But enough about the ring, I have some important news."

"About what?"

"The Crimson Circle are going to try and arrest the Wereding Ambassador for your father's murder."

"What!" Robin shouted, shooting from the seat as if a rocket had been lit beneath her. "When?"

"In the next few hours," Luna said, a bemused look on her face, as she watched Robin pacing round the room like a caged Tiger.

"I must be there," Robin snapped, as she stopped before Luna. "Luna can you arrange it so that I am there, when she is arrested?"

Luna looked up at Robin, studying her face closely.

"It might be possible," she mused, as if talking aloud. "But I am not sure it is wise."

"I must be there," Robin insisted, reaching out to Luna and resting a hand on the smaller woman shoulder.

"But why?"

"Why?" Robin asked, taken aback by this question. "I must be there."

"But why?" Luna asked again, her face suddenly closed and unreadable. "The Crimson Circle will be able to penetrate the tower and arrest Bright Eyes or their magic will keep them out and the

Crown will then have to get involved. Either way you will serve no one by attending a siege."

"I have to know," Robin insisted stubbornly.

"Granted," Luna conceded. "But what is it you have to know so urgently?"

"Whether it was them."

"Ah, that's it; you believe you will know on sight whether someone is guilty."

Robin turned away, angry and disappointed at the scorn in Luna's voice.

"I know it's ridiculous."

"It might be ridiculous," Luna said, placing a hand on Robin's arm. "But it is a need of the heart and therefore not to be denied."

For a long moment Robin did not understand what Luna had just said, then it sank in and she span to stare down at the shorter woman. Who was grinning up at her, a mischievous glint in her dark green eyes.

"You mean it?"

"Of course I mean it," Luna said, grinning at Robin. Though her expression then turned serious. "We will go with the Crimson Circle strike force, if we can catch them, but you must not act Robin, we can only watch. You must promise me Robin that you will not interfere."

"I'm not sure I can do that," Robin said, in a shaky voice.

"Then we will not go," Luna said, her voice becoming steely, her green eyes becoming hard and unflinching.

"I promise," Robin cried, as she felt the chance slipping through her fingers.

"That's better," Luna said, the smile returning. "Come you will need to dress for riding and I will need to make some preparations of my own, I will meet you outside in twenty minutes."

THE TOWER UNGLOVED

"The most dangerous blade, is a dagger from the dark."
Tomas Healm to a soldier of the north from the Watch Wall records.

Halmer was studying a new spell Tigress had sent him, when the scuff of boot alerted him that he was not alone. He looked up nervously, half expecting to see a black robed brother of the Crimson Circle in the door, but to his immense relief he saw that it was Sky. He also observed that she was bent almost double, her hands on her knees as she tried to regain her breath.

"Sky are you alright?"

After a deep breath, the girl straightened and nodded her head.

"The Circle, is their news?"

Believing that if anyone were to move against him it would be the Crimson Circle Halmer had set Sky to watching their main barracks and to report to him any movements. Sky had once again taken up her role as a street beggar and had watched the large stone building for the last day. Now she was here, it must mean that she had seen some significant movement. Sky nodded in response to this question.

"Are they coming here?"

Sky shook her head.

"Then where?"

Sky pointed to the scroll, spread out before Halmer and twisted her face into a snarl.

"Tigress, you mean Tigress, they're going to attack the Tower of the Glove."

Sky nodded so fast, Halmer thought her head might fall off.

"Quick Sky, we must warn them."

The girl nodded and followed Halmer, as he made to leave the room, but at the door he rushed back and grabbing up the scroll shoved it into his belt.

Halmer questioned Sky as they dashed through the street to where the Tower of the Glove stood on the edges of the city. Even though Halmer had learnt much of Sky's sign language, it was not easy to understand what she was saying, but he managed to make out that a high ranking member of the Circle had led a handful of the Black Fists (the Crimson Circles militant arm and their assassins) out of the gates and had made off in the direction of the Tower of the Glove. Added to this, Sky had heard on the street network that the brotherhood would no longer put up with the Weredings and would kill or drive them from the city. However, by the time they made it to the tower there was no sign of the dark spell casters. Either they had taken a roundabout way to come to the tower, or they were already in place and hidden from sight. Halmer did not enter through the main gate, but through a small wooden door at the back of the property, for which Tigress had given him a key. Once through the door, they were in the grounds and the herb gardens at the back of the tower. Halmer left Sky here and went to find Tigress. As he moved along the narrow gravel path that ran between the fragrant herbs, an animal growled at him from the dark. Halmer froze, he had been to the tower only once after his first meeting with Tigress and had entered this way that time, but there had been no animals that might have snarled at him. The snarl, was followed by a gruff voice out of the dark.

"Who goes there?" snapped the voice and a silver light shun out, catching Halmer in its moon like light.

Halmer found himself raising his hand and he called out in a surprised squeak.

"A friend. I am Halmer, I have come to warn Tigress of an impending attack."

From behind the light, there came a familiar husky whisper.

"It's alright Gildor, it is Lord Healm, a pupil of Tigress."

"Cole, is that you?"

"Yes Lord Healm," the stocky messenger replied and a moment later he moved into the light, his yellow eye glowing in the dim light. "Please forgive our watchfulness, but we are under siege."

"Then you know about the Crimson Circles attack?"

"Their attacking now?" the question was barked by the holder of the lamp, which Halmer now realised was being held close to the ground.

"My servant Sky saw a group of the Black Fists leave the Temple of the Circle not twenty minutes ago. She believes they are coming here to try and drive you out."

"To exterminate us you mean," snapped the growly voice.

"Peace Gilder," Cole whispered. "Please lead Lord Healm to Tigress, Biter can stay with me."

"But what about the lamp?" Gilder growled.

"Take it with you, I do not need it."

"Follow Lord," growled the short form of Gilder.

Halmer followed the bobbing lamp, as it led him along a path and through the towers front door to where Tigress stood in a hall, brightly lit by lamps that glowed with a silvery light that did not seem to be oil or tallow, for they did not flicker. However, for the moment Halmer did not notice these lights, for he was now able to see Gilder clearly. Gilder was a dwarf, a perfectly formed man, who stood only two feet tall, but who never the less looked formidable in a shirt of gleaming ring mail. His shoulder long main glowing golden, in the bright light.

"The Lord Halmer to see you Tiger." The Dwarf growled and turning moved back out into the night.

Halmer could not help but stare after the tiny man.

"Gilder is your first dwarf isn't he my friend?" Tigress' voice, purred in Halmer's ear and made him jump as he remembered himself. "Yes."

An answer that made the tall Wereding laugh heartily.

"Well he has a father and several brothers round here somewhere, so I should get used to him, but come it was not to learn of dwarfs that you have come to see me or am I wrong?"

"I came to warn you that the Crimson Circle or rather the Black Fists are about to launch an attack on this tower."

Halmer took a step back, his hand dropping to his belt, where his dagger was sheaved. For at these words, Tigress' green eyes seemed to blaze with an unearthly light and his top lip curled back revealing long fangs, as an animalistic snarl roiled out of his large body. But as soon as the beast had appeared, it was gone and Tigress face was touched with regret.

"I am sorry about that my friend. I am usually in control of the beast, but sometimes my control slips."

"I am sorry I doubted you," Halmer said, quietly removing his hand from the daggers hilt. "But as I say the dark brothers are coming to attack you."

"Thank you for risking them to warn us," broke in a new voice, that of a tall woman dressed in dark robes, a large silver disk at her throat. "But it is not entirely new news to us Lord Healm."

"Healm the Lady Bright Eyes," Tigress said and he accepted from her the black staff, that Halmer had seen in the cabernet.

"What will you do?"

"Stand and fight," Bright Eyes said.

Halmer opened his mouth to speak, but anything he might have said was drowned out by a great voice that echoed round the tower.

"Weredings you are charged with the death of the Lord Robert Canduss and the disappearance of his daughter. Come out and surrender, or we shall be forced to come and arrest you."

"It is Calador," growled Tigress, "he is one of the Master's right-hand men and is very powerful."

"Well we shall soon see how powerful," Bright Eyes said, as the large moonstone atop her staff flared with a bright silver light.

The feather cloaked form of Kit appeared at Tigress' side, a long wand in hand.

"Will he stand with us?" she whispered, her yellow eyes making Halmer shiver, as they rested on him.

"You needn't," Tigress said, to Halmer. "You have risked much already, in bringing us this news. You might still be able to slip away."

Halmer considered this offer, but the idea of slipping away now, made him feel like a coward. Tomas would probably tell him to run, but Tomas was not here, so Halmer must make his own decisions and live with the results of those decisions.

"I will stay and give you what help I can, though I fear that I can offer you little aid."

"The world is moved by small hands, doing small deeds," Bright Eyes said, between whispering spells. "Still the dark brothers need not know that you helped us."

"How?"

"I will make them think they see another," Tigress said.

"Then hurry," Kit whispered. "We have little time."

As if to underline her point, the night was filled with a huge explosion that rocked the floor below them.

"They've found my flame ward then," Tigress said, as he planted the but of the black staff on the ground.

"Hurry," Kit said, as she and Bright Eyes rushed out of the tower.

"This may tingle," Tigress said, as the staff seemed to darken and the silver seemed to shine brighter. "But will not hurt."

As Tigress chanted, Halmer felt a slight tingling sensation flow over him. At first Halmer thought that nothing had happened, but glancing down a this hands he gasped when he saw that his skin had turned pitch black.

"Come my friend the spell will only last for so long and time is against us."

Tigress made to pass him, but Halmer gripped his arm.

"But what can I do to help?"

"For a start, put your ring on. It will protect you from electrical attacks. You have the scroll I sent you?"

"Yes," Halmer said, slipping the ring from round his neck and onto his finger.

"On that scroll there are spells for lightning, you may have to use them. Now come."

With these words, Tigress rushed out into the night. Halmer followed him, but came to a halt on the fresh hold, as he baulked at the heat and light of the great red fire that blazed along the top of the grounds outer wall. Silhouetted against these dancing flames, were the twisting bodies of two things that might have been men.

"They tried to come over the walls," Tigress said, from the top of the steps "Only to trigger my fire ward spell."

"That won't hold them long," Bright Eyes said, from where she stood at the foot of the steps.

She was proved right, as from beyond the walls a voice began to chant loudly.

"A counter spell," Kit said, as she quaffed a dark liquid from a pewter vile. Halmer could not be sure in the uncertain light, but he thought that Kit's skin became darker and took on a knobbly, knotted appearance, as if it had turned to wood.

Even as Kit remarked this, the flames flickered out and the blackened figures fell from sight, leaving the smell of burning flesh behind them. The disappearance of the fire also leaving the stones glowing with residual heat, but a moment later three or four figures appeared atop the wall. As soon as they did, Tigress, Kit and Bright Eyes all cried out, and Halmer was dazzled as bright lights flashed from the two staffs and Kit's wand. When his sight cleared there was no sign of the figures atop the wall.

"What happened to them?"

"Bright Eyes got one," Tigress informed him, as he drew from a pouch at his hip a small bag. "He fell back off the wall, but three more made it."

"So let's see what they are doing." Kit hissed.

Pointing her wand into the air, she screeched a word of power and a bright, white light shot into the sky and hung high above the tower. Its light spreading into a large rune that hung like a full moon, casting its light over the grounds below.

"Gildor has taken care of one of them," Bright Eyes said, pointing off to the right where near to the wall a flower bed had become a gaping pit. Whether the pit had been dug before and covered like some hunter's dug when catching big game, or if the Weredings had used magic to create it, Halmer was about to ask, when a dark figure that seemed no more than a great shadow moved on the path that led to the steps. As it did there was a creak of wood and suddenly there was a huge spiders web stretched between the lines of trees that shaded the path and trapped in its strands like a huge fly was a figure clad in glittering mail.

"Yes," Kit hissed in triumph, as she ran forwards her wand spitting a flare of fire at the trapped man.

"Kit no! There's another one," Tigress shouted.

Tigress was right; even as the trapped figure's cloak ignited under the fiery attack, a second shadow stepped from behind one of the trees and fired a tiny hand crossbow at Kit. The tiny dart, sending the wand spinning from her hand. Tigress fired a crackling bolt from his staff's tip and Halmer's nose was filled with the smell of ozone, as the crackling electrical blast scorched the air that the figure had occupied. The shadow had stepped back behind the tree, probably to reload the hand bow, for it was suddenly there again and firing it at Kit. However, Kit must have cast some kind of magic upon herself, for the dart bounced off her body and even before the shadow could react, Kit slammed her hands together and from her fists there arched an electric charge that stabbed into the shadow. But whether Kit's magic had no effect, or whether the shadow was immune to her attack Halmer could not tell, but the figure seemed unaffected by her magic. For when the charge failed, the shadow stepped through the web as if it wasn't there and lifting an shadow arm extended it towards Kit. As if Kit weren't already in trouble, the first shadow had hissed words that made the air around it crystallise as if they were freezing and the web quivered and then vanished, as if it had never existed. The second shadow shed its burning cloak and stepped forwards to join its brother in attacking Kit.

"Kit," Tigress screamed in rage and leaping from the steps, he landed beside his lover to face off one of the shadows.

Halmer was about to join him, when he spotted movement from the corner of his eye and turning saw something he had not expected. He had expected to face the Crimson Circle mages and their assassins the Dark Fists, but he had not expected to face ten feet high clouds of fire. The apparition before him seemed to be a living cloud of fire, cast in the shape of a serpentine human. Long tendril like arms of fire reached out for him, while from the crackling flames two spots that burnt brighter than the rest of the thing fixed him with a baleful gaze. As its fiery gaze lit on him, Halmer felt as if a hand of fire caught hold of him and he felt as though he was burning up from inside. Then Bright Eyes was beside him and her staff moved through a mystic pass and her words seemed to bulk the fiery cloud, for it hissed like a spitting cat and turned its attention to her. Now free of the burning sensation, Halmer fired his crossbow at the apparition, for no better reason then it made him feel better. The bolt however, had no effect on the living cloud, for it simply passed through the cloud. Having no more effect then making the cloud ripple, as if it had been stirred by a cast stone. Halmer feeling helpless cast his bow aside and pulling the scroll from his belt unfurled it at squinting at the spell recited the words he saw there. As he did, he plucked from where he wore it round his neck in a small pouch flint and steel and striking them together as if to conjure a spark, he felt the ring on his hand pulse like a heart and from the flint and steel there leapt not a spark, but a stroke of lightning that blasted the fiery cloud. But the stroke seemed to do no more than annoy the cloud, for hissing with rage it either spat an answering lightning bolt at Halmer or, through some magic of its own, it sent Halmer's lightning bolt back at him. Halmer cried out in fear and flung up an arm to protect his face from the blinding bolt. Fortunately it was the one upon which he was wearing the ring, for instead of hitting his body the bolt twisted in mid-air to be drawn like a needle to the magnet of his ring. So although Halmer felt a jolt of shock pass through his arm, he shook it off to see the electricity riving in the heart of his rings stone. It appeared that Tigress had been right, the ring would protect him from electric attacks. Still the snake like cloud was still there and from its riving and hissing Halmer feared a second attack. Bright Eyes once more interposed herself between them; her staff shooting a blue beam of cold that froze the air, but seemed only to dim not quench the clouds flames. The snake hissed and coiling itself as if to strike, flung its flaming body around Bright Eyes. Its fiery coils wrapping her body tightly, as the flaming cloud attempted to either constrict her or burn her with its body, but for some reason that Halmer could not divine the cloud seemed to be suffering just as much as Bright Eyes must be. For it hissed, as if in great pain and its brightness seemed to dim, smoke pouring off it as though its fire was failing.

"Water," Halmer cried helplessly, for he did not know what else to do, but shout, "Water."

However, his cry for water was answered by a tiny form that darted out of the tower entrance to hurl a bucket of water over Bright Eyes and the flaming serpent like cloud that girded her. Whether the water was the last blow, or whether Bright Eyes' magic had succeeded Halmer did not know, but even as the water splashed over the entwined combatants there was a great plume of smoke and the fires of the cloud were finally quenched leaving Bright Eyes free. As the smoke cleared Halmer could see why the cloud had been in pain when it bound her with its coils. Bright eyes appeared to have become a figure of living ice, for her body was encased in a skin of crackling blue ice, which glowed through her burnt and slashed robes. What was more, was that now that the heat of the cloud was gone, he could feel the cold radiating off her in waves. Halmer was about to ask her if she was alright, for he feared that she had been turned into a frozen statue, but before he could she rushed from the steps to rush past Tigress and Kit as she rushed to the gates. Halmer wanted to follow her, but before he did he turned to see who had throne the water and where they were now. Halmer found that it

120

was a tiny woman, her black cap of hair barely coming up to Halmer's waist.

"Thank you. . ."

"Clover my Lord," the girl if she was a girl said, demurely her eyes cast down.

"Thank you Clover," Halmer might have said more, but a crash from the entrance to the grounds drew his attention.

"The gate is down," Tigress shouted, as he slashed a blade of fire at his shadow.

"My bow?" Halmer asked, looking about for his discarded weapon.

"Here my Lord," Clover said, as she held out his bow to him. "My Lord your skin is changing."

Halmer looked down at his hands, to see their inky shade paling.

"Tigress said the magic wouldn't last long."

Quickly arming the bow Halmer rushed to help Tigress, only to find that the shadow lay at his feet in a crumpled and chard heap. Halmer shuddered, as he looked down at the blackened body of the thing that must have been a man. He turned to see if Kit needed any help, but she too had killed her opponent. Her hands were now long cruelly curved talons, that were dripping blood.

"Quick the gate," Tigress said and with a flair of silver light and a muttered word, Tigress seemed to become a streak of motion, as he moved with blinding speed.

"Have they broken in?" Halmar asked Kit, as he tried to focus on her face and not her cruel hands and their dark stains.

"I did not think it possible, but yes. Come let us see what we can do."

THE CIRCLE TIGHTENS

"A snare will choke you, but it can still be cut or slipped."
K. to Moonstone from The Wereding Chronicles.

When Robin (now clad in britches, boots, leather jerkin and long riding cloak), emerged from her home it was to find the giant mute Wolf waiting for her. Luna's tongueless servant, was holding the bridles of three horses. Robin recognised her own Horse and the giant horse that had born Wolf that day.

"Where is Luna?" Robin asked the giant, not expecting an answer. However, she received one. The giant pointed to the house, and even as Robin turned to look where he was pointing, Luna emerged from the house, a large pouch in her hand.

"Are we ready?" She asked, as she strode up to them. Wolf boosted her into the saddle and taking the reins, she dug her heels into the horse's flanks and with a neigh the horse galloped into the night. Leaving Robin to leap into the saddle and gallop in the smaller woman's wake, with Wolf bringing up the rear.

"Where are we going?" Robin shouted to Luna, when she brought her mare alongside Luna's.

"The Crimson Circle will have begun the attack on the Weredings, so we go to the Tower of the Glove and see what we shall see."

Luna led them to a sparsely inhabited region of the city on its northern outskirts, where a large tower stood in its own walled grounds. In front of the tower's main gate there stood a cluster of about ten men and women, dressed in black. As the trio rode up, the leader a tall emaciated figure was speaking in a voice that echoed off the walls of the tower.

"Weredings you are charged with the death of the Lord Robert Canduss and the disappearance of his daughter come out and surrender or we shall be forced to come and arrest you."

"Who is this that acts in my father's name?" Robin asked, as she looked on the tall almost skeletal figure wrapped in his black robes.

"His name is Calador," Luna said, as she slid down from her horse. "He is high up in the order of the Crimson Circle; he appears to be in charge of this group. Shall we see how he does?"

Robin who wanted to confront the Weredings herself, dismounted and would have strode to the skeletal man, but Luna sensing her mood impose herself between them.

"You promised not to interfere," Luna said, as she slid between Robin and the group of black clad figures.

Robin nodded, as she watched two of the black clad figures run up the stone wall that marked the grounds boundary walls. As she watched the two figures ran up the stone, as if the vertical plane was horizontal.

"Is that magic they are using?" Robin asked, as she watched them reach the top of the wall.

Luna turned, to consider the two black clad figures standing atop the wall.

"Yes, the Black Fists have certain amounts of magic at their disposal," Luna agreed. "Though, whether it is enough to match the Weredings remains to be seen."

As if to enfosice Luna's point, the wall upon which the two black figures stood suddenly burst into flames and the two figures screamed horribly as they were wrapped about by the burning flames of a magical fire.

"Calador should not use his assassin's as cannon fodder," Luna sighed. "He should know better than to send his men straight at the Weredings, that will only get them killed."

Once again Luna seemed to have guessed the spell casters mind, for the tall thin man raised a silver skull tipped black staff and began to chant in a strange tongue.

As Robin watched fascinated, she felt the air around her thickening and a wind shrieked strangely around her.

"What exactly is he doing?" Robin asked, as she felt a coppery taste at the back of her mouth.

"I believe that he is casting a counter spell that should banish the flames and any other defensive spells on the wall so that he can send in more fighters."

Even as Luna said this, the flames blinked out and the burnt corpses that had been the attackers fell from the wall. Robin felt sick, as the smell of burnt flesh washed over her like a dragons breath. Calador however, was unaffected by the loss of his men, for with a shriek of his high voice he ordered four more of the black clad figures towards the wall.

"Will they make it?"

"Perhaps," Luna replied, as she watched the four figures run up the wall like it was a gentle slope. "But I doubt that all of them will make it over."

Once again Luna predicted the events correctly, for as the four figures reached the top of the wall, voices from beyond the wall called out and Robin had to blink as bright lights flashed, silhouetting the four cut-outs that were assassins. With a cry of pain, one of them fell backwards, toppling to land at the feet of the tall spell caster that was leading the assault. The three remaining figures disappeared from sight and Robin realised that they had leapt down into the towers grounds.

"Will they succeed?"

"Probably not," Luna said and then she grinned wickedly. "Unless we help them. Would you like to see me cast magic Robin?"

"Is it illegal?"

Luna's response was a deep laugh.

"Wolf get me some fire wood," Luna ordered, as she began to scratch a symbol in the ground before her with a long, if gnarled stick.

Robin watched as the giant strode to a nearby sapling and wielding a long handled axe, cut several boughs from the tree. She switched her attention between Wolf and Luna, as she was scattering packets of herbs over the circle she had drawn around her and the tall black clad Crimson Circle leader as he too began to cast a magic. Robin wanted to concentrate on Luna, but her attention was drawn to the black clad sorcerer. Robin watched fascinated, as his silver skull tipped staff glowed with sickly green light and before his thin frame there appeared a great green saw-toothed ring that span towards the wooden gates of the wall and like some great serrated knife spun on the spot. Its jagged teeth biting into the wood and spitting splinters in all directions.

But her attention was drawn back to Luna, by a bright flash of light. Robin turned back to find that Luna had lit a small fire within the circle and as she watched Luna began to dance about it. Capering about, her long cloak fluttering and floating about, as her small form leapt into the air to land perfectly balanced. Her hands flicking in mystic gestures, as she chanted and cast. Robin was captivated by the grace of Luna's movements. Luna moved with the speed and grace of a dancer and the agility of some great cat. Robin could hardly bring herself to look away from the lithe form of the woman she loved-lusted for. But difficult as it was to tare her eyes away, the fire blazing up and filling the area with light snapped her eyes back to the conflagration. Even as Robin watched, the fire that now stood taller than a man twisted and rived until it resembled a huge snake like form that lowered its head towards Luna, as if it was enquiring what she wanted.

"Enter and consume." Luna said, to the fiery cloud that detached itself from the fire and floated towards and then over the wall.

"What was that?"

"An elemental, a spirit of fire," Luna said, as she leaned on her gnarled stick.

"You summoned it?"

Luna nodded, her head bowed, her sweat matted hair hanging down into her face and Robin realised that Luna was using the stick to hold her up.

"Luna are you ok?"

Luna lifted her head, though it seemed to take all her strength to do it.

"Summoning is never easy," Luna wheezed and Robin was shocked to see just how old and grey Luna looked. "Fire spirits are particularly difficult to bend to the will, as they are so quicksilver in nature."

"Wolf," Robin cried and the giant, seeming to sense too that his mistress was unwell or drained, strode to his mistress' side and lifting her in his arms carried her to where the horses had been tethered. "Will she be alright? Is there something I can do?"

Wolf did not reply, not that he could with words, but pulling a flask from his belt he thrust it into Robin's hands while, lifting Luna into a sitting position.

"What is this?"

"It will give me the strength to carry on," whispered Luna in response to Robin's question to Wolf.

Understanding Robin unstoppered the flask and kneeling at Luna's side, held the flask between her teeth and Luna gulped the sweet smelling liquid down. She lifted a hand when she had enough and Robin removing the flask looked at her face, to see that much of her colour had returned though Luna still looked very tiered.

"Better?" Robin asked.

Luna opened her mouth to reply, but whatever answer she meant to give was drowned out by a great grown and crash that shook the earth beneath them. Robin glanced over her shoulder, to see that the Crimson Circle had succeeded in penetrating the Tower of the Glove. For the great gate that had held against them, was rent and fallen at Calador's feet, as the tall wraith like spell caster stood upon its fresh hold, his assassins ranged behind him.

THE TRIAL OF WATCHING

"Sometimes, watching is not enough sometimes we feel we must act,
but sometimes to act is not the right thing. We watch, judge and only
act when we must."
K. to Moonstone from The Wereding Chronicles.

When Halmer and Kit reached the gates it was to find Bright Eyes stood just inside the ruin that had been the gates. Her staff held high, its crystal head glowing with a flickering silver light that resembled moonlight. At her side Tigress crouched, his hands weaving, his voice snarling through the fraises of an incantation. On the other side of the gate, a tall figure clad in black robes stood its own skull tipped staff glowing with a light that reminded Halmer of marsh gas. Lined up behind this black brother were about four black clad assassins, some clutching daggers and short swords others were casting their own spells.

"We have to help them, they can't stand alone against them," Halmer said and made to rush forwards, but Kit clutched his arm.

"Wait," the short woman hissed. "Tigress' spell of concealment has faded the Black Brother and his servants will see your face, wait here by the trees. If they get past Eyes and T. use your crossbow, but do not move from here."

Halmer opened his mouth to protest, but Kit rushed (feathered cloak billowing), to Tigress' side, her own voice now raised in chant.

"They will not stand alone," Halmer whispered, as he made to rush forwards, but he was restrained.

As he made his mind up, a hand reached out of the shadows and gripped Halmer's arm. Surprised Halmer followed the arm that held him back, to find Sky staring white eyed back at him. It appeared from her signs that she had overheard Kit's words.

"No stay, hide."

"Very well Sky for your sakes," Halmer said gently, for he realised that Sky had no way to protect herself and she was in the middle of this battle because of him, so he would protect her as best he could. If that meant hiding and hanging back then he would do it.

A cry drew Halmer's eyes back to the standoff, to see one of the black clad assassin's had screamed as he leapt through the air at Bright Eyes. Halmer tried to get his crossbow up for a shot, but before he could the figure's foot connected with Bright Eyes' body and a scream of pain rang out to cut the night. The assassin fell at Bright Eyes' feet, his body curling into a ball, as it tried to deal with the pain that had overwhelmed it when its foot had connected with the Wereding's ice-encrusted body. Halmer grinned with relief as he saw this, but his grin of triumph was wiped from his face as with a crack like fracturing ice the spell ended. The blue glow that radiated through her skin vanished and she was a flesh and blood woman again.

The tall skeletal spell caster must have believed that this attack had weakened Bright Eyes, for he ordered another of his attackers forwards. Bright Eyes however, was not quite spent yet and with an imperious sweep of her arm she flung out her arm to point at the black clad assassin and the man froze rigidly in place, as though he had been caught by a sudden frost that had turned him into a statue. The Black brother snarled and hissed words of power. Halmer felt them vibrate through the air and suddenly he was blind. He blinked and found that his sight cleared, to reveal that he had not gone blind, but the gate had been engulfed in a cloud of utter darkness.

"They won't be able to see in there," Halmer said, to Sky, but turning to her he found her squatting on the ground attempting to light a torch. "Good girl. Let's see if I can do as well."

Pulling the scroll out of his belt, he squinted at the spidery writing and found the words of power that would conjure light. However, before Halmer or Sky could finish their attempts the cloud of darkness began to drift away as a strong wind began to move it. Then a brilliant, blinding flash of light wiped the cloud away.

When Halmer's eyes had recovered from the glare, it was to discover that the last two assassins were lying either dead or incapacitated at Kit's and Tigress' feet. Though it appeared that Kit too was injured, for her robe was torn at the shoulder and her arm was drenched in blood, though she still appeared to be standing.

With all his minions taken care of the Black Brother was left no choice, but enter the grounds and face the trio himself. He chanted words of power and twisted a silver ring on his left hand. Halmer's eyes narrowed, as he saw a nimbus of black light flicker into existence around him. Halmer realised that the dark brother had cast some kind of defensive magic's upon himself. A fact that he confirmed minutes later, for as the dark brother glided forwards and through the shattered gates Halmer fired his crossbow at him. The bolt bounced of some invisible shield that surrounded the man and several inches away from his body the bolt was turned aside effectively as if the sorcerer were wearing a suit of plate armour. Halmer decided to try again, in the hope that his second bolt might have more success, or that a second attack might at least weaken the spell, but his second bolt too was turned aside. Halmer still had plenty of bolts, but by now the dark brother had come too close to the trio that stood to block him.

"Bright Eyes get back," Tigress snarled, as he straightened to his full height.

"No Tigress, he is mine," Hissed Kit.

"Neither of you are fit to face him now." Tigress snarled, as he held his staff before him. Its rune tip glowing, with unleashed power. "Bright is drained and you are hurt. Bright tend to Kit while I deal with this insect."

Bright Eyes did not argue with Tigress, but taking hold of Kit's uninjured arm, drew her back to the tree line. Where she began chanting over the smaller woman's bleeding arm. While Tigress stood in the dark brothers path, his staff head glowing brighter as he drew upon its power to cast a spell of his own. Sensing perhaps that Tigress was casting an offensive spell, the tall black robed figure began to chant in response. Tigress however, was strengthening his own defences, for as Halmer watched, a nimbus of flames haloed the tall cat-man. This fiery shield however, could have been the best defence that Tigress could have cast, for as he reached the end of his casting and the halo formed around him the black brother finished his own casting. From the eyes of his silver skull staff tip there shot twin beams of black energy that must have been freezing, for icicles formed in the air which the rays passed through and a spray of steam was thrown up as the beams splashed against Tigress' fiery halo. The black robed sorcerer cursed and cast another spell. Tigress too began chanting and they finished almost simultaneously. Tigress' spell sent a crackling stroke of lightning at the black brother, but the sorcerer's spell seemed to make Tigress' shape flicker and shift. For a long moment Halmer did not see Tigress standing within the flames, but another form entirely. Tigress had appeared to transform into a tall figure wearing black armour, his head encased in a full helmet crafted to resemble a snarling wolf. Halmer could not believe what he was seeing and realising that the black brother had cast an illusion over Tigress, shaded his eyes and looking more closely could see a flickering between the two images, one flicker of the fiery shield and he saw Tigress, the next it was the tall black wolf helm. Halmer could not understand why the black brother had done this, the spell seemed not to effect Tigress other than make him look like someone else. Tigress' spell however, slammed into the black nimbus that protected the sorcerer and seemed to penetrate it, for the spell caster was sent several steps back. His arms jerking, his lips snarling his pain.

Then a new figure came screaming into the gate, its long sword flashing in the light. Its red hair flying out behind it, as it charged at Tigress.

Robin had kept her word to Luna, she had watched and stood by as the gate fell and the assassins battled with the Weredings, even though she was itching to draw her sword and plunge into the fight. But her word held her in place at Luna's side, until the flickering light of crisscrossing spells light up the black wolf helm that Robin knew and hated. Then it did not matter that she had given her word to Luna, she thought of nothing but revenge on that dark figure. Before Luna or Wolf could stop her, she had ripped her sword from its back sheath and was sprinting through the shattered gates her voice raised

130

in rage and triumph, as she closed in on her enemy.

Tigress saw the red haired figure charging at him and redirected his spell at it. Robin's charge was brought up sharp when a crippling hand of ice grabbed hold of her and squeezed her in its fist. Robin's breath seemed to freeze in her chest and she thought she was going to die. Then from somewhere deep inside her a voice seemed to whisper words in her ear and Robin thought past the cold in her throat to hiss the words she heard in her minds ear. The cold fist that clutched her was gone, as suddenly as it had appeared and she was charging the wolf helm once again.

Tigress saw the ice that his spell had conjured melt away from the red hair girl, as red flames kindled around her mirroring his own fire skin spell. He realised that this girl was a powerful spell caster, though she did not wear the usual black robes of the Circle. Still she was coming to Calador's aid and that meant she was an enemy. Tigress drew more from his already taxed staff and began to chant the words of one of his most powerful harming spells. However, as his voice rose in volume, Kit heard his chant and recognising the spell for what it was and realising who it was aimed at intervened.

"No Tigress, she is the Canduss girl we need her alive."

Tigress did not stop chanting, but refocused on the black brother and moment's later claws of fire reached out to tear at the man. The black brothers spell sent a bolt of black lightning at Tigress. The Wereding expected that his ring would absorb the electrical attack, as it had done dozens of times before, but the stroke must have consisted of some darker magic. For although Tigress felt the electricity arch to his ring and sink into the stone, the darkness however, flowed through Tigress' arm and slammed into his body. Washing over him in a wave of soul numbing pain.

Leaving Tigress curled on the ground, his voice a wordless hiss that could not form words of magic no matter how much he tried. His opponent however, seemed little better off. For he had fallen to one knee, his black robes burnt away. The rents in his cloth revealing blackened flesh.

Robin however, was not affected and she was still convinced that

Tigress was Kain and so she charged at him and might have attacked him, if Bright Eyes had not hit her with a ray of frost from her staff. A ray that warred with the flaming halo and although it did not snuff out the flames, it did seem to freeze Robin in place.

"Kit get them outside the walls," Bright Eyes shouted, her teeth gripped as she seemed to paw strength into the attack.

Kit hunkered down and grasping her medallion began to cast a spell. Even as Bright Eyes' ray sputtered out and she fell to her knees drained of strength, a great wall of wind appeared from nowhere and Robin and the black brother found themselves being forced backwards. Robin screamed and tried to force her way back to the fallen Kain, but the wall forced her away and as soon as they were outside the broken gate the portal sealed itself with a great wall of stone that blocked the gap so that the breach was sealed leaving a tall wall keeping them out. Robin realising that she had been denied her revenge, howled in anguish and hammered at the wall with her sword. Then Luna was at her side and was holding her by the wrists.

"Enough Robin, enough," she shouted into Robin's face, as she tried to restrain the taller woman.

"I was so close," Robin moaned and then she collapsed into Luna's arms sobbing, as she broke down.

Luna did not reply to this, but simply rocked Robin trying to comfort her with her presence until the exhausted girl fell unconscious.

"Wolf," she ordered her servant. "Take Robin back to her house."

Luna watched as the huge man carried Robin's limp body and draping her across his horse rode away. Only once she was gone, did Luna turn like an enraged Tiger on the black brother.

"You tricked her into thinking that Kain was in there!" she snarled, her green eyes blazing, her voice as cold as ice.

Her rage was met by cold laughter.

"You are a one to talk about elusions."

"Speak your mind Calador."

"You are tricking her into thinking you love her."

"There is no lie in my love for her," Luna spat back.

"Ha, lie to me, but not yourself."

"Enough," spat Luna, her rage flaring in her eyes like lightning on the horizon. "You endangered her, that I will not allow."

"You will not allow," shot back the tall sorcerer. "You are a bystander in this war, my master is yours too."

"I am my own master, and now you will learn it."

Before the black brother could act or do anything to stop her, Luna drew a dagger from her belt and leaping across the distance between them plunged its glowing tip into the man's breast.

"I protect my own," Luna hissed, as she watched the man's spirit fade from his eyes.

THE LICKING OF WOUNDS

"Wolves lick their wounds when hurt, but we burn our flesh to make it whole. Perhaps the wolves have the right of it!"
Lor to Kye, The Wereding Chronicles.

I nside the grounds of the Tower of the Glove Bright Eyes and her fellow Weredings were counting the cost of the battle.

"Bright Eyes how is Tigress?" Halmer, asked as he looked down at the tall man, who was still curled in a foetal position.

Bright Eyes did not reply for a long time, her concentration focused on Tigress. Her hand placed on his cold sweaty forehead.

"Eyes," whispered Kit who knelt on Tigress' other side, a thin line of blood trickling down her arm from under the bandage ignored in her concern for her lover.

"He has been wounded by some dark magic," Bright Eyes said, in a distant voice.

"Will he recover?"

"He is already recovering, but he will do better if we can warm him."

At this Kit called into the dark.

"Clover, stoke up a fire."

From out of the darkness there emerged Cole, (his arm in a sling).

"She has already done it," he said, his voice revealing his own pain.

"Come then help me carry him into the tower," Bright Eyes said, though she struggled to get to her feet. She too was drained of strength and it was Cole who supported her, as she struggled to her feet.

Kit, Halmer and Sky helped to carry Tigress into the tower where they placed him before a roaring fire and Clover gave Kit a mug of mulled wine.

"Can he drink it?"

"I think he can Kit," Bright Eyes said, as she too accepted a mug from Clover.

"Bright have you any healing magic's?"

"I know some of course, Cole, but I am not strong enough to cast them and besides the moon is only just beginning to wax, they may not work. I cast two spells tonight that never worked. However, I do have a stock of healing potions. Clover the satchel on my work bench."

Halmer was aware of the tiny girl leaving the room, but his attention was on Tigress. Who had recovered enough to sit up and swallow the mulled wine, though his gaze still seemed vacant.

"Howes he doing Kit?"

"It might take a time, but I think he's coming round."

"What's the score? Is anyone else harmed?"

Gilder entered at this point, two dwarfs that by their resemblance must have been his sons in tow.

"Well you can all sleep safe in your beds," Gilder snapped, as he surveyed the room "Me an me boys have swept the grounds. There is none of that stinking Black Fists left."

"What about the one you dropped in the pit?"

"AR did I forget to tell thee that hole just closed up. He just needs a marker now and he well buried."

Halmer shivered at the grim, but cold way the dwarf referred to the death of a man. Though Halmer could not blame the dwarf for the death, after all they had been attacking him.

"That raises a point," Cole said, as he accepted a small silver vile from Clover. "What do we do about the bodies?"

He chinked the vile with Kit and they both quaffed the thick milky looking liquid.

"We drop them outside the grounds and let the Black Brotherhood deal with them," Kit said, as she fed Tigress the same milky liquid.

"Regarding the Black brothers and the rest of the Kingdom," Cole said, as he unwrapped his sling to inspect his healed wound. "What happens now, I mean we have killed them."

"What are the consequences?" Bright Eyes asked, as she watched Tigress look up at her with focused eyes and when she helped him to his feet he stood unaided looking about him.

"Tigress can you hear me?" Kit asked, her eyes fixed on her lovers.
Tigress did not answer her with words, but instead swept her up
in his embrace and hugged her to him. Kit cried out in pleased relief
and flung her arms about his neck. Embarrassed Halmer turned
away, to meet Bright Eyes' intense gaze.

"What is it?"

"Did any of the Black Fists or the Crimson sorcerer see you
properly?"

A knife of fear twisted in Halmer's bowels, but he shook his head.

"At least I don't believe so," Halmer said hesitantly. "Why would
it matter, if they did?"

"What about the Canduss girl? Did she see you?"

"She had eyes only for Tigress, she seemed to hate him! Why was
that? Was it something to do with the illusion cast upon him?""

"That will keep for the moment, did she see u or not?"

"Once again I don't believe so, but why do you ask?"

"Because, if they did what I am about to propose could be very
dangerous for you."

"Bright what will happen next?" the tiny girl asked, as she
collected the vials.

"I will protest the invasion of the Crimson Circle and the Crown
will deny that it had anything to do with the attack."

"But we have killed them!" Cole objected.

"Yes Cole and for that I expect the Circle will try to destroy us
utterly. So I don't suggest that any of us go out into the city or the
Fists will be stabbing you in the back."

"But will they attack again?"

"No Clover I don't think so, or at least not tonight anyway.
Which may give us the chance we need?"

"What chance," Halmer said, drawing Bright Eyes' attention back
to him. "What is it you want me to do?"

"We must attempt to find out what the situation at court is. Is the
King about to mobilise the city guard against us? Has he sanctioned
a private war between us and the Crimson Circle and a hundred
other details before I can decide what our next move should be."

"And you need me to do that?" Halmer asked, though he already knew the answer.

"It will mean great danger for you and I cannot order it, but if you could try and find out what the court is thinking it will help us immensely."

"If it will help you decide," Tigress's voice broke in, from behind them. "I promise to teach you any spell it is within my power to teach."

THE ROAD TO REVENGE

"Vengeance is a poison that can consume you and blind you to the truth."

Lightning to the Red Wizard from The Wereding Chronicles.

When Robin finally woke, it was with a blinding headache. "Where am I?" she croaked, her voice hoarse, her throat dry. Her mouth felt furry, as if she had not drank in many days.

"In your own bed my Lady," Imp's voice, whispered at her side. "Here drink this."

Robin accepted the cup and gulped down the blessedly cold water.

"Please my Lady sip. If you drink too quickly you will be sick."

"What happened...Oh yes the Tower of the Glove...How long have I been out?"

"An entire day," Luna's voice, came from the other side of the bed and when Robin glanced in her direction, it was to see that the girl was still wearing the same clothes that she had gone to the tower in and Robin realised that the little woman had not left her bedside in all that time.

"Thank you," Robin whispered.

Luna shrugged and smiled tiredly at her, but the smile was somehow sad, not relieved.

"Robin much as I am glad to see you awake, I have some bad news for you."

"It's not Rose?"

"No, no there is no news about your sister. No it concerns you and your. . ." Luna groped for some elusive words. "Condition."

"My condition...What's wrong?"

"The patch has grown," Luna said, her voice flat and emotionless.

"Luna what is happening to me? What is the magic changing me into?"

138

"I do not know Robin! I am sorry, but I don't. I wish I did, but I don't. You need to leach the magic off, only then can you prevent it from spreading." Luna's expression grew grimmer, "It might have helped if you didn't go charging into a magical jewel."

"I am sorry about breaking my word," Robin said, suddenly ashamed and abashed.

Luna's face was suddenly lit up, by a sunburst of a smile.

"You were thinking with your heart and that's why I love you."

Robin's mood brightened, as she realised that she was forgiven.

"But why did you charge in like that?"

"I saw him," Robin said, her face growing darker. "In a flash of light I saw his wolf helm."

"Kain?"

"Yes Kain," Robin spat, her face twisting with anger. "I didn't think, I just wanted to kill him and I might have gotten to him, if it wasn't for that big Witch."

"That big Witch was Bright Eyes Silverbrow, the Wereding ambassador and an old and powerful Werewolf. But even if she had not intervened, you are no match for Kain. He is too powerful for you yet."

"But I will have his head!" Robin snarled.

Luna chuckled at that.

"Perhaps, but not until you are more powerful in magic."

"But I need to learn anyway, to stop this poison in my blood," Robin said, as she grasped at any means to obtain her vengeance. "Please Luna help me get him."

Luna looked sceptical, and then with a shake of her fiery head, she grinned.

"Very well, we will see what you can do."

Robin through back the sheets, to find that she was still wearing the same clothes she had had on that night, save of course her boots. Which she found at the side of the bed.

"Slowly my Lady," Imp said, concernedly. "Scholar Vyman says you may still be weak from the events."

But Robin didn't feel weak quite the reverse, she felt buzzing with energy and felt that she could face any task that Luna might set her. Luna however, was more cautious.

"I warn you that magic draws on your own reserves of strength. You can cast the simplest of spells, but if you are not ready or are tired or weakened by illness it can draw too much strength from you. So we will try a small spell and see if you can manage it. If you feel too weak, let me know at once and we will stop. Do you understand?"

"Yes I understand," Robin said, eagerly for although she had been led to believe that magic was evil, she no longer believed that and besides she was being driven to learn magic so that she could stop the growth of the dark skin.

Luna considered her closely, as if she was not sure she believed her. Then with a shrug, she removed from her belt pouch a small clear crystal, which she placed in Robin's hand.

"What is this for?"

"It is a component of the spell, you are about to cast."

"Oh, what do I do with it?"

"The spell I am about to teach you, will tell you if there is any magic in the area."

"Will it tell me what the magic is?"

"Possibly, it depends how good you are at it, but if you can sense where magic is concealed it will be a start. Now concentrate on the crystal."

Robin looked deeply into the heart of the stone, her mind noticing the way that the light seemed to flicker like a tiny flame.

"Focus on the stone and speak the following words. Speculum revealum."

Robin felt a little ridiculous as she said the words, but concentrating on the stone she willed the spell to work. But no matter how she concentrated, nothing happened.

"Concentrate," Luna hissed, in Robin's ear, but Robin could not have been more distracted by the alluring sensation of Luna's lips only inches from her ear.

Still she tried to focus on the stone, but still nothing happened.

"You need more power! Think of energy flowing from you to the

140

stone and then out into the room," Luna whispered again.

Robin focused on the stone and although her eyes were staring into the stone, her mind's eye imagined a beam of energy flow from her head and into the stone. As she did this, she felt something like a door crack open and she felt a wave of power flow through her. The crystal seemed to turn red and then a red beam of energy stabbed out from the crystal and swept the room before her. The beam flickered back and forth, as if it were seeking something, but it seemed to find nothing and Robin wondered if she had somehow failed. Then Luna stepped before her and the beam immediately moved from one side, to focus on Luna. The beam hovered over her and then touched several spots of her body. Robin saw a medallion, a ring and the dagger at her waist all appear as if the beam had surrounded them in a halo of light and then the beam vanished and Robin felt drained of strength. She might have fallen, but Luna was there to catch her and help her back to her bed, where Robin slumped looking up at Luna. She remembered what the revealing ray had shown her.

"You have a neckless, a ring on your right hand and your dagger are all magical in some way," Robin whispered.

Luna's face broke in a grin.

"Congratulations, you have cast your first spell. You have taken your first steps towards revenge."

Robin smiled, as she faded into unconsciousness. For she now knew that she would be able to claim her revenge.

When Robin came round this time, it was to find that she had only been out that night and it was the next day. She also found that this time Luna was not waiting for her, but Imp, who brought her tea at once told her that she had gone to the Crimson Circle and would return soon.

"Is there any news of Rose?"

"No my Lady," Imp said, sadly. "If I had heard anything, I would have told you as soon as you woke."

Robin changed into leggings and a shirt and going to her father's library, began to read the book she had found the day before. It turned out to be a kind of Bestiary, listing the different kinds of Weredings and listing their notable members. Robin found a large illustration of seven figures. One of them being the tall, robed woman who had frozen Robin last night, not two nights ago. The illustration even showed her holding her tall staff, with its large crystal like cap stone. At the top of the illustration, was written a caption that said this were the seven siblings of the Silverbrow clan. Below the figures were their names. The woman, was as Luna had said Bright Eyes. To her right, was a tall man holding a great, black longbow, and to her left was a woman that could have been her twin, save for the fact that her arms were silver and her hair was all but silver.

"So these are the creatures that Rose is with?" Robin muttered, as she looked at the cruel wolf like features of the group. Noting their yellow eyes and long teeth.

"Yes and not one of them is to be underestimated," came Luna's voice, from behind her. "Even the youngest, Moonstone is more accomplished in magic than you."

Robin jumped when she heard Luna's voice, for she had not heard her enter, but she relaxed when she realised who it was.

"I wish I had seen this before, it would have at least let me know who my enemies were."

"And I might have shown it to you, if I had known of it. I did not know that your father possessed a copy."

"The Lord Canduss knew much about the Weredings and their magics," boomed a new voice that seemed to fill the small book lined room.

Robin turned to see that filling the studies door was a huge man, draped in the robes of the Crimson Circle. A huge red chain hanging about his neck.

"Robin may I introduce Lord Alden Scarison the Grand Master of the Crimson Circle."

Robin shivered to meet the man that had been called a dark spell caster, but when she looked at his face she did not see the face of a monster. Rather she saw a broad, flabby face that had the broken blood vessels look of a heavy drinker, but who still war a look of dignity.

"Please to meet you my lord," Robin said, though she did not move to shake his hand or bow to him.

The giant Grand Master, though did not seem to notice or care as he rumbled on.

"Luna tells me that you want to learn magic?"

"Need, not want," Robin replied, though she could not bring herself to meet his eyes, as she answered him. She did not fear the man's rumoured evil, but she did fear the power he wheeled. This was a man that had the power to crush her and her house.

"Well I imagine that Luna has already begun to teach you."

"A single spell," Robin said, quietly.

"Well we will have to do better than that, won't we?"

Robin looked up, with surprise when the dark man burst into deep, throaty laughter.

"It will take a couple of days, but we can have you initiated into the order as soon as you like."

"And then I can practice magic?"

"My girl then you can wheel magic that can move mountains," boomed the giant and he burst into more laughter.

Luna turned, from where she had been examining the illustration, to stare directly at the giant.

"I wish to be Robin's tutor," her green eyes boring into the giants own.

"Oh, really," the giant said grinning. "I would have thought that my Ladies duties would prevent her from teaching, our young friend. I was thinking that Calador would be her teacher."

"That cadaverous skeleton," Luna spat, contempt clearly written on her face.

"He is my greatest spell caster," Scarison shot back.

"He might be, but he is probably the worst person to teach," Luna snarled back.

"My dear Luna it has long been known to me that you hate my lieutenant. But you cannot fault him in his duties. He is the master of the school of novices."

"A rank he abuses," Luna snarled.

The big man's face changed from jolley, to serious.

"Luna you are one of my favourites, but even my patience is not limitless."

"Neither is mine," Luna shot back, her green eyes filled with a sparking light. Her hand falling to her belt.

"Luna I do not wish to fall out with you, perhaps a compromise is in order," rumbled the big man.

This seemed to make Luna hesitate.

"What did you have in mind?"

"Robin can serve her first period with Calador and if he thinks she is progressing well, you can take over her training."

Luna turned away from Scarason and towards Robin and when her back was to the giant, she gave Robin a wink. that told robin that this was exactly what she had wanted. Robin got the impression that Luna had just manoeuvred the giant into the position she had wanted him to be in, without letting him know.

"I agree, but will Calador?"

"He will if I order it."

"And will you?"

"If The Lady Canduss is agreeable to this arrangement."

They both looked at Robin then, seeming to ask her permission, though they had been talking about her as if she wasn't there. She had not liked the tall skeletal sorcerer, she was aware that he had attacked the Weredings who she considered her enemies and she had witnessed that he was very powerful. So she supposed that he would be able to teach her. She shrugged.

"When can we begin?" Robin said, reluctantly.

"Calador is still healing and my brothers are waiting for the full moon, but then we can bring you into the fold."

"I can't wait," Robin said, though in truth she was uncertain and almost afraid of what this path might lead to.

The Grand Master bowed to them and was gone, with a swirl of black robes. As soon as he was gone, Luna was in robin's arms. Her own wrapped round the taller girl's neck.

"We've done it Robin," she purred, into Robin's ear. "You'll have to spend a week or so at the temple and then you're all mine."

Robin didn't know how she felt about that, but she could not resist Luna's sunburst smile and when Luna began kissing her face, Robin could not resist the fire that flared up inside her.

BAITING THE LION IN HIS DEN

"Sometimes the only way to catch the spider, is to enter his parlour."
Eloo to Kye, Kye's journal.

Halmer not for the first time, wondered if he had gone mad. He glanced about nervously, he was in the throne room of the Kingdom. He had not come here to see the King, and in deed the King was not on his throne. It was rumoured that he was ill and abed. In such cases the Queen and his council ruled, in his place, but Halmer had not come to see them other than to find out if they were openly making war against the Weredings. No Halmer had come to meet a member of the court, but even so he felt like the Lion would pounce on him and devour him. It was not the King that he felt now, but the huge stone lions that seemed to line the long hall. They flanked the entrance doors they lined the steps up the dais. They snarled at him from the throne's arms. As Halmer crept into the hall, a tall man in the red cloak of the city watch standing against one of the walls caught his eye and although the guard was at attention, he slightly nodded his head. Halmer scuttled across to huddle beside him.

"Kevin good to see you," Halmer muttered out of the side of his mouth, as he looked about him.

"And you too Hal. You said you wanted something, what is it?"

Halmer wondered if he was doing the right thing, after all he and Kevin were childhood friends, but could he trust the man all the same?

"Kevin how do you feel about the Weredings?"

Kevin glanced about him and lowered his voice a notch.

"Are you still grubbing about for Wereding magic?"

"Not anymore," Halmer whispered back. "But you didn't answer me."

"The official line is that the Weredings are not to be trusted."

"And your line?"

"Why are you asking Hal?"

"Answer my question, and I'll answer yours."

Kevin did not answer Halmer at once; instead he stared across the room, his gaze fixed on a carved lion opposite him. Halmer thought he wasn't going to answer and was just about to turn and flee, when the taller man spoke in a voice barely above a whisper.

"I don't know H. I hear all kinds of stories about the Weredings and yet...I have spoken to that messenger Cole he seemed alright."

Halmer gulped and then plunged ahead.

"Kevin what is the Crown's position on the Weredings? Are we... at war with them?"

"At war! Halmer what's gotten into you? If we were at war the whole realm would know. Besides which, as far as I am aware, there is no reason for us to be at war with them."

"What not even all the terrible stories?"

"There just stories. Halmer you are beginning to scare me. What have you gotten into?"

"A private war between the Crimson Circle and the Tower of the Glove."

"By the Triple Fold God." Kevin nearly cried out. "Halmer you had better be careful."

Halmer nodded and looking about him whispered some more.

"Kevin I've got to go, but do me a favour."

"What is it?"

"If you hear anything about the Weredings, let me know will you?"

"If I can, Halmer I'm still a member of the city guard."

"I know Kevin and thank you."

Halmer slipped out of the large hall and gave a sigh of relief when he emerged into the day light. He felt he was safe now. As he began to feel free, a large heavy hand fell on his shoulder and held him locked in place.

"Lord Healm, jus the man I was looking for."

Halmer's heart nearly leapt out of his chest, as he imagined a huge

Crimson Master or a city guardsman standing behind him. He taw loos of the hand and spinning round stared up at the large man that looked down at him. Halmer sighed with relief, when he saw that the man was wearing the white of a Scholar.

"I am sorry my lord, I did not mean to frighten you. I just wanted a word with you."

Halmer recognised the man now, it was Ragnar the head of the Scholar's. A man that Tomas had spoken about in the past.

"My pardon Lord Ragnar, you took me unawares."

"No apology is required my Lord, the fault was mine. I merely wished to have a word with you."

"And what word would that be?"

"A word that might be better said in private. Perhaps you would like to come back to my rooms and we can talk about it over a cup of tea or something stronger if you like."

Halmer wondered if he should, if the Scholar knew about his involvement with the Weredings, but after a moments consideration he agreed. The large man led him only a short distance, not to the Temple of Learning that was the Scholar seat of power, but to a small town house that was comfortably furnished. Ragnar led Halmer into a small, but well-appointed study that was lined with books. Halmer had expected servants, but the large man himself lit a fire and set the kettle over the fire. Perhaps sensing Halmer's thoughts, he smiled and answered them.

"My man is off today, so I am afraid you will have to put up with me."

"I thank you kindly for your hospitality," Halmer said, as he accepted a biscuit. "But you did say that you had something to say to me."

"Firstly, how is your brother? I miss him at the council?"

"Fine, as far as I know. I have not heard from him, since he left for the wall."

"Ah, that is a shame, but never mind. You are quite correct, I did not bring you here just to exchange small talk."

"Why did you bring me then?"

"To ask you to pass on a message to your Wereding friends."

Halmer nearly choked on his biscuit, as he sputtered a denial of this. Ragnar held up a large hand and smiled at the smaller man.

"Please my young friend don't deny it, I have my own sources and I know that you have visited them at least twice. Do not worry, I am no enemy to you or the Weredings. I know what the Weredings are and I know them of old. So have no fear of me. It is because, I am a friend to you and the Weredings that I have brought you here."

Halmer decided to choose his words carefully, for he could not leave without knowing where he stood and if he did leave at once he might confirm the old man's suspicions of him being an Elf Friend.

"If I were a friend of the Weredings and I'm not saying that I am. What would the Throne say about you passing messages on?"

The large man laughed loudly.

"The Crown has turned a blind eye to my dealings with the Weredings for many years, though that may be changing and that is why I feel the Weredings need to be warned."

"And what would you warn them of...if I were to carry a message to the Weredings that is?"

The white clad giant laughed heartily at Halmer's continued denials.

"The warning is that the Crimson Circle are gunning for them..."

"Gunning, what does that mean?"

"Forgive me Lord, I am so old that sometimes I slip into the past way of talking. Guns were weapons of the past, what I am telling you Lord Healm is that the Circle wants to wipe them out."

"That is not news."

"No it is not, but this is. The Crimson Circle have been gunning... hate the Weredings, but until now the King has staid their hand, but the King is despite my best efforts nearer to death each day and his influence dies with him. The Queen waxes in power and she will not withhold the Crimson Circle. What is worst, is that a growing number of the army commanders are beginning to listen to the Crimson Circle."

"I am sorry if I appear thick my Lord, but why is this so dangerous to the Weredings?"

"It is dangerous because, there has been a growing argument among certain quarters that says that the Weredings own too much of the land."

"Land! We need land from the Weredings?"

"We are a growing people Lord Healm and the people grow larger every year. Soon they will be too many people for us to cope with, but to the north The Weredings live sparsely across a vast land that could be turned to feed and home the growing population."

"But the land belongs to them?"

"Now it is," the giant Scholar said, as he took the whistling kettle off the fire and poured them both a large cup of tea. "Before the great burning our people lived all over Albian and possibly the Weredings did too, living alongside us. Though they were we believe practically unknown at that time. After the great burning however, we abandoned most of the north and they populated what we believed we no longer wanted. They claimed the land as their own perhaps they were right to do so, but now our people say that the land still belongs to us and the Weredings should give it back to us."

"And this is the message you wish me to take to them?"

"I wish you to warn them that the people grow restless and that the Weredings should be on their guard."

"I will warn them."

"You mean you would warn them, if you were their friend," the Scholar said, smiling though his tone was not mocking.

THE CIRCLE CLOSES

"The road to hell, can start with small steps."
The Prophecies of the Grey Pilgrim.

Robin had seen the Tower of Crimson from afar many times, but she had never been near it and now she stood at its entrance waiting to pass within its dark red stone walls. She was a little nervous she realised, even though Luna stood at her side. They were waiting to be let in, for although Luna had given them a token the men of the Black Fists would not yet let them enter.

"Could you just pass them invisibly?" Robin asked, remembering a most pleasant magic lesson-game that she and Luna had played. When Luna had turned herself invisible and Robin had used magic to find her, Robin eventually finding a naked and wanton lover waiting for her at the end of that hide and seek.

"I could try," Luna grinned back, clearly remembering that lesson with equal pleasure. "But I would probably not be able to get past the wards that are in place."

"Wards?"

"Magical protections."

"Could I see them?"

"You might, you have practiced the Wizard Eye spell. Use it now, if you want."

Robin removed from her belt pouch, the tiny crystal that Luna had given her. She had practiced it many times over the last four days and was very skilled at it. She performed the spell without even a twinge of weakness and when the beam of the sensor reached out, it showed her that the two guards halberds blades gleamed with magic, as did the rings they war. But their magic's gleamed palely in comparison to the web of magic that crossed and re-crossed the doors and as Robin swept the light of sensor to either side of the doors she realised that the walls too were laced with magic. The very mortar seemed to be magical. Robin looked up, to see that the web of magic ran up the tower and as she watched it throbbed with power.

"I never realised that so much power could be gathered into one place," she gasped, as the spell failed and her sight returned to normal.

"The tower was made over a hundred years ago and over time the black brothers had renewed and strengthened the magic. It is likely, that you will spend some of your apprenticeship bolstering the wards."

Robin was about to ask Luna more about her service, when the great dark wooden doors opened inwards to reveal a dark hallway beyond. From that darkness a voice whispered, as cold and quiet as a breath from a tomb.

"Enter, if you wish to learn."

Robin looked to Luna, who nodded encouragement.

"Robin I cannot follow you yet, you must go on alone."

"I must enter alone?"

"For now, but I will not be far behind you. Be brave, my Red breast and all will be well."

Robin looked from Luna's face, to the dark portal and gulping, she slowly walked into the darkness. As soon as she crossed the fresh hold the doors slammed closed behind her, plunging Robin into the deepest darkness. She almost cried out in fear, but she managed to control it, though she did draw her dagger and hold it up before her.

"Would you cut the dark?" Came a disembodied voice, from out of the darkness.

"I would cut any who attacked me. Show yourself."

"The dark is both your enemy and your friend; would you learn of the dark?"

"If it will aid me."

"Then take the first step and join the circle," said the voice.

Robin had learned a spell from Luna that would conjure light, but the tiny woman had warned her to cast no magic in the tower unless she was bad to. Though she could feel the fingers of her free hand twitching, as if they wanted to twist through a mystical casting.

Robin gathered her courage and stepping forwards stepped

through a curtain and into a lighted corridor. She blinked, as she stepped out of utter darkness into smoky torch light. The torch light was not strong, but coming as she did from utter darkness she was half blinded. Her blinking eyes made out two shadow figures dressed in black robes; they reached out with only half seen hands and steadied her. They did not speak, but taking firm hold of her guided her along the smoky tunnel.

"Where are you taking me?"

But the guides would not, or could not speak, so she let them guide her on into her future.

Eventually, the corridor opened into a huge circular chamber. A chamber that was occupied by a great circle of the black robed figures that Robin took to be the rest of the assembled Crimson Circle. The ring however, was not complete. There was a gap in the circle. A gap that her guides led her to and once they had joined and closed the circle, they released her arms and let her stand on her own. She looked around her, looking for a familiar face among the black brothers, but they were all wearing cloaks with deep cowls that were so low that their shadow depths hid all features. She looked across the circle to the opposite side of the circle. The other side of the circle was the same as her own side, a wall of dark clad figures unmoving and silent. Her eye was drawn to the centre of the circle. Here there rose from the floor an altar or kind of dais, a tall slab of black stone. Upon which there lay a chain of red metal and a long rod or staff of black metal. Her attention was drawn from the alter and its items, by the same haunting voice that seemed to come from everywhere and nowhere at the same time.

"You have closed the circle, but you are not part of it yet. Would you join and learn?"

Robin feeling that she was at the centre of a crossroads, felt that she was about to make a crucial choice. A choice that would define her life and her future. She felt fear then. Fear of the unknown, but she reminded herself that this step would take her closer to Rose.

"What must I do?"

"You must swear."

"What must I swear?"

"Advance to the alter of learning," came the voice, that was a whisper in her mind. "Don the emblem of our order, take the rod of truth and swear your pledge to the order. Once you have given your word, you give your mind and body to the Circle."

Robin moved to the alter and the circle closed behind her, seeming to shrink as the hooded figures drew the circle tighter around her. She ignored them and moving to the slab, she lifted the chain from the stone and lifting it before her eyes examined it. It was a neck chain, from which there hung like a badge of office a flat ring of red metal that gleamed dully in the torch light. The circle reminded Robin of blood and for a moment she was seized by the idea that she was holding a chain of blood. That if she donned it, the chain would bind her to these faceless shadows. Then the face of Rose floated before her and the clasp of the chain clicked, as the cold circle enclosed her throat. As it did a gust of wind, like a breath from the circle or the tower itself seemed to sigh through the room. As though a long held breath had been released in relief at her decision. She looked down at the alter and seeing the staff of black metal, she picked it up and held it up before her. As she did, she felt Roses presence. She could not have put it into words, but she felt Rose, she saw her face swim before her and heard her voice in her mind calling her name. The circle of black robed figures stirred and some of them turned on the spot to face outwards. Some of them even made the waving gestures of spell casting.

"Swear to serve the Crimson Circle," whispered the voice. "Swear to learn and we will give you power to bend the world to your will."

"Rose, I do this for you," Robin muttered, under her breath and then razing her voice spoke so that the whole room could hear. "I swear to serve the Circle and to learn what they will teach me."

As she said this a charge shocked her from the rod, as though it was too hot for her to hold. Her hand fell open and the staff fell to the black stone of the alter and Robin felt charged by the energy. She felt it flow up her arm and into her blood and she felt then as if she could tare the walls of the tower down brick by brick.

"Then welcome sister, to our circle," whispered the voice and Robin found herself being embraced by Luna's strong arms, her familiar face beaming up at her.

"I am proud of you," Luna whispered, in Robin's face. "Wait till later and I will show you just how proud."

That promise conjured up erotic images, before Robin's mind's eye, until the Crimson Master appeared over Luna's shoulder and smiled broadly at her.

"Welcome sister of knowledge," he said, his voice a steely purr. "May I present your new master of the arts, Calador."

The giant, black clad figure turned to his left, where the tall skeletal figure of the sorcerer that had attack the Tower of the Glove stood. Robin met his dark glance and although she felt the shock of his glance, she managed not to flinch. She knew that she did not like him, but she also realised that he was now her teacher and that she would have to be pleasant to him. She managed to gather her curtesy and dipped a curtsy at him.

"I look forwards to your teachings master."

The curtesy seemed to amuse the cold man, for a cold thin smile touched his lips.

"We will see," was all his reply, as he turned away to speak to another brother.

Then Luna recaptured her attention.

"Come on and I'll show you to your quarters," Luna said, with a lusty wink.

MESSAGE AND MESSENGER

"When receiving news, it is important to inspect the messenger as much as the message."
The Book of the Druids.

When Halmer arrived at the Tower of the Glove, it was to find two remarkable changes. The first change, was that the stone wall that had sealed the gate was gone and the wooden gates were back. Though they looked thicker and were now bound. The second remarkable change, was that the gate was flanked by two members of the city guard. Their presence made Halmer hesitate. They would no doubt report his visit and he couldn't allow that. Hopefully they had not observed him, but he decided to circle the tower and entered the grounds through the small gate. To find one of the dwarf Gilder boys, armed with axe and shield standing guard. Halmer nodded to him and the blond boy who looked more like a child than a man nodded back and let Halmer pass into the gardens. Halmer followed one of the paths to the small kitchen garden, where he found Cole cutting firewood.

"Greetings Cole," Halmer said, holding out his hand to the short man.

"Well met Lord," returned the Wolfblood, as he put his axe aside and clasp Halmer's forearm, as if they were brothers in arms.

"Where is the Lady Bright Eyes? I have tidings and a message for her."

"I believe she is in her study," the stocky youth said, as he glanced up to where a strange light was flickering in a window. "Though it looks like she might be too busy to receive you. Still, let's go and see. This way my Lord."

The youth led Halmer to where a small door entered the towers lower sections, and they passed down a short flight of stone steps to enter the kitchens. Where Clover, Cole's sister was baking bread, her apron covered in flour.

"Greetings Clover," Halmer said, bowing to the tiny woman, who blushed at his curtesy.

"Greetings my Lord," she stammered back.

Cole laughed at her embarrassment.

"If you can find time, perhaps you could brew us some tea Clover."

"You could brew it yourself," she shot back.

"It's for the lord Healm not me," Cole explained.

Leaving Clover blushing and speechless, they passed up a longer flight of steps that brought them through a door into the towers main entrance. From their they climbed to a landing, where a single thick wooden door stood. From behind its thick dark wood, their came a deep voice chanting, words that even hear seemed to thicken the air.

"She's casting," Halmer said, shivering with what, fear, anticipation?

Cole did not answer, but wrapped on the wood. The chanting stopped and Halmer could have sworn that he heard a curse, growled by the tall woman. Then the door was flung open, to reveal the tall woman glaring at them.

"What?"

Halmer took a step back, for the sight of the tall Werewolf standing there, scowling at him was an intimidating one. Her yellow eyes glairing balefully, her lips curled back from teeth that to Halmer seemed longer and more fang like than ever. However, whatever angry words she might have spouted, died on her lips when she saw who was standing before her.

"Halmer, I am sorry, I thought it was Cole interrupting my scrying."

"You were scrying?" Halmer asked suddenly interested, for he had heard of the practice, but never seen it.

"Trying," growled Bright Eyes, the look of frustration returning to her face. "I have been trying to contact someone, anyone in the north, but have had no success. I suspect I am being forded. But enough of my failures, what is it and what news do you bring me?"

"As far as I can find out, the Crown is not moving against you yet," Halmer said, as Bright Eyes led him into her study.

Halmer's eyes darted about, as he took a seat opposite a large wooden desk that dominated the room. To one side he saw a long work bench, littered with parchment, crushed and discarded herbs and bottles and vials. Though as he sat down, he spotted on the desk a large, silver basin filled with water or some darker liquid.

"You were using this to scry?"

"Yes, yes," Bright Eyes said, dismissively. "You say the Crown is not moving against us that still leaves the Crimson Circle."

"That is trouble enough," commented Cole, from his place near the door.

"I have more news for you and it is not so pleasing," Halmer said, as he tore his attention from the rune carved basin.

"Let me hear the worst," Bright Eyes said, as she held her silver medallion up before her, as if fortifying herself.

"As I was leaving the palace I was approached by the Grand Scholar..."

"Ragnar?"

"Yes, you know him?"

"I have exchanged knowledge with him," Eyes said dismissively. "But what did he want with you?"

"He seemed to know that I knew you, though how I don't know myself..."

"That one has his own contacts and sees far," Tigress' voice came from the door, as he entered carrying a tea tray.

"No doubt, no doubt."

"Well however he may or may not know it, he wanted me to pass on a message to you Bright Eyes. He says that the people are looking to the lands in the north."

"The people," Bright Eyes asked, as she poured tea for them. "What people and what do they want with the land?"

"He was not specific, but he seemed to hint that the people of the south thought that the Weredings had too much land and that they could give some up for them."

"We took the land once it was abandoned," objected Tigress.

"Peace Tigress," the Wereding ambassador said, holding up a restraining hand. "Does Ragnar think this belief will lead to immediate action on the souths part?"

"No, he just wanted to warn you that there are mutterings."

"The land is ours," Tigress snarled.

"Peace Tigress. We no more own the land than the lords of the south do. We manage it is true, but the powers own the land and the land owns itself."

Halmer would have liked Bright Eyes to explain these words, but Cole interrupted her.

"Surely the Crimson Circle are the immediate problem."

"For the moment," Bright Eyes agreed.

"I spotted the guards on the gate," Halmer said, as he gingerly sipped the tea which turned out to be mint and very pleasant.

"They are of the city watch," Bright Eyes remarked, smiling faintly. "I am informed that they are to keep the peace, not to spy on us."

"But they will report your movements," Halmer pointed out.

"A similar arrangement has occurred in the past," Bright Eyes dismissed.

"Did the Grand Scholar or any other source inform you what the Crown intends?" Tigress asked, as he passed back and forth behind Bright Eyes.

"As far as I can tell," Halmer said, hesitantly. "The King wants no trouble with you, but the Queen is a different matter."

"What of the Black Hag?"

"Well she is young and the King is old. It is likely that she will grow in power..."

"And she loves us not," said Bright Eyes, in a flat no nonsense voice that made it a statement not a question.

"It is likely that she will encourage the black brothers and turn a blind eye to their prosecution of you."

"Then we are at war," snarled Tigress, his voice becoming almost inhuman.

"Not with the Crown!" Halmer objected, in a high squeak of a voice.

"Aren't we," Tigress shot back.

"Be still," commanded Bright Eyes, as she gave both of them a steely glance.

"You are both right and wrong. Yes we are not at war with the Crown and yes we are at war with the black brothers."

"What will you do?"

"What we will do, is a very good question though I admit at the moment I do not know the answer."

"What do you want me to do?"

"You wish to continue your association, with us?" Bright Eyes asked, her gaze suddenly penetrating his soul.

"As far as I know, the Crimson Circle do not know about me and so I am not threatened by them."

"And if they did know about you, what would you say then?" Tigress asked, his green eyes pinning Halmer to his seat.

Halmer paled and looked to Bright Eyes, understanding she answered him.

"No as far as we know they are still ignorant, Tigress is however, putting a poignant question."

Halmer gathered himself and feeling Tigress' eyes on him, looked up from his cup to meet them.

"I would like to think, that I would despite their knowledge stand by you."

"Bravo," croaked a voice, behind him and turning he found the feather clad form of Kit. Watching him, with her yellow hawk eyes that made Halmer shiver, for he always felt she was sizing him up for a kill.

"You have a plan?" Tigress asked her, a new light flickering in his green orbs.

"Fortunately for us all, I do."

"Well don't keep it to yourself."

YOUR HEART'S DESIRE

"When asked what your heart's desire is, take careful thought. It may not be what you think it is!"
Epitaph of the Red Rage.

Robin had to wait for three days after her initiation, to practice magic. She had thought that she would learn earth shaking magic's and power as soon as she joined, but she had only seen miner spells and felt unseen energies echo through the tower. Her first night had been a wonder, as Luna and she had said a special goodbye, but when she was woken before the dawn Luna was gone and it was her fellow novices that waited for her. Robin was sharing a small dormitory with two other new students, but they had left her alone the night before. Now they woke her and she found that she would be training with a tall willowy girl, who like Robin's white blond hair was all but shaved, as was the hair of the boy that was with her. The boy who seemed no older than ten, was Alfred and the willowy girl was Carra. They told Robin that they would have to attend to several chores, before they could break their fast. It turned out that these chores included lighting fires, drawing water and serving their teacher (Master Calador), his breakfast. Robin was given this task, as she was the new student (the other two having been a the tower for the last month). When Robin knocked on the cell door, the man's cold voice bad her enter and she found that the tall, thin man was already up and dressed in his black robes, and was sat at a narrow desk examining a large leather bound book by candle light. Robin placed the tray of bread, butter, honey and several duck eggs on the edge of the desk and stood uncertain, as she did not know if she had to wait on the man or not. After a moment, he seemed to become aware of her. Looking up at her he raised a thin, black eyebrow.

"Yes Canduss?"

"No one told me, do I wait on you?"

A thin smile came to his cold, lean face.

"Not unless you wish to be late to your first lesson. Go and break your own fast and then return, I will be ready for you then."

"Yes master," Robin said, though the words felt strange in her mouth, for she had never had a man who could be called master hold claim over her before, even her tutors were servants.

Robin returned to the kitchen, to find her fellow students gathered round a small trestle helping themselves to a small cauldron of porridge.

"What mood was he in?" Alfred asked, a fearful look on his pinched face.

"Cold," Robin offered, not sure if that was right.

"About normal," Carra said, as she added salt to the porridge and then tossed a pinch over her shoulder.

"What did you do that for?" Robin asked, wondering if it was some kind of magic, she needed to learn.

"For luck," Carra said, surprised that Robin did not know of this almost comical ritual.

Robin did not like the thought of salt in her porridge, but she need all the luck she could get so she too flicked a pinch over her right shoulder. She was going to ask the other girl what the lesson might entail, but the other girls next words were addressed to the young lad Alfred and they drove any thoughts of the lesson out of her mind.

"Alfred have you heard any of these rumours about the Wereding tower?"

"Which rumours? That the tower has vanished into thin air, that the Shadow Master shattered it with a single word, or that the tower has burnt to the ground?"

"When did these rumours start?" Robin asked, suddenly afraid that the enemies that were within the reach of her arm had escaped her. "I have heard nothing of this?"

"I heard the gate guards talking about some attack launched against the Weredings and all kinds of rumours are flying among the students."

"Never mind that," the small youth said "We had better hurry up or we'll be late, and you know how he hates it when we're late."

"Would he punish us if we are?" Robin asked, for she had noticed that the child sported a black eye and bruises on his knuckles.

"He has in the past," Carra said, softly though she could not meet Robin's eye.

Robin was so nervous that she could only manage a few mouthfuls and then the other two were sweeping her along to her first lesson of magic. Though if Robin expected to cast lightning bolts or fire balls, she was bitterly disappointed. The Black Dragon as Robin learnt Calador was known among his peers, did not meet them with rods of power or wands, he was not even carrying the skull tipped staff Robin had seen him wheeled on the attack of the Tower of the Glove. He met them in the second level of the circular tower, in a large library-scriptorium, where he directed Robin to a desk. To which was chained, a large battered leather tome. Though Robin tried not to show it, the disappointment must have shown on her face.

"Before you can cast magic, you must know how to say it," lectured the tall skeleton. "Learn the runes of power and you can create a spell that can split mountains, but in this school you will not cast a simple cantrip until I am satisfied that you know what you are saying, when you speak the old tongue."

When Robin opened the heavy cover of the book, it was to find that it was a dictionary of the old tongue. The ancient language that had been used in the mists of time and which was sometimes used by the noble houses to embellish their coats of arms. Robin knew a few words of this language, she had been taught her own family motto by the late Scholar Galmor years ago, some many of the symbols and words before her felt familiar, even if she could not actually recognise or interpret them. Her own motto "Rosa ess Swarvace, bet Falcos fallow laz t'e dona balt," meant the rose is sweet, but the eagle falls like a thunder bolt, helped her to pick out the words that made up this motto, but other than that she found most of the rest of the words unfamiliar. She glanced across at her two fellow students, who sat on either side of her at identical desks, studying from what Robin could make out identical books to her own. Though by the look of it, they were both further along. Robin was about to look back at the book, when Calador who may have spotted her glance decided to test her.

"Canduss the words for the four elements?"

"Terra, Ventus, Insendium and aqua," Robin heard herself say, almost amazed that she knew the answer, but she did.

"It seems we have a prodigy," Calador sneered at her and Robin was not sure if he was pleased or angry.

"Perhaps she can give me the words to the ignite spell."

Robin of course had no idea what the master was talking about. Though she felt she could tell him given a little more time. she had been surprised that she could tell him the names of the element's and realised that she suddenly understood many of the characters that had until that moment mystified her. It was as though a door or window in her mind had just opened and shown her some hidden key. The key was not revealed to Robin, but somehow it gave her the understanding to interpret the complicated symbols and she knew what the word was and how she could take individual characters and make them words that were now clear in her minds-eye. It was as though the words were written in fire across her mind.

"Incendium..." Robin heard her own voice say, the words escaping her lips before she could stop them.

The effects of these words were remarkable, the tall man narrowed his eyes and staring coldly at her, he turned away and left the room.

"We may all pay for that," Alfred whispered.

"I'm sorry! I didn't mean to say it," Robin whispered back.

"It doesn't matter Robin," Cara said softly. "If you can read, you will soon please him."

"I don't want to please him," Robin spat "I want to cast magic."

"You will, you will," soothed the other girl.

But it was another two days, before she was allowed to cast a spell. She had gone leaps and bounds with the old language and before very long Calador was speaking to her in the old tongue and Robin who had grasped an almost magical skill with the language answered him easily, as if she had been speaking it all her life. This meant that he was by the third day, willing to let Robin practice a spell. She and her fellow students, were gathered into the central courtyard that formed a well round which the tower circled. This lesson took place at night and the moon which was just past full, shined down on the small pool that sat at the centre of the paved yard. Robin felt a frill, as she anticipated the upcoming magic. Though Calador had not told them what he would be teaching them. She wondered if it would be some kind of elemental spell, as he had talked about the manipulation of fire with an almost loving tone in his voice. That thought however, made her frown, as she stared down into the almost mirror calm waters. If he wanted to teach them about fire magic, wouldn't' they have been better practicing that in one of the magically protected chambers that Cara and she had had to clean out once.

"Do you see anything in the water Canduss," Calador's voice whispered in her ear, making Robin jump, for she had not heard him approach. "Do you intend to learn the lesson without me?"

Robin bit back a retort and managing to control her anger and gather her curtesy, spoke in a voice devoid of a tremor.

"Master Calador how can I learn a lesson without you, when I don't even know what the lesson is?"

Her only answer was one of his cold egmatic, smiles that Robin found infuriating.

"What are we here to learn master?" Alfred asked, as he looked from Calador to Robin and back again.

"We are here to learn how to scry," Calador said, as he stood on the opposite side of the pool from the three students.

"Scrying, what shall we see?"

"That depends Alfred, what is your heart's desire? What would you wish to see? Who do you seek?"

Robin suddenly thought of Rose. This would be her way of finding her, but even as she thought this, she was distracted as the desire to see Luna almost drove Rose from her head. Both their faces were driven from her mind, as Caladors cold voice cut into her thoughts.

"Canduss, perhaps you would like to join us."

"I am sorry master," Robin apologised and averted her eyes from his own cold gaze.

"Concentrate," the master said. "I am about to teach you something important, so watch me carefully or you might miss a vital component."

Robin watched, as from a belt pouch the black master removed a small leather bag, from which he took a pinch of dried leaves.

"This is dried Rosemary," he said, as he sprinkled it over the pool. "Now remembering to summon the power from within you, visualise what you wish to see and speak the words of power. Speculum revelum."

As he said this, the mirror of the lake seemed to mist, as if a giant had breathed on a mirror. Then the mist cleared to reveal to them all an image of a high mountain pass, silvered by the moon. Then the image was gone and the pool was a blank silver disk.

"Very well, who wants to go next?"

Alfred accepted the bag of rosemary next and when he cast the spell, an image of a young girl lying in a bed appeared, but the image only lasted a second before a single tear fell from Alfred's eyes to send ripples spreading across the image. The ripples distorting and then shattering the image.

"Control," Calador snapped, at the little boy, "You will never gain mastery, if you let your emotions rule you boy."

Carra's scrying was misty and seemed to show a castle tower, but either it was surrounded by fog or for some reason the casting was not working.

"Did I do something wrong master?"

"Uncertain," the master sighed. "Something maybe interfering with the scrying."

Cara did not respond to that, but passed the bag to Robin. Robin hated herself for doing it, but she thrust all thoughts of Luna from her and summoned Roses face before her mind's eye and spoke the words. She watched as the water clouded and could not believe it when the mist cleared to show her sister lying in some grey room, was it a cell? Robin thought that Rose was dressed in strange leathers, but the image was not clear and even as she watched a curtain of clouds rolled across the image. Robin felt the power coiling inside her, as she commanded the magic to show her Rose. The cloud cleared, but the image that appeared suddenly was not her sister, but a large horned, reptilian head covered in bright red scales. Robin felt its glowing red orbs meat and lock with hers. She heard the beast roaring in her ears and then all was black.

In her own tower, Luna watched as Robin fell to the slabs of the court and she too swooned as she felt a pain stab through her heart.

A PRAYER TO THE MOON

"The problem with priestess of the moon is that they have to consult their goddess before they make a decision."
Lightning to the Red Wizard, The Wereding Chronicles.

Halmer watched as the sun set, in an inferno of reds, that promised a glorious day tomorrow and wondered if he would be here to see it.

"Well you wanted to see magic," Halmer muttered to himself "Be careful what you wish for."

Halmer turned away from the window, to look across at where Bright Eyes was meditating, in readiness for the right that she was about to perform. Kit had explained her plan and Bright Eyes was interested, but she would not implement it without first consulting her Silver Goddess. Only after that, would she help with the great magical right that Kit's plan would need. Bright Eyes intended to speak directly to the Silver Lady and ask her to judge the plan, but she wanted as much magical protection while doing it as she could and so Halmer was here waiting for the moon to rise and the ritual to begin, so that he could add his meagre magical talents to Kit's and Tigress'. Who would attempt to protect Bright Eyes from what?

"Lord Healm," whispered Clovers voice, at his elbow.

Halmer turned, to find the tiny woman standing there with a tray of bread, cheese, butter and a flagon of wine.

"Thank you," as Halmer took a hunk of cheese, he looked across to where Bright Eyes was stood, her eyes closed her face turned upwards as she prepared herself mentally.

"She is fasting," Clover said, as though reading his thoughts.

"Fasting?"

"She must purify herself, before entering our Goddess's presence," Clover explained, as she handed him a cup of wine.

"How long will it be before she is ready?"

"We will begin now," interrupted Bright Eyes' voice, making him jump and almost spill his wine.

Looking across, he saw that she had ended her self-imposed trance and was staring back at him with eyes that glowed with an intense further. Almost a feverish gleam to the yellow eyes that glinted in the dying light.

"Do we do the right here?"

"No the prayer must be made in the open air beneath the light of the moon," Bright Eyes explained, as she gripped her silver pendant with both hands.

"We will perform the rights on the tower top," Tigress said, as he closed a heavy spell book, which he had been studying for the last hour.

"Come then, let us begin," Bright Eyes said, as she swept out of the study.

Halmer followed her out of the room and up at least four flights of stairs, that eventually led to a trapdoor that was open to the night air. When Halmer looked about him, he found himself standing on a narrow platform at the very top of the tower. Halmer shivered, as he realise that they must be very high up and the castellated battlements were only waist high, though in places they rose like spears to blade like pinnacles. He looked to where Bright Eyes was standing, in an effort to distract himself. Bright Eyes was already beginning the ritual, she swept her silver medallion through mystic passes. As her voice rose in a chant, a silver glow, like a gleam of moon light radiated from it to light the ground before her. Turning on the spot, she drew a circle of glowing light around her. When she came back to where she had started, there was a circle of faintly glowing light drawn around her, as if she had drawn it with a stick of phosphorescence. She then made more magic casting and as her pendant followed by handfuls of herbs and powders passed over the circle, her form shimmered and dimmed, as though he were seeing her through a thickening air. As if smoke or water were distorting her form. Once this was done, Bright Eyes stopped casting magic and lifting her head to the sky closed her eyes, as if listening for a sound on the edge of hearing. Halmer was not sure what she was listening for, nor did he know how she would be able to hear it over the spells that Tigress and Kit now cast. As Tigress stalked round the circles outside, he sprinkled what looked like ashes, so that a white-grey circle was formed outside Bright Eyes' silver one. While Tigress was doing this, Kit was moving in the opposite direction, touching the battlements with the tip of her glowing wand. So that she drew a glowing red circle, that lit the stones. Halmer realising that his time had come, red out the spell on the scroll that Tigress had given him. As Halmer pronounced the words of the spell, he felt the ring on his hand grow warm and glancing between the scroll and his ring, he saw that the stone glowed. With its bright blue light and he felt strength being drawn from his limbs and pass through the ring to form a cloud of blue energy that formed in the air before him. Even as he pronounced the last syllables of the spell, this cloud rose spreading out to cover the whole of the tower and then it became a transparent dome that covered the whole top of the tower and then the magic dome was gone.

Halmer leant against the parapet and watched Tigress's and Kit's castings. As they no doubt had planned, their castings finished simultaneously and they met one another at the same moment their spells activating at the same time. A wind sprang up from nowhere and Halmer felt himself being pushed towards the battlements, as the wind circled Bright Eyes forming a Minnie whirlwind and the stones of the battlements ignited into bright red flames. But Bright Eyes seemed to notice none of this, as she stood silently chanting to herself; no not herself Halmer corrected himself, to her Goddess. Halmer could see that the flames and the wind were meant to shield Bright Eyes from any attack, but what could reach her at the top of a tower.

"The wards are to protect Eyes from magical and spiritual attacks," Tigress said over Kits head, for the two lovers were wrapped in each other's arms.

"But who or what would attack her?"

"Such a casting, as Bright Eyes is making can attract spirits and beings from other worlds. If she does not protect herself they may claim her body."

"Could such spirits attack us?"

Tigress grinned broadly.

"It is a possibility, but we have each other."

Spirits were not the only eyes watching the Tower of the Glove however, from the street a pair of eyes watched as the top of the tower seemed to ignite into flames. The shadow that watched it, felt a wind sweep past him as its swirling dust cloud made straight for the tower top.

"The bitch is speaking to the Goddess," Kain growled, to a smaller shadow.

"What does that mean Lord Kain?"

"It means that she is unable to contact the rest of the Weredings, so she turns to her Goddess for guidance. Tell the Crimson Master that if he intends to attack the tower, he must do it now while they are all distracted with the casting."

"I go," squeaked the small hooded figure and it scurried away, leaving the tall wolf helmed figure staring at the tower with glowing red eyes.

"Perhaps it is time for me to take a hand. Lord Erebus give strength to my arm."

Bright Eyes' vigil seemed to last for hours to Halmer, though it was probably only minutes. As he waited the full moon rose behind him and cast its bright light on the seen before them, as it did the wind that had stirred the ashes that Tigress had scattered was suddenly gone and the flames that flickered on the battlements snuffed themselves out.

"Is that supposed to happen?" Halmer whispered, for as when a loud sound stops, the silence seemed a physical presence, listening and watching ready to pounce.

"Yes," Kit said, as she moved towards the circle. "Bright Eyes must have contacted the Silver Goddess, she has ended the wards."

As Kit approached the taller woman, Bright Eyes opened her yellow orbs and stared sightlessly at Kit. Then she swayed and would have fallen, if Tigress had not reacted and leaping past Kit grabbed hold of the Druidess's shoulders.

"Bright Eyes can you hear me?"

"What's wrong with her?" Halmer asked, as he rushed to join them.

As he moved towards them, Kit span on him and flung up a hand to warn him off.

"Stay back, until we know who she is?"

"Know who she is?" Halmer asked stupidly, until he remembered that the wards had been erected to prevent some demon or spirit from invading Bright Eyes' body and possessing her.

"Bright speak to me?" Tigress said, shaking the tall woman.

"Here, see if she will take this?" Kit said, as she handed Tigress a small flask.

Tigress held it to Bright Eyes' lips and she gulped the liquid down, spluttering as she gulped and some of the liquid flowed over her chin and fell onto her medallion that now the moon was hidden by clouds, was glowing with its own radiance. Kit and Tigress stood back from Bright Eyes, both with a hand on their own medallions, as if they were readying themselves to cast spells at Bright Eyes. Bright Eyes swept them with a gaze that shilled Halmer from where he stood, then she flung her head back and laughed.

"Wholly water; you gave me holy water Kit! Do you think I am possessed?"

"Are you?"

"Look at my pendant."

Bright Eyes held her silver disk high before them and the silver glow brightened to an almost blinding dazzle.

"Would I be able to bear and wheeled the Ladies power, if I were possessed?"

"Alright Eyes you are not possessed, now can you lower the light?"

Bright Eyes chuckled and although the light did not disappear altogether, its intensity dimmed so that it was like the sliver of a new moon.

"Is that better?"

"Much, now could you answer a few questions?"

"No, but I will tell you what you are dying to know, though the news is not good," Bright Eyes said, her voice suddenly filled with pain.

"You actually spoke to a God?" Halmer broke in, not able to believe that Bright Eyes had talked to a deity.

"Yes Halmer, I spoke to our Silver Lady and she showed me many things, many visions. Most of them I did not and still do not understand, but the one thing I did understand is that we must leave these lands. We are no longer wanted here."

"So we put my plan into effect" Kit croaked, from where she was staring down into the grounds.

"Yes and no," Bright Eyes replied cryptically.

"What?"

"Yes Kit you are right we must evacuate the tower, but no we will not do it the way that Kit has planned."

"Well whatever we do, we had better do it fast," Kit said as she looked beyond the walls of the tower. "Someone is approaching with many torches and I don't think their coming to give us a feast."

"It is the Black Fists and they are being led by the Crimson Master."

"You can't be certain..."

"Yes Tiger I can," Bright Eyes cut him off. "That was one of the things our Lady showed me. They are coming to wipe us out and I do not think that we can stop them this time."

"What do we do?"

"You cannot help me with this Tigress," Bright Eyes said, as she placed a comforting hand on the tall Wereding's shoulder. "If there were time I might have been able to teach you the right, but we have run out of time."

"Speaking of time," Halmer broke in, "in case anyone has noticed they are breaking the gates in."

"Yes time is the difficulty," muttered Bright Eyes, as she looked to the sky.

"How much do you need?"

"As much as you can give me."

Tigress strode from the tower and with a swirl of feathers, Kit too had disappeared.

"Can I help," Halmer asked hesitating, for although he wanted to give whatever aid he could to the defence of the tower, he felt as if he were abandoning Bright Eyes.

"Yes, as a matter of fact there is," Bright Eyes said, as she knelt in the middle of the fading circle. "Ask Clover to bring my staff."

Halmer turned to go, but as he did she called him back.

"Halmer, thank you."

"For wat?"

"You did not have to stay, in fact you might still leave."

"I rather think it's too late for that." Then Halmer gave her a deep bow. "Besides how could I live with myself, if I left a damsel in distress?"

"Bless you," she cried after his retreating form.

When he reached the ground floor, it was to find that Tigress and Kit had not gotten outside, for the enemy had either avoided the wards or broken them. For they were at the bottom of the entrance steps, the three short but broad forms of the dwarfs blocked their advance. Their axes clashing with the blades of shadowy attackers. Tigress lifted his staff above his head and aiming its rune shaped tip over the dwarf's heads, unleashed a lightning bolt at the shadows. The blinding stroke dazzled everyone, as its light filled the hall, but it hurled the shadows back from the besieged trio. Halmer's howl of triumph died on his lips, as some unseen spell caster unleashed a terrible spell. The air around the trio seemed to explode and they were suddenly flung back. Their cloaks and hair on fire, as if a dragon had spat them out. Kit screamed and ran to where the three lay smouldering just inside the doors. Tigress snarled, when he saw the fire toss them back, but he held the steps, as a cloud of darkness flowed towards them. Tigress held his staff high and sent the pronged lightning bolt into the shadow.

"Halmer the door," Tigress snarled, from between gritted teeth, as he swayed as if locked in a struggle with an invisible enemy.

Halmer rushed to the great wooden double doors and even as he wondered if he could move them an inch, the door swung on oiled hinges. Even as he moved the left door into position, a crossbow bolt slammed into the wood. Then when he darted across to the opposite door, he felt an invisible, but icy hand grasp at his heart, but somehow he was able to shrug it off and began to swing the door across. As he did black figures rushed from the dark and up the steps. A spear rushed at Halmer through the rapidly closing gap, and thrusting between the narrowing gap prevented Halmer from shutting it. He put his shoulder to it, but the door refused to shut and Halmer's heals slipped, as he was slowly but relentlessly forced back. Then Tigress was at his side and he gripped the spears shaft with a glowing hand and with a loud crack the shaft split. With Tigress' added weight and strength the door was forced shut.

"We can't keep them out, before the bar is in place," Halmer gasped.

Tigress however, had other ideas. He touched his staff to the doors and spoke a word of power. The hinges and handles glowed.

"That will hold them for a moment only," Tigress gasped, "Quick halmer help me with the locking bar."

He and the tall Wereding lifted the large bulk of wood and slotted it into its mountings, but even as they did, the great door boomed as something large struck a mighty blow upon them.

"Will it hold?"

"Not for long. If there were just armed men then I would say hours, but the Circle is with them and they have spells that could open this tower like a tin."

"So what do we do?"

"Keep them out as well as we can, but for now we look to the wounded. Kit how are they?"

Kits voice was a grim hiss, but at least it boar good news.

"They live, but they are not going to be of much use for hours to come."

"They must be made of strong stuff," Halmer muttered.

"They are Dwarf's," Tigress said, a crooked grin briefly touching his lips, though his face was covered with sweat. His eyes showing the pain of some struggle.

"Tigress are you alright?" Kit asked, as she moved to his side and placed a hand on his face.

"You're burning up." she exclaimed, her voice unable to disguise her shocked surprise.

"I only just beat off a mental attack," Tigress admitted, as he leaned heavily on his staff.

"Clover," Kit cried.

Halmer had not seen the little woman, since he had passed her on the stares during his head long rush to the doors; though he had not needed to tell her to take the staff to Bright Eyes. For the tiny woman was struggling up the stairs with the dark wood stave. Halmer had stopped to offer his help, but the girl had waived him off. Now the little girl appeared at the top of the steps that led down into the entrance.

"Water, wine," Kit hissed, her yellow eyes flashing.

Clover vanished with such speed that Halmer wondered, if she had used magic to transport herself through time and space.

"What about the back doors?" Halmer asked.

"Cole was out back last I saw," panted Tigress.

"Halmer would you go and see what's happening on that front?"

Halmer opened his mouth to answer, but he was forestalled by a great vibration that ran through the entire tower. It was as though the tower was a huge bell and someone was striking it. As Halmer felt the stone beneath his feet vibrate, he wondered if the Crimson Circle had unleashed some unbelievable magic.

"I never realised the black brothers were so powerful!"

"That wasn't them," Kit said, as she fed Tigress water. "That's Bright Eyes' doing."

"But how?" Halmer asked, after a long pause as he took that fact in.

"Please Halmer there isn't time now, please go and look to the kitchen doors."

Halmer nodded and turning ran up the stairs to the next landing, but once he got there he was lost. For he could not find the door that he and Cole had used to ascend from the kitchen areas that was until Clover appeared at his side and pulling back a wall hanging revealed the low door. Halmer was about to tell her to wait here, but even as he formed the words Clover slipped through the door and was gone from sight. Halmer cursed and followed her into the gloom beyond. As he groped down the stairs he heard a groaning in the darkness. A sound that made him freeze momentarily, was it the groans of Cole injured or dying or was it the chanting of a spell caster. Then someone, probably Clover lit a lamp and the kitchen below became clearer. The room was empty of bloodthirsty assassins or black clad sorcerers. For that Halmer was grateful. It did, however, hold both Cole and Sky. Both of whom were bloody with wounds.

"Cole," Clover squeaked, almost at the same time as Halmer spoke Skies name in shock.

Halmer rushed down the steps, to where Clover was fussing over her brother. Who sat with his back against the steps that led up to the low door that led out into the gardens. Halmer let out a long breath when he saw that Coles left arm ended in a bloody stump that was leaking blood through, the make shift bandage Cole had wrapped round it. Sky was not much better off, when he glanced at her. Sky's dark tunic was covered in blood and when he tore the cloth away it was to reveal a deep stab wound in her side.

"They're not going to live, unless we can do something quickly," Halmer whispered, to Clover.

Cole cried out as clover tried to examine the stump. His eyes flickered open and he looked up into Halmer's face.

"The door, he's trying to get in through the door."

Halmer glanced up at the door and as he did, it shivered as a mighty blow struck the wood.

"We can't stay here," he muttered to clover. "But I'm not sure they will survive, if we move them."

"My axe," Cole moaned, as if he would die with it in hand.

"Kit and Tigress, will have healing potions," Clover said quickly. "Then wait here."

He taw back up the stairs and stumbling down into the entrance hall, to find Tigress weaving a web of ice across the wood, which was steaming as if some heat was being applied from the outside. While Kit was muttering spells over the dwarfs.

"Cole and Sky are hurt," Halmer wheezed, out of breath, "Clover said you would have healing potions."

Kit did not stop chanting, nor did her right hand stop its gestures, but her left hand dove into a pouch at her belt and she thrust a couple of small pewter flasks at Halmer. Who grabbing them, turned on the spot and ran back to the kitchen hoping that he was not too late. Fortunately both the wounded were still breathing, though both looked on the verge of death.

"Did you bring the healing drafts?" Clover asked, her face almost as pail as her brothers, as she tried to staunch the blood running from his stump.

Halmer all but taw the stoppers from the flasks and forced the tube between Coles teeth. The man's eyes flew open and he spat some of the green liquid back out, but once he understood what was required he drank it down and almost at once a look of calm slid onto his face. When Halmer looked down at the stump, it was to see that the thick blood had stopped and the stump had formed a scab over the wound.

"Remarkable," Halmer muttered "Let's hope that this works for you too Sky."

The girl opened her eyes, for she must have heard her name and she opened her mouth for the draft. So she swallowed the liquid better and she too became better the pallor left her skin and her ragged panting steadied. Halmer had not realised till now, but the stab wound in her side must have damaged a lung. It was a miracle the girl had lasted this long.

"Remarkable," Halmer repeated, as he stared down into the metal flask, his curious mind wondering how the draft was brewed and what went into it.

His ruminations however, were distracted as another heavy blow struck the door.

"Quick Clover, we've got to get them out of here before he comes through, or he'll kill them..."

Clover made to help her brother to his feet, but she fell to one knee, as the floor beneath them gave another quake. Halmer stumbled and almost fell over Sky, but managed to steady himself and was about to help Clover up when a nerve paining splintering filled the room and the door fell in pieces on top of them. Halmer looked up from under where a large plank had driven him to the stone floor, to see standing in the open door a tall dark figure outlined against the nights sky. In one hand this figure held a long object that was a blade of some kind, but in the other it held a crackling ball of energy that gave off a sickly green light that seemed to cast more shadows then illuminated them. From somewhere under the debris of the door Cole moaned their attackers name and it brought a fist of fear to Halmer's stomach, for he knew it.

"Kain!"

THE TOWER OF THE MOON

*"Some people are like lanterns, light can shine through their flesh. It is
their souls that are the wick."*
The Druids' Hand Book.

Tigress watched as the wood and the sheen of ice he had used
to fortify it began to melt and run onto the ground, as the
doors glow intensified. It might have been because of this
glow he did not at first notice the change around him, but Kit who
was trying to recover the Dwarf's glanced up at where he stood,
gathering strength and power for the next attack noticed the change.

"Tigress the walls, their glowing."

Tigress thinking that they were burning through somewhere
else, looked around worriedly, but he saw that the glow that Kit was
referring to was a soft silver glow, like the gleam of the moon on a
cloudy night that seemed to be leaking from the stones of the walls
themselves.

"I think this is Bright Eyes' doing, not the circle."

"Can we stop them, from getting in in time?"

"I don't know, but they will be through any minute."

"Not if my beard is burnt they won't," groaned the familiar gruff
voice of Gildor.

Kit had been trying to revive the three dwarf's and although
Gilder was still badly burnt, his hair burnt off his beard singed he
still seemed to have some fight left.

"Rest Gildor," Kit said, trying to press the old man back down,
but he would not lie still.

"Have yaeh any ail?"

"Ail no, but I do have healing drafts," Kit said, as she pulled
another flask from her pouch.

"Ail would be better, it tastes better and does just as well at healing
me."

"I don't mean to be rude, but we're not having a party," snarled Tigress, as he tried to cast a spell on the doors, but he had taxed himself overmuch and either someone was counter spelling his magic or he was to week or tiered to cast it properly made no difference, as with a great crack the locking bar snapped in half and fell at his feet and the doors disappeared in a blinding flash of light.

When Tigress looked up from where the magic had frown him, it was to see the vast bulk of the Crimson Master standing beyond the doors shattered remains. Kit screamed and spat a flair of fire at him, but the line of fire twisted round the man without touching him, as though he was enclosed in an invisible shield. He lifted his hand and with a word a silence fell over the hall and tigress could hear nothing, the man had cast a spell that deadened sound and therefore prevented the casting of magic. The Master was about to stride in and claim his conquest, when Gildor unable to utter a curse mouthed it and pressing hands to the stone of the ground summoned up his own innate magic. Even before the Master could put a foot over the fresh hold, the portal vanished as the doorway was filled by a wall of stone that shot up to block the breach. Gildor unfortunately, was not able to laugh at the look of shock and anger that had flashed across the man's face, as he realised that this prise had just been snatched from him, for the use of his own magic had drained whatever strength he had left and had passed out.

"Is he still alive?" Tigress asked, as he tried to gather his feet under him.

"He is still breathing," Kit said, as she checked his pulse. "Will the stone last?"

"It is still there, he is not manifesting it with his will. He must have summoned it or manipulated the stones themselves, it will last until they batter it down or melt it away."

Even as Tigress said this, a huge blow slammed into the stone.

"They are stubborn aren't' they?"

"That isn't the only problem, Halmer has not returned, they have probably entered through the kitchen door."

"Can you hold here for now?"

Tigress smiled wearily, at his slim lover.

"For the moment."

"Then I will see what is happening below." Before Tigress could object, or add a comment, she was a swirl of feathers.

"May the Goddess protect you," Tigress whispered, after her. "Bright Eyes I hope whatever you are doing works soon."

As if in answer, the tower gave a third tremor and the light emanating from the stones seemed to glow brighter. Although the brightening told Tigress that the Werewolf was having success it also seemed to drive their attackers to greater efforts to break in. As Tigress watched a giants fist seemed to be hurled against the stone and a web of cracks spidered across the new wall. Cracks that Tigress watched spread with every blow.

"May the Goddess protect me too," he whispered to himself, as he gathered what he knew were his last reserves of strength and magic.

Halmer stared up at the hated Kain, a Wereding assassin that even Tigress feared. For he was the vilest Wereding to have crawled out of the north and a trader to his kind. The wolf helmed assassin stared down at them with glowing yellow eyes and sneered at their weakness when he snarled at them. His voice hissed words of cold power and clovers lantern was snuffed out.

"Is this the best Bright Eyes could dig up."

"Burn in hell," shouted Clover, as she flung her lantern at him.

Galvanised into action by Clover's act of defiance, Halmer cried out the words of a spell and struck the metal flasks together. From his striking hands, the lightning bolt he had expected did not leap. Instead a thin spark of energy arched to ignite the oil that the shattered lantern had spilled at Kain's feet and before the black blade could react he was engulfed in a wave of dancing flames that drove him howling like a banshee back out of the door and into the night.

"Well that went better than expected," Halmer said, looking down at the flasks that were now twisted and blackened lumps of metal.

"Let's get out of here, before he or someone else comes," Clover said, as she helped Cole to his feet.

"I'll drink to that," Halmer said, as he dropped the twisted flasks and gave a hand to Sky.

They were just about to climb the steps out of the kitchen, when a black form appeared at the shattered door and a crossbow bolt whistled, like some lethal bird over their heads. The bolt however, was answered by a cry neither bird nor woman and from the steps above them their flared a blast of light and Halmer's hair crackled as a breath of winter passed over his head. The bowman screamed and disappeared from the opening.

"Get up here," came Kit's harsh croak, as her cloak flared around her retreating form.

"Yes mam," Halmer muttered under his breath, as he helped Sky limp up the steps.

Once they got to the top of the stares, they closed a heavy wooden door behind them and Clover drew two bolts to secure it.

"But that won't hold them for long," Clover said.

"This might help," Kit said, as she held up a scroll, as she red magical words the parchment crumbled away and a strong metal chain wrapped itself round the door and sealed itself to the stone of the wall.

"What now?" Cole asked, as he regarded the stump that had been his arm.

Before any of them could answer, the tower gave a final teeth rattling shake that made them all feel as if the tower was about to fall off the planet and spin off into space. At the same time, the light pouring from the walls intensified until the towers walls seemed to be made of moonlight not stone. As the shaking reached its crescendo, the light began to pulse with the rhythm of a heart and Halmer felt like he was inside the body of a giant rather than a stone tower.

"What is happening?" Halmer shouted to Kit, as he fell to his knees, though the stone he fell onto was pulsing as if it longed to break free of its mortar and join some dance.

"Whatever Bright Eyes is doing has reached its climax," Tigress replied.

"Well if the black brothers don't kill us, her magic might," Halmer said, though his words were lost in the tolling of some great bell that seemed to be ringing all around them.

Then almost as suddenly as it began, the vibrations stopped and the tower was plunged into a silence so deep it was almost a physical presence. Though although the vibrations had stopped, the light that shimmered from the walls like a full moon still gleamed with its cold light.

"It's gone quiet," Tigress whispered.

"Your point?"

"The Crimson Circle," Kit croaked, catching onto Tigress' meaning.

"They've stopped attacking," Clover said.

"Bright Eyes must have stopped them," Tigress said, though his voice said that he didn't quite believe that.

"Let's go and see," Kit said.

Before anyone could reply or react, Kit was running up the steps.

"Follow the lady," Tigress said, as he limped after her.

Halmer watched them go and then turning to Clover gave her a look that as much as said "should we follow them?"

"Go, I'll tend to these two," Clover said, tears glistening in her eyes as she watched Cole holding his shortened armed before him, as if he didn't believe it was missing its hand.

Halmer turned and slowly followed the two spell casters up the tower. At one of the landings he glanced out a small window and saw a sight that he didn't quite believe. The land outside the window had changed drastically since he last glanced out. The gardens were gone, the walls were gone and everything that had lain beneath his gaze, it had all disappeared. To be replaced by a sea of rolling grey mist that seemed to cover the whole of the world, in its ghostly vapers.

"Bright Eyes, what have you done?"

Halmer would have like to put the question to Bright Eyes in person, but when he reached the towers top it was to find her laid out on the stones her eyes staring sightless into the sky. Her iris's no longer yellow, but a glowing silver the same colour and shade as the light that shun from the walls.

"So that's why they call you Bright Eyes," Halmer said to himself, and then speaking aloud, "Is she alive?"

"As far as I can tell yes," Kit said, as she slipped a mirror back into her cloak. "She is still breathing."

"Then what's wrong with her?"

"Probably she's spent herself in the casting," Tigress said, as he looked at the strange shrouded world through a mounted telescope.

"Will she recover?"

"I certainly hope so Halmer," Tigress sighed.

"Good because, I would like to ask what the hell she has done and where she has taken us!"

"You think that too then?" Tigress asked, taking his green eye from the lens to regard Halmer.

"You believe that we have moved?"

"Yes, but how and where is beyond me."

"It's beyond me too Halmer," Tigress said, his voice showing the mental and physical exhaustion he was in.

"I can tell you where you are," a voice said softly beside them, though its tone was gentle it sounded strange as if it echoed.

Halmer turned to see a strange image, the figure was that of a short, slender girl about Kit's height and frame, though her hair was a flame red and her eyes were green. Halmer would have been welcome to see her, if it hadn't been for the fact that he could see the towers battlements through her transparent body. He was, he realised looking at a ghost.

"Are you a ghost?"

"Of a kind," she replied.

"Are we dead then, is this the world of the dead?"

"You are not dead, but this is a world of spirits yes."

"We are in the Other World," Tigress said, staring at the girl, "you are a spirit blessed by the Goddess!"

"The Other World," Halmer said allowed. "Another world, then how do we get back?"

LUNA'S SURPRISE

"Never read a book by its cover, it might turn out to be a dragon in disguise."
Lightning to the Red Wizard, The Wereding Chronicles.

When Robin came back to herself, it was to find herself laid out on the stones of the courtyard. Her eyes looking up the central well of the tower, the many candle lit windows merging with the stars above them. Where was she? Then it all came flooding back and she remembered the glowing eyes of the dragon. Had it been a dragon's head she had seen replace Roses face? Then Cara was bending over her, a damp cloth in hand.

"Robin can you hear me?"

"Yes," groaned Robin, for she suddenly felt a pounding headache.

"See Carra, all your fussing was unnecessary," rasped Calador's voice, from the other side of the pool.

"Unnecessary, maybe, but not unwelcome," Robin said gently to Cara, whose look of concern for Robin's health and safety was genuine. "What happened, why do I feel like a horse has run over me?"

"Something interrupted the scrying," Calador said, as he towered up behind Cara's kneeling form.

"It looked like a red dragon," Robin groaned, as Carra and Alfred helped her to sit up.

"Well, whatever it was, you reacted," Calador said, sneering though his expression might not have been as cold as it was before, "Well whatever it was, you reacted to it and from somewhere conjured a fire skin spell."

"Oh no not again," Robin moaned and she reached around to feel at her back.

"Will she be alright master?" Carra asked.

"She has not done herself any real harm," the cold man said, his eyes freezing Robin as they seemed to burn into her soul. "She will be fine in the morning, but the lesson is over, we will try again tomorrow."

With that he turned on his heal and strode away, his robe flapping behind him like the wings of a giant bat.

"He warms you with his presence doesn't he?" Robin groaned.

"Seriously Robin are you ok?" Carra asked.

"I think so, but I would like to get to my bed."

"Come then, to bed it is."

Actually what Robin wanted was to be in private so that she could examine her back and the extent of the scales spread. Once Carra and Alfred were certain that she was alright, they left her alone in her small curtained off space in the large room that was their dormitory. Robin stripped down to her pants and feeling around, she felt the slightly raised shiny scales that were replacing her skin. She hung her head, when she realised that the scales had spread over a considerably larger portion of her body. The original patch had been a small coin sized spot on her left shoulder blade, but now it had crept up to the top of her shoulder and was creeping towards her collar bone. She closed her eyes and moaned. It seemed despite her efforts she was still transforming into what? Would she still turn into the scaly woman from the book. Robin collapsed onto her bed and burying her face in her pillow, silently cried into it. At that moment, she longed for Rose, her sister could comfort her. Luna too, flittered into Robin's mind, but Robin did not want her lover to see her cry, so she reached out for Rose with her mind.

The next day they did not reassemble in the courtyard until after noon and Robin reluctantly accepted the bag of dried Rosemary. She was not aware of it, but Calador gave Carra a look, that was a prearranged signal and the other girl moved to stand behind Robin to catch her if she fell this time. Robin, however, was not aware of this; she was wholly focused on the small pool before her. She scattered the powdery leaves onto the water and spoke the words of power and felt a surge of strength flow from her to the mirror of the pool. Which clouded and remained clouded, Robin stared at it until her eyes felt like they would pop out, but the clouds hardly faded. They seemed to thin at some point, to show the silhouette of a figure that she could swear was Rose. She knew it was Rose, but the outline of her sister was all she could make out. No detail could be made out, it was as though Robin was seeing her through a fog. Then the water swirled, as though something beneath had stirred. It was as though a fish had disturbed the water and when the ripples were gone, the mirror was gone and the pool was still.

"Well that was less dramatic, if as disappointing," hissed Calador. "Still at least we don't have to pick you up off the floor."

"It was Rose," Robin whispered, her voice suddenly strengthless and her emotional strength drained.

"Perhaps it was, perhaps it wasn't," the master said glaring at her, "But if it was, she appears to be masked."

"What could do that?"

"Another spell caster could be shielding her, or she could be in a place of magic."

"The North," murmured Carra.

Carra had said this under her breath and Robin was probably not supposed to hear this, but as Carra was standing at her shoulder she did anyway.

Carra had better luck this time and the tower she sought appeared clear and defined. Alfred too saw the young girl riding in a wood. The fact that her fellow students had achieved to see what they wanted did not upset Robin, she felt certain that she had seen Rose. It was the company of Werewolves and the Triple Fold god knew what had enmeshed Rose, in a net of webs and this was why she could not see her. As she ate her beef stew at the evening meal, more than ever she wondered if being here learning these miner spells and weavings would help her save Rose. She wished that she could speak to Luna, she would know what to do. Perhaps she would be powerful enough to see through the Weredings' nets. So she was delighted and amazed when Luna appeared in her sleeping cell the next morning. Robin had had a disturbed night, tossing and turning as she saw Rose wrapped in spider webs, a huge and monstrous spider looming over her, poison and blood dripping from its fangs. Then she had felt a gentle hand on her shoulder and opening her eyes expected to find Carra waking her for the chores that they would have to perform before they broke fast, so when she opened her sleep filled eyes to see Luna's square jawed face grinning down at her she was delighted.

"Luna, am I still dreaming?"

"No, I am here," Luna said, her smile widening.

"Then why are you here," Robin asked, a flush of lust flaring up and she flung the sheets back in the hope that Luna would join her in the bed.

"Not now my lover," Luna said, her face suddenly becoming serious. "I have come because, a development has occurred that could be of great use to our cause, but we must act now, if we are to take advantage of it."

"Luna what are you talking about?"

"I will explain on the way, now dress and pack whatever possessions you may have here. You may not be coming back."

"I won't be coming back?" Robin was not sure what that news made her feel. She longed to be free of the cold Calador, but she had come to like Carra and Alfred and she might not see them again.

"Can I say goodbye to Carra and Alfred?"

"No, we must leave in secret. No one must know that we have gone yet. Now no more questions, pack dress."

Luna added to Robin's quick exit by sweeping round the curtained corner of the room, not that Robin had much in the cell anyway. When they entered the sleep room, both Cara's Alfred's and the other two students that shared this room all had their curtains closed and Robin realised that they were not awake yet and she wondered what time it was. She wanted to ask Luna, but the tiny woman who was not baring a lantern, but who seemed to glow with a subdued light that hung around her like a hallow and that must be magical, put a finger to her lips and led Robin through the silent halls of the tower. Only once they had passed through the great double doors of the tower and were standing beneath a still dark sky, did Luna speak.

"Robin I know you have a thousand questions, but please wait until we are clear of the city."

Robin opened her mouth to protest, but changed her mind and nodded. She looked around for some kind of transport, to find Wolf standing nearby with their horses.

"Put up your hood," Luna said, as she gently drew the cowl up over Robin's head. "I don't want anyone knowing who you are."

Robin mounted and Wolf boosted Luna into the saddle, then the big man watched as they trotted away. Robin was bursting to ask her questions, but she held her tongue until they had passed over the river bridge that marked the northern boundary of the city. Then after a quick look around, Robin cast back her hood and stopping her horse turned to Luna.

"Are you going to tell me what this is all about?"

"Put your hood back up," Luna snapped.

"Not until you give me some answer!"

"Please Robin, put your hood back up," Luna said, in a soft whisper.

"Not..."

"Put your hood up and I will tell you what you want to know, but I do not want anyone to see who we are."

Robin muttered a curse under her breath, but pulled the cowl back up, so that her face was a light sliver of skin under the deep cowl.

"You have been chafing under the Black Dragon haven't you?"

"Yes," Robin said, not surprised that Luna knew the nickname of the master. "I don't feel like I am learning anything that will help me get Rose back."

"Well in that case, you will be pleased to hear that I am taking you to meet a new ally. One who might just be able to help you get Rose out of the Weredings' clutches."

"Who?"

"His name would mean nothing to you," Luna said cryptically, as she made her horse trot on.

"But how can he help us?"

"Robin please, you don't want me to spoil the surprise do you?" Luna said mischievously.

"You know sometimes Luna, you are infuriating."

"Just the way you like me," Luna came straight back and urged her horse into a gallop, so that she outdistanced Robin.

As Robin spurred her own horse, she realised that she recognised an old twisted tree in the brightening gloom of the dawn.

"We're nearly home," she called out to Luna.

"Of course we are, I am taking you to meet him at your home where else do you think I would take you for such a meeting?"

Luna would not say a word more, but spurred her horse to greater speed. Robin tried to ask her more questions, but was forced to spur her own steed to catch up with her. Luna had said that they were going to meet this mysterious new ally at her home, but Luna did not stop at the house, but rode past it and towards the long wood. Here she dismounted and tied the horse's reins to a branch.

"We're meeting him in there?" Robin asked, as she vaulted out of the saddle and bound her horse to a second branch.

Luna did not answer, but strode off into the dim half-light that was brightening steadily, as the sun climbed higher up the sky. Robin sighed, but followed her into the dim half-light. The light beneath the canopy was dimmer, as the sun had not climbed high enough to truly penetrate the trees and in parts where the leaf cover was thickest it was almost pitch black, but in others the light was bright enough to see by. Luna who seemed to be able to see very well in this half-light flitted from tree to tree like a ghost, and Robin was hard pressed to keep up with her.

"Luna slow down, I haven't got cats eyes."

Luna giggled as if this was some big game, but when she reached the next clearing Luna was lounging against a tree, a silly smile creasing her face.

"That's better," Robin muttered, then more louder. "Are you going to tell me now what this game is all about?"

"I have brought you to meet our new ally and there he is," Luna said, pointing leisurely to one side.

Robin looked about her a the very large clearing that they were in, to find that it was true they were not alone.

THE TOWER OF THE EAGLE

"Secrets are simply truths hidden, but there is always a reason why they are hidden."
Takana the Harpy, The Wereding Chronicles.

The same day, but many hours later and several hundred miles away, Rose was looking out over a lake and wondering where her sister was, not knowing that she had been asleep recovering from a poisoned dagger wielded by their father's attacker, while Robin had seen her father's funeral.

Rose looked out over the lake and promised Robin that they would come for her, unaware that her sister had no knowledge of her doings and she too was unaware of what had become of Robin in the days between their father's death and that moment. Though she had seen Robin in a vision and had been told that this may mean that Robin was a member of a dark cult so she had sworn to rescue Robin. All this went through Roses mind, as she looked down at the lake and the area that faced it. Just outside the city of Care Diff, the city of the Weredings, the Fairy people. Behind her stood Lightening, the tall fire mage that had sworn to help her and around her were the four Werewolves and the Elf Eloo, who had all agreed to help Rose fulfil that promise.

Her thoughts were interrupted by the hoarse whisper of Kye's voice.

"I must leave you, for a short time."

"But Robin!" Rose began to object, fearing that Kye's absence would prevent them from setting out and she was already chomping at the bit to be gone.

Kye held up a hand, to forestall her.

"What I must do, will only take the night and as The Hunter will not give us a decision till dawn, it will not interfere with your plans."

Rose bit her lip in uncertainty. Kye stepped close to her and locked his blue eyes with her own.

"I have given my word to help you Rose, I do not break my word!

Please Rose, trust me, I will not fail you, but I must do this."

Rose stared into those bright orbs that changed from dark blue to a baleful yellow according to the phase of the moon and sensing the Werewolf's iron will, she believed that he would not break his word. She nodded and Kye was gone. Disappearing as if he was a ghost.

"I do wish he wouldn't do that," she complained.

"Why don't you wish for raining mushrooms," Eloo said.

"Now that would be something to see," Lea smirked.

"Knowing my luck, they'd be poisonous," Lor his brother, grumbled.

"What do we do now?"

"Takana would it be alright, if we stayed with you for tonight?" Silver Skin, the tall Werewolf Druidess asked, as she looked to the lake as if she was looking for Kye.

"Be my guest Silver Skin, though if you are asking for permission to stay in the Tower of the Eagle, you should ask your young friend there, as she is probably the owner now." Said the Harpy, a creature that although having the shape of a woman, had feathers sprouting from her arms and legs. Those wings had been much larger hadn't they? They must have been, for the small feathers that sprouted from her skin could not have born her aloft. Perhaps she had shrunk her wings, Rose would not have been surprised at all. After all she had seen stranger things. However, what was she talking about now.

"I'm sorry, but I don't know what you're talking about!"

"I am staying at the Tower of the Eagle, but I don't own it, it belongs to your house."

"My house?"

"The Tower of the Eagle was gifted to the Weredings by the Canduss house long ago," Takana said, her green eyes regarding her closely.

Rose just stared at her.

"I had no idea, Lightning, Silver Skin did you know this?"

"No Rose, I swear I had no idea your house had Wereding connections," Lightning said, in amazement.

"Well whether you knew or not, the tower is yours," Takana said calmly. "Come let me show you your tower."

Takana led them back towards the city that they had moved through only an hour or so ago, to arrive at the meeting of the

Wereding nations. They passed through the great boundary wall, passed by the large hill that was at the centre of the dwelling and passing through the wall of trees to come to the ring of towers and buildings that formed one of the outer rings of the city, where a single large tower stood apart from the rest of the buildings. Looking up Rose understood why it was called the Tower of the Eagle, for the top of the tower was mounted by a huge statue or Gargoyle shaped to resemble a giant golden eagle. Rose squinted at the huge statue and gasped, as she realised that the golden Eagle was standing on a rose shape plinth. The golden Eagle standing upon a rose, was the symbol of her house.

"This tower bears my household emblem!"

"Of course it does, it belongs to you. It is your tower," Takana explained, as she stalked stiff legged towards the steps that led up to the single narrow door that stood at the base of the tower.

Rose for a long time could not move, as she took this in. What was a tower belonging to her family doing here? She had always suspected that her father had been fascinated by the Weredings, though he would not let them know about them, but an actual tower in the heart of the Weredings' city?

"Rose are you alright?" Lightning asked, at her side, his green eyes peering at her closely.

"Yes I think so, I'm not sure."

"All this must be very confusing for you!"

"Just a bit," Rose said, smiling back a the tall man.

By now Takana had reached the top of the steps and had knocked on the door which was opened by someone inside. Takana passed inside and Rose could now see who had opened the door. It was a troll, but the smallest troll that Rose had yet seen, the small grey figure hardly came up to Rose's knee.

"Is that a Troll?"

"Yes, her name is Emerald," Lightning said, grinning at Rose. "Shall we go and see her?"

"Why not?"

Lightning gently took hold of Roses arm and guided her to the steps. As they approached, they were watched by the tiny Troll, who considered them with a pair of bright green eyes that told Rose how she got her name. When they reached the tiny balled figure, it bowed its smooth hairless head and spoke in a soft sigh.

"Mistress Rose, I am pleased to see you again. It has been many years since we saw you here."

The small dwarf like troll's words shocked and surprised her.

"I have been here before?"

"Yes my Lady," whispered Emerald. "Though perhaps you do not remember it. You and your sister were very young, perhaps not long out of your mother. Still this is your house, please enter and partake of what we can offer you."

Rose stared at the tiny troll and then shaking her head in disbelief, she walked past the woman and entered the tower that she did not remember. Past the door, Rose found herself in a small lobby that had a door to the left and right and a twisting flight of spiral stairs before her. Takana had climbed several of the steps and turning back to look down on Rose, beckoned her to follow. Rose nodded back, but before she did, she noticed that carved into one of the doors were her coat of arms. Not just the eagle and rose, but her family motto, if Rose need any more proof that this tower belonged to her family, this provided it. Sighing in resigned exasperation, Rose began to climb the seeming endless spirals of steps. They were however, not endless and after a long climb, she came to a landing or balcony that ran round the inside of the tower and although the steps continued to climb into the gloom above, Rose was drawn to an open door from which a pool of light spilled forth. Going to it, Rose saw beyond a large study or library warmly lit by a large fire and lit with many candles. Takana was sat behind the desk, her hands, from which quill like feathers sprouted, was holding a candle before her.

"Light it," she said, her bright eyes locking with Rose's.

"I'm sorry?"

"Lightning has taught you the fire lighting spell, use it."

Rose stared at the candle in its holder for a moment, before she recalled the kindling in the woods that she had lit with the spell that Lightning had taught to her. For an instants Rose doubted that she could do it, she could not remember the words, but somewhere inside her a feeling of power seemed to leap up within her and she felt like a well of energy was surging to her brain. Her hands seemed to perform the gestures of their own and the magic word was on her lips before she was conscious of it.

"Incendium." As she spoke the word, a spark seemed to leap from Rose's fingers, to the candles wick and suddenly the candle was burning.

"Very good," Takana said, as she put the candle to one side. "How do you feel?"

Rose realised that she felt ok. The last time she had cast the spell, it had drained her and she had to sleep after its casting, but now although she had felt the spell draw off some of the spring that she could feel flowing through her, she realised that it had not had the same drain on her and she only felt a little dizziness.

"Not too bad."

"That's good, but I still suggest that you sit down before you fall down." Lightning said, from the door.

Rose agreed with him and looking around moved to the fire, where a comfy chair stood and Lightning took the seat facing her across the fire.

"Are you hungry?" Takana asked, from the desk, where she was sharpening one of the quills from her arm and having crafted a quill pen dipped it into ink and began to write on a scroll.

"Yes you could probably do with something." Lightning said.

"Yes I'm starving," Rose said, suddenly realising just how hungry she was.

Even as Rose said this, Emerald appeared at her side, with a tray of bred, butter and honey, cheese and a bottle of a red wine.

"Vitels my Lady."

"Thank you." Rose said, as she took bread and cheese.

"Well Lightning, it seems that you have your first student," Takana said, as she stalked up and down behind the desk.

"Does this mean that I have graduated to the next level?" Lightning asked, a piece of bread half raised to his mouth forgotten, as he stared into mid-air.

"It does, give me your ring."

Lightning slid the large gold ring off his hand and placed it on the desk. In her turn, Takana handed Lightning a tightly wrapped scroll that was held together by a similar ring. Though from where Rose was looking, it looked like this ring had more runes or design on it then the ring Lightning had been wearing.

"You have progressed to the fourth level of the Fire school, may you learn more as you teach," Takana said, her grim mask only now cracking into a smile.

Lightning bowed his head to her hand and kissed the hand that held out the scroll. Then he took the scroll and slipping the ring off the parchment, slid it onto his hand.

"Now that is over, we must initiate a new student into the fire school."

Rose looked around the room, expecting that she was referring to Eloo or someone else, but the little elf and the other werewolves had not come with them and so there were only the three of them in the room.

"And who is that?" she asked, as she lifted a cup of wine to her lips.

"Why you of course Rose Canduss," Takana said, her face once more a beautiful, but stern mask.

Rose involuntary spat the wine out, as she realised what Takana had just said.

"Me!" she squeaked, staring with disbelief at Takana.

"You need to learn magic don't you?"

"Well yes..."

"You are willing to learn from Lightning are you not?"

Rose looked across to Lightning, who was watching her with those large, luminous, green eyes and she saw uncertainty there. She realised that he was not sure if she did.

"Well I suppose so," Rose said uncertainly, she liked Lightning. She had come to trust him, but was he the best person to train her in magic she was not sure.

"Then it is settled," Takana said, "Prepare to receive your ring of rank."

Rose watched, as Takana picked up a ring from the table and to Roses amazement and shock held it in the flame of the candle, she herself had lit. Takana showed no pain, as her fingers held the ring in the heat of the candles flame. As she heated the ring, she chanted and Rose realised that she was casting a spell and she recognised the word "Incendeum," the word for fire among Takana's muttered incantation, but the rest of it was unintelligible to her. Lightning who must have watched her closely and understood her shock a the sorcerers putting her hand into a fire, explained how she felt no pain.

"Takana is the most powerful fire mage I know, she is totally immune to fire of all kinds."

Rose nodded, as she watched Takana withdraw an unburnt hand from the flame and although the ring glowed red hot in her hand, she seemed to feel no pain. She stalked to stand in front of Rose and held out her palm to offer the glowing ring.

"Take it and join us in the fire school."

Rose stared at the ring that lay in Takaana's palm like a glowing red eye. Its dark runes and symbols standing out from the glowing metal like black cracks in the metal. It was still glowing hot, surely it would burn her. She hesitated reached out then stopped, her hand hovering over it. Strangely, although the ring glowed red hot, it gave off no heat.

"Take it Rose it won't hurt you," Lightning said, encouragingly.

Rose's fingers closed round the ring and it was cool to the touch, not hot at all. She held the circle of metal up before her eyes. The rune that stood proud was a symbol that reminded her of the letter I.

"Put it on," Takana advised.

Once again Rose hesitated, did putting this ring on make her a spell caster? Rose felt that she was at a crossroads in her life. The acceptance of this ring, might be an irrevocable act. A step too far, a step down a road that she might never be able to turn back from. Should she put the ring on or would it be better to find out more about it and don it later. Before she realised what she was doing, or before she could change her mind, she slid the ring onto the ring finger of her right hand. She had expected to feel some reaction when she donned the ring, but all she felt was a slight warmth as if she was only now feeling the heat of the red hot metal.

"There now you are an apprentice in the Fire School, as you learn more and advance in the school you will receive new rings and the powers that are linked to them."

"Powers?" she asked, as she regarded the gold band and the red stone that was set in it.

"The ring you bear allows you and I and Lightning to communicate telepathically."

"By the mind?"

"Yes, but don't try it now," Lightning said, arresting her hands assent to her forehead. "You're not ready for that yet."

"The ring I have just given Lightning has that power, but it also grants Lightning the ability to defend himself."

"Defend himself how?"

"Ah, you are running before you can walk," Takana said smiling "That is a secret you must learn later."

"Well is there anything else I should know?"

"There are many things you will need to learn," Lightning said, as he gave her a refilled cup of wine. "But they can keep, for now welcome to our brotherhood."

Rose smile back and clinked her glass with his. Sitting back, she held up her hand and regarded the ring. Admiring how the gold glittered in the fire light.

"Do you have questions for us Rose?"

"Yes, but the first one has nothing to do with your brotherhood."

"Then what is burning away your tongue?" Takana asked, grinning wickedly.

"Can you tell me about this tower? Before today I never knew it existed."

"Those questions are better put to Emerald than to me," Takana said, and moving to the fire she pulled on the bell rope that hung there. Barely had Takana released the rope, then the tiny grey figure was at her side.

"What do you wish Lady?"

"Not I Emerald, Rose wishes to know more about her home."

Emerald turned her gem like eyes on Rose and bowed to her.

"My Lady, what do you wish to know?"

"First of all, does the tower really belong to me?"

"It does my Lady," the tiny woman whispered. "Your father had it built over thirty years ago and commissioned me to be its care taker. So it belongs to your family."

"If that is the case, why didn't he tell me about it?"

"You will have to ask him this my Lady, I do not know."

"My father...My father is dead," Rose said, her voice hitching as she said it.

"Dead?" Emerald said, her own voice breaking. "When, how?"

"It appears that Kain slew him," Lightning said, as he moved to stand behind Rose and she started, when he began to massage her shoulders.

"Relax Rose, I am just trying to relax you."

After the initial shock of his touch, Rose realised that she did feel relaxed. She also realised that she liked Lightning's touch.

"You said you saw me when I was young, tell me about that."

"It was one of the few times that your Lord father visited us. He and your Lady mother may she rest in peace, came to visit the court and they brought you and your sister with them."

"I don't remember it."

"As I say you were barely born, but you are here now and I am ready to give you the key and the other items that your father left ready for your return."

"Father left things here for me?"

"Yes my Lady, the keys and a scroll that was to be given to you, if you ever came here without him."

Emerald gave Rose a large set of keys and a scroll sealed with wax and stamped with her family crest of the eagle mounted on a rose. Rose took a deep breath and broke the seal. When she unrolled it on her knees, she recognised her father's small, but precise hand.

"Rose, Robin, if you have received this, then I am probably dead and you will have had to step into my shews. Emerald can be trusted, put yourself in her hands. I know that you know nothing of her or this tower and probably I died before I could tell you of your heritage and responsibilities, I am sorry for that! You will have to find your own way among the politics of the Kingdoms. I hope that you can forgive me for not telling you about your Draconic history, but I had to protect you from it. I hope that I have given you some start in the race you will now have to run. Please forgive me, your loving father Robert Canduss."

Two huge tears dropped onto the parchment and Rose suddenly realised that she was crying. Lightning stopped his massage and simply hugged her from behind. His warm presence reassuring her and letting her know that he was there for her. Eventually she stopped crying and pulling herself together, turned to a still and waiting Emerald.

"What else did my father leave for me?"

"The tower and its armoury," the small woman replied.

"Armoury, this place has an armoury?"

"Yes my Lady, within it lie many magical weapons including

several swords crafted to bear your arms."

"Not Eagle swords?" Rose asked, not quite believing what she was hearing. The eagle sword had been her father's greatest possession, a sword forged from the best steel and its hilt was crafted to resemble an eagles head the cross guard being a pair of golden wings. It was an air loom of the house and rumoured to possess special properties.

"There are two my Lady. One crafted for you and another was set aside for your sister. Would my lady wish to see it?"

"Not just now," Rose decided. "I think I've had enough for now, thank you Emerald. On the other hand I would like to know where Eloo and the rest of them have gotten to."

"Oh sorry Rose, I forgot to tell you," Lightning apologised. "Silver Skin said they would go to their hall and make the necessary preparations for our journey."

"If it happens," Rose sighed and suddenly she was exhausted.

"If my Lady would wish to rest, I have prepared a room for you."

"Go on Rose, get a few hours' sleep," Takana advised. "You will need all the rest you can get, you may not have the opportunity in the days to come."

"Very well, Emerald lead me to bed."

THE RAIN OF HEAVEN

"The words of the Goddess fall like rain from heaven. Though they may hurt like hail."
The Book of the Wolf.

Once the meeting with the Queen had finished, Kye had left the group and had gone to the great lake that lay beside the amphitheatre, where the court of the Sylvan Throne had taken place. He had known for a long time that things were moving, powers were gathering that were beyond his understanding, but he felt that some ancient power was rising and it was a threat to his people and perhaps even his Goddess. So he had resolved to invoke a right that would allow him to speak with his Goddess, if she was so willing. As he knelt at the lakes side and prepared himself for the ritual, he became aware of another's presence. Looking up he found himself being regarded by a pair of bright blue eyes.

"Mother," Kye asked, as he rose from his kneeling position, to stand facing the tall form of Great Mother.

"You desire to commune with the Goddess?" Great Mother asked, in her gentle voice that often reminded the listener of running water.

"I need answers," Kye stated flatly.

"You misunderstand me Kye," his mother said gently. "I do not come to stop you, but to aid you."

Kye lowered his eyes, clearly rebuked and slightly ashamed.

"I thought as a Druidess, you had come to prevent me."

"I am a Druidess it is true, but as a priest of the Silver Lady I will help you. Though I warn you, she may not answer and if she does you may not understand her or you may be hurt by this right."

"I understand."

"But you will continue."

"I place myself in the Ladies hands, she will treat me how she sees fit."

"And you accept that judgement, even if it is death?"

"She is the Goddess I am her servant," Kye whispered reverently.

Great Mother laughed gently, her laughter feeling and sounding like rain spattering against stone.

"You know Kye you are only a lowly Ovate in the order of the Druids. You have little standing, but you have more faith and reverence than others high in her church. It gives me hope."

"Hope for what?"

"Hope that the Lady will treat you kindly."

"Will you help me?"

"I cannot add more to the right than you," Great Mother sighed. "You must make the blessing and sacrifices yourself, but I will watch over you, while you leave your body and travel into the other world."

"For that I thank you mother."

"Shall we begin?"

Kye went back to his knees and making a cup of his hands, scooped water from the sacred lake and spilt it into a stone cup, richly carved with runes and symbols of the moon.

"You do of course realise that she is waning?" Asked Great Mother.

"Then I will have to prey twice as hard," Kye said, as he took a blade and sliced his palm and let a few drops of his own blood fall into the cup. Even as he did this the wound was healed and Kye seemed not to feel the wound. He took a moonstone (the stones precious to the Goddess), and dropped it too into the cup. Then he stirred it with a silver rod and lifting it to the rising moon, spoke the words that were required to complete the right and send his spirit into the domains of the Goddess.

"Great Lady, Silver One, Lady of the Healing Light. I ask you for audience, please listen to my appeal." With these words he knocked the potion back in one draft and the cup fell from his hand as he swooned.

Great Mother stood over him and checking his pulse, nodded to herself.

"Swift journey my son, may the Silver Lady take you to her bosom."

THE SUMMONS OF A WYRM

"The oldest of Wyrms are like forces of nature. They like a volcano lie dormant for hundreds sometimes thousands of years, but when they eventually wake they can break upon the land like a tidal wave."
Lightning to the Red Wizard, The Wereding Chronicles.

Rose had only just left the study, when a short figure entered the room. Rose would have recognised the figure as a Minotaur, but this powerfully built man with a bull's head must have been a child or a dwarf, for it barely stood five feet tall, though he was almost as wide.

"Please forgive the intrusion," the Minotaur said, in a surprisingly musical voice.

"Yes Tore," Takana said, as she stared at the bowing Minotaur. "What is it? I thought you were studying the movements of the stars tonight."

"And so I was my Lady," the bull man said, bowing again, "But as I watched the stars from the top of the tower, I was approached by a messenger seeking Lightning."

Lightning, who had been dosing in his fire side chair, jolted up in his chair suddenly fully awake.

"A messenger, looking for me?"

"Yes my Lord," the Minotaur called Tore said, bowing again to Lightning.

"Oh for the Fire Lord sakes Tore, stop dipping and get to the point. Who wants Lightning?"

"My Lady it is a young dragon, who says her name is Flint."

"Flint," Lightning cried, as he rushed out the door. "I didn't even think she was old enough to fly!"

Tore watched Lightning rush from the room.

"I hope I have not done wrong, in bringing this to Lord Lightning."

"Why would you need my approval Tore," Takana said, as she poured the short if bulky Minotaur a cup of wine. "If Flint has come with a message, why shouldn't you bring it to the attention of the one sort?"

"I thought that perhaps you would want to know first, before the Lord Lightning," Tore said, his dark brown eyes cast down.

"Tore you are surprisingly shy for a Minotaur," Takana said, smiling a thin grin as she handed him the wine. "If I wished to know Lightning's every move I would give orders to that effect, but I do not ask that much of my students. As you should already know."

"Yes my Lady, sorry my Lady," Tore said, as he gingerly accepted the cup.

"Do you wish me to continue the star watching my Lady?"

Takana cocked her head at this, as if considering the question, but then she smiled and shook her head.

"No Tore that won't be necessary, you get to your bed."

"My Lady," as the short minotaur turned his broad back, Takana considered the dark muscular back and wondered if she should join Tore in that bed.

Lightning rushed from the study and up the twisting steps of the tower to where the steps ended, just below a trapdoor that led out onto the towers top and the battlements that surrounded the platform from where Tore had been watching the stars. As Lightning reached this trapdoor, it was to find hanging from the lip of the open portal a creature the size of a large cat. The creature did have the shape of a cat, with a long whiskered snout and head of a cat, but most cats did not have a pair of short curved horns sprouting from the back of their heads. Neither did they have the large leathery bat like wings of this creature. The creature which was unmistakably a small dragon, regarded Lightning with a pair of glittering flint yellow eyes.

"Flint," Lightning said, with delight. "What are you doing here?"

The small dragon called Flint, fluttered its Smokey wings and its bright red scales seemed to puff up, as the small dragon flexed its body.

"Mother sent me with a message for you," Flint said, in a soft sibilant whisper that seemed to rustle in time to her wings and flexing scales.

"A message for me from your mother? I thought she was still in hibernation! Did she speak to you from her dreaming?"

"Yes from mother, she has woken and sent me and my sisters to seek you and the Red Woman," hissed the small dragon, as it finally released its grip on the trapdoor lip and spreading its wings half dropped and half glided to the ground. Where she padded round Lightning's feet.

"The Red Woman?" Lightning asked, as he stepped back to give the large cat like creature room to move. "Who does she mean?"

"I was told by my mother Lady Firethorn to seek you and the Red Woman you would be with."

"Does she mean Rose?" Lightning asked, thinking out loud.

"That I do not know" hissed Flint, as she flicked her tongue at Lightning's boots. "All that mother said was to find you and tell you to come to her with this Red Woman as quickly as possible."

"She did not tell you why?"

The small dragon that was Flint, hissed and a small spout of fire gouted from her nostrils.

"Since when, has our mother needed to explain her reasons? She commands and we obey."

Lightning bowed his head, as if scolded by the dragon.

"You are quite right, but the Red Woman is one who desires to go south, not north. I am not sure that she will come, if I cannot provide a reason."

Flint hissed at that, but seemed to think upon it, as she stalked round the top of the stairs. Finally she spoke.

"I cannot explain why she must come, only that she must, but perhaps you can convince her as to the urgency of this mission."

Lightning did not looked convinced a this. Seeming to sense Lightning's doubt, she lifted a forepaw to her throat to touch and lift into the light a small, sparkling, red jewel that was hanging about her neck.

"Mother wished me to convince you that you should come, so she has sent you the shield scale you left behind with us."

"I gave it to her in payment for a scroll she gave me. If she sends it now, it must be urgent."

"She gives it back to you, without obligation so that you may bring this Red Woman to her safely," growled Flint.

"Then I am very grateful to her, perhaps I can give her something in exchange for it," Lightning said, seeming to be speaking to himself.

"No doubt she would be pleased, if you would replace this with something of equal wealth."

"I will see what I have to hand," Lightning said, as he bent and gently unclasped the chain from around the small dragons long neck and held the chain up to the light. To behold a small round shield like disk that was not a couple of inches across. Which hung from a red metal chain. Lightning hung the chain about his own neck and kneeling down before the dragon he scratched the place where the chain had been. From the cat like Perring and the way that Flint half closed her eyes, it was clear that she enjoyed this. After a few moments of this petting, Lightning stood and looking down at the small dragon spoke to her softly. "Are you to escort us to your mother?"

"Yes, she wishes it."

"Then if you are rested, I will take you to Rose and we shall see if we can convince her."

"We must," hissed Flint.

"We shall see," was all Lightning would allow, for he was sure that Rose would be difficult to convince to the need for this trip, as she was desperate to go south and find her sister Robin.

Lightning descended the steps and as he did, he heard the clack of Flint's claws, as they clicked against the metal risers of the steps. Lightning found Rose in one of the small bedrooms, a floor down from the tower top. She was lying sprawled on a narrow cot, her sheets flung back from her, as if she had cast them aside, her body thrashing as she was clearly in the grip of a nightmare.

"What is wrong with her?" Flint asked, as she leapt into the air and hovering above her flicked her long tongue at Rose's struggling form.

"She is having a nightmare, I would guess." Lightning said, as he gripped hold of Roses out flung arm and shook it. "Rose please wake, you are safe. You are in the Tower of the Eagle. Please Rose come back to me."

Rose had not undressed, when Emerald had led her to the narrow cot in the small room, but had simply kicked her boots off and sprawling onto the bed had pulled the blankets over her. She had fallen asleep, almost as soon as her red head had hit the pillow. Her sleep had been deep and for the most part unbroken, but even as Lightning was meeting with Flint, Rose was gripped by the nightmare that Lightning found her in moments later. Rose found herself in a dark, stone valley, strange stunted trees shadowed against the dark sky. Rose moved towards a large still pool and looking down into its dark, mirror like surface saw her reflection in the waters. Her face stared back at her, though it was a tired and drawn face and dark circles showed beneath her eyes, as if she had little sleep for many days. Then even as she watched, Rose saw her face ripple and shift at first she thought it was the water that was shifting her reflection, but as she watched she realised that it was not the water that was moving and shifting, but her face that was changing. She was seeing that change in the mirror of the waters. Rose cried out, as she watched glittering, red scales spread across her face, turning it into a red mask. From which her own eyes stared back at her. She felt a motion behind her and spinning saw that Lightning, was standing only a few feet away.

"Lightning," she cried and her voice sounded inhuman and bestial to her own ears.

She moved towards Lightning, but as she did he gave a huge monstrous roar and burst out of his clothes, as he transformed into a huge glittering monster. A monster that unfurled its smokey wings and glared hatefully at her, with glowing coals. Rose screamed, as the creature's jaw swung open and a wall of flame reached to engulf her. It was in the grips of this fiery nightmare that Lightning and Flint found her. Lightning shook her and called softly to her. Rose eventually opened her eyes, but when she saw that it was Lightning for a moment she saw overlaying his bird like features the red jaws of the winged monster from her nightmare. She pulled away from his grip and brought her knees up to her chest, as she pushed away from him.

"No get away," she cried, as she covered her eyes with her arm.

Then Emerald was there, her hands which Rose had expected to be cold and stony, were surprisingly soft and gentle, as they took hold of Roses shoulders and shook her.

"My Lady Rose you are safe, you are among friends! It was only a nightmare," the little woman said gently, as she first shook Rose and then cradled her in her small arms and Rose buried her face into the tiny woman's breast.

As Rose gathered her wits about her, she withdrew and shook her head.

"Thank you Emerald I am fine now."

"Very well my Lady, would you like some mulled wine or hot milk," the little woman asked, as she stepped back and was the impeccable servant again.

Rose looked down at the little woman's hands, as she remembered how soft they had felt and was surprised, but not shocked to see that the little troll woman's hands were covered in a fur of green. It looked like it might be moss, but whether it was moss or not, the soft fur made her hands feel gentle and even normal.

"Yes, that would be nice thank you Emerald." Rose said, and turning was shocked to see a tiny red dragon sitting on the foot of her bed. For a moment she thought that the nightmare had come true, but she managed not to react so violently and as she inspected the cat sized creature she realised that the eyes that regarded her back, were a yellow rather than red. The red, cat like dragon flicked a long, forked tongue at her and after rustling and settling its wings it hissed something that sounded like words, though Rose did not recognise them.

"Flint asks if you are ill?" Lightning asked, his large, green eyes still concerned, as he kept his distance from Rose. He did not know what Rose had seen, but she seemed to be frightened by his presence, though she had never been before. "I too am concerned to know if you are ok?"

"I am now, I had a nightmare, oh such a vivid nightmare," Rose shuddered, as she recalled the images that she had seen.

"But you are ok now?"

"Yes I am, but who or what is this?" Rose asked, as she watched the cat like creature half unfurl and then close its wings to its body. She could see that this creature was a dragon of some kind, but she was attempting to move the conversation away from herself.

"This is Flint," Lightning said, as he scratched at his neck. "She is as you might perceive a Fire Drake and she has come seeking me with a message from her mother."

"Her mother?" Rose asked, as she watched the dragon stretch and then lift a hind leg to scratch behind one of its long, mobile cat like ears.

"The Lady Firethorn," Lightning said, nodding. "The Lady Firethorn is a very old dragon and very powerful. She knows things that are hidden to the rest of the fay."

"And it is something that she knows that had made her send this drag...Flint to find you?"

"Perhaps," Lightning said, fidgeting in the bedside chair. If Rose could have put a name to Lightning's attitude, it would be embarrassment. "It is more complicated than that Rose..."

"What's complicated about it?"

"Rose I am sorry, but Firethorn wants us to go and see her."

"What now?"

"As soon as possible," Lightning said, once more squirming in his seat and Rose began to feel a dread rising in her mind.

"Well how far is it? Is she in the city?"

"Ah there is the complication," Lightning said, lowering his eyes. "She does not live here in the city, but in the hills to the north..."

Rose suddenly understood why Lightning was nervous and her own anger flared up.

"No, we can't go north Lightning, Robin is in the south not north."

"Please Rose, hear me out?" Lightning implored.

"No I won't listen Lightning! Robin is south not north. Going to see this Firethorn will take me further from Robin not get me to her."

Rose might have said more, but the dragon in miniature broke in. It had half closed its eyes while Lightning had begun talking, but as Rose began to argue with him, those yellow eyes snapped open and the wings that looked like they were made of smoke snapped open and the tiny dragon seemed to swell to twice its normal size. Its tail lashed from side to side, as it spat a small Colum of fire into the air. Then it spat several words at Rose that Lightning translated for it.

"It does not matter, whether your goal is in the south or on the moon. If you wish to find it, you must go north to speak with my mother. She alone can help you reach your goal."

Rose was not sure, she felt that she had to go south. Robin was south and from what everyone was telling her, Robin could be in very bad trouble, but what could this dragon know? Could it be some knowledge that could help her and Robin?

"How far is this Firethorn?" she asked grudgingly.

Lightning tensed and could not meet her eyes.

"At least two days travel from here."

"But that's two days from Robin," Rose burst out.

"I know Rose and I'm sorry, but I feel that we must go and see her."

"Is there no other way of contacting her than going to see her?"

"I'm afraid not, with others we could probably contact her via a scrying spell, but Firethorn does not like to be spied on and she has wards in place to prevent such contact. That is why she has sent Flint, rather than contact us by another means."

Rose exasperated, turned away from Lightning and stared at the blank stone wall. She did not want to go north to see a Dragon for god's sakes, but Lightning was saying that they had too and Rose had come to trust the tall fire mage. Rose summoned up Robin's face before her mind's eye and summoned all her courage.

"Very well Lightning we go and see this Firethorn, but we must leave now."

Rose felt his hand on her rigid back and when he spoke, it was in a very gentle voice.

"Thank you Rose, I know what a difficult decision this is for you."

"Just get us there and back, as fast as you can," Rose muttered, as she went limp with exhaustion, for the decision had drained her emotionally and she felt sleep pulling at her senses, but she could not give in. She had to get ready to go north.

It might have been thirty minutes later, but it felt like an eternity to Rose, before she was mounted on a small horse, in front of the Tower of the Eagle. She wondered what the others of her company would think of her departure and she turned to ask Lightning.

"I have told Takana what has happened," Lightning said, guessing her question. "She will let them know what has happened and where we have gone."

Rose nodded and turning her head back to look forwards, watched as the small dragon Flint fluttered back and forth before her, snapping up the large moths that were still flitting about in the predawn night.

"I presume you know where you're going?"

"Yes, just follow me."

Lightning led them back through the tree ring, past the stone ring and its encircled hill and back out of the north gate. Where two of the giants waited, with their weapons and gear.

"I thought we left them at the west gate?" Rose asked, as she gratefully accepted her long sword from eh giant.

"Takana sent a message for them to be fetched to this gate, so that we could pick them up here," Lightning explained, as he received his own short sword.

Rose nodded and felt better, as she felt the familiar wait of her long sword settle against her back. She had come to learn that sometimes steel was not enough to defeat an enemy in this land of spell casters, but she would still have its hilt in hand, wen going into battle.

"Lead on," she said, and Lightning rode his horse along a well built road, that lead as straight as an arrow north.

"Did your people build this road Lightning?"

"Yes, but they only rebuilt what was already there, that is why this road only goes for a few miles north, before it fails, but it will take us faster than any of the other tracks that lead north."

"Then I am grateful to your people."

"Unfortunately, the tracks after this or few and far between and are much harder than this."

"But you know the way?"

"Yes I know the way and so too does Flint, if I do loos the way, which I should not she can guide us."

"Then let us hope that we don't lose the way, the more time we spend looking for deer tracks the longer we are away from Robin."

"We will go as fast as we can Rose, but the land north of Care Diff is a hilly and even mountainous land and traveling is not easy at the best of times."

"This just gets better and better," Rose muttered under her breath.

After that they travelled along the paved Corse way in silence, and this was how the rising sun found them.

HOMUNCULUS

"Spell casters can give an echo of life to unliving things and make them their agents."
From a page of a Grimoire from the Wereding records.

Great Mother had stood vigil over Kye's prone form for the whole of the night and but for a few movements of his hands or lips that mouthed silently, he had not moved. So it might have shocked her, when as the sun rose to guild the waters of the lake, he suddenly snapped open his eyes and sprang to his feet.

"Where is Rose? She must not go north."

"What did you see my son?" the giant silver haired woman asked, her voice as calm as a lake.

"I have no time to tell you now mother," Kye whispered, as he cast about him. "The Lady showed me things that I may be able to prevent, but only if I can find Rose in time."

"Well before you go take this." Great Mother handed Kye a short sword in a black leather sheath.

"A Fang of the Wolf!" Kye breathed, as he held up the sword, its pummel gleaming silver in the dawn light.

The swords pummel was crafted to resemble a silver wolf's head, its eyes yellow stones, its silver fangs grasping between them a large moonstone.

"But why?" Kye whispered, as he gazed at the silver wolf's head. "I thought that they had all been presented to other members of the Silver Shield."

"All but this one and I give it to you now because, I believe that you may need it in the moons to come."

"Thank you mother, this is a great gift you give me, but I have not time to thank you properly."

"Wheeled it against our enemies Kye, that is thanks enough."

Kye nodded and turning he ran towards the city. Great Mother watched him go and raising a large hand, wiped a tear from the corner of her eye.

"Take care my son, may the Wolf's Fang protect you, for I cannot."

North of the Fairy city, Rose and Lightning were scrambling through a rocky and broken land. Several miles along the paved road had dwindled into a gravelled path and then a dirt track, that lasted another half a mile and then the ground had rose steeply and the land changed radically. It became rocky and dry, great cracks split the land and the ground itself rose and fell in steep ridges and gullies. They could not ride their horses in this land of rock and cracked clay, so they led them up and down, until they came to a ridge higher than any they had climbed before and looking north Rose saw before them like a wall raised by the hands of giants, a line of mountains that stood jaggedly against the sky like a row of giant teeth.

"Is that where we're headed?"

"The Roaches, yes," Lightning agreed distractedly, as he seemed more interested in something closer at hand.

"What is it Lightning? Is something wrong?" She asked, her hand subconsciously drifting over her shoulder to grip her swords hilt.

She followed his eye line, to see that he was looking at the small valley that lay before them and for a long time could not see any cause for concern. The only difference to this small shallow valley, was that unlike many of the ones they had stumbled through before, there was more than the thick mosses and lichens that carpeted the stones. In this valley there was a very thin copse or line of tall bushes or stunted trees. That were despite their height, were stunted twisted things their branches either bear or covered in dead dry leaves that rattled disturbingly in the teeth of the wind.

"What's wrong Lightning, I can't see anything wrong."

Lightning who had drifted into some kind of trance, shook himself, as if waking from a dream.

"I don't know Rose, like you I can't see anything wrong and yet I don't like the feel of that yonder valley."

Rose glanced down into the dell and shivered, as she realised that although the sun was high, it did not seem to penetrate the shadow valley.

"Can we avoid it?"

"How?" Lightning asked, pointing to the large vertical pillar of rock that rose on one side and a crack that seemed to fall away for ever, on the other side. There was only one way forwards and that was through the shallow valley.

"Would Flint scout for us?" Rose asked, looking about for the small dragon, who had disappeared into the blue sky moments before.

"She might," Lightning said, his eyes looking north. Rose could see nothing, but he seemed able to see something that she could not and seemed to have some mystic link to the dragon. For even as she watched his lips form words, a black dot against the sky grew larger and seconds later like a stooping hawk, Flint descended to grasp Lightning's arm, as she considered his face with those glowing yellow eyes. Lightning whispered to it and the dragon hissed, lashed its tail back and forth and with a beating of wings it took to the air and swooped towards the valley and disappeared against the gloom.

"If there's anything to find, Flint will find it."

"Do we wait for her, or do we go after her?"

"We will go after her," Lightning decided, after a slight pause.

So they led their horses down into the shallow valley and slowly moved towards the thin line of trees. As soon as they entered the valley, Rose knew that they had made a mistake. As soon as the shadows fell across them, Roses heart was gripped by a cold hand of dread.

"Where's Flint?" Rose whispered, for she felt a need to speak quietly in the dead air that seemed to hang like a fog about the dell.

"I'm not sure," Lightning said, in an equally low voice. "I can't see her."

As they plodded closer to the line of twisted trees, the less Rose liked the look of them. For some strange reason, she couldn't get the idea that they were being watched out of her head. Perhaps it was the illusion that the bent and naked trees had almost a human look to them. The way they held their branches and bear crowns made them look like frozen statues, just waiting to come to life. Just as they reached the treeline, they saw her dark form hovering above the line of boulders that marked the far end of the valley. Just as Lightning opened his mouth to call to her, what resembled a stroke of black lightning, forked from the boulders to snatch the small dragon from the sky and hammer it to the ground.

"Flint!" Lightning cried, as he saw his small friend plucked from the air.

"Lightning look out, the trees," Rose shouted, as her worst fears became reality and the skeletal trees suddenly lurched to life.

Uprooting themselves, the men like trees lurched towards them, long branch like arms reaching for them with long cruel thorns reaching to tear flesh.

"Homunculus damn them!" Lightning cursed, as he drew a long slender wooden wand from his belt and spitting a word fired from its tip a scream of sound that split the wood of one of the tree creatures like an axe striking it.

The tree creature paused in its lurching strides and seemed to lower its lump of a head to consider the dark liquid, leaking from the breach. Rose was not sure if it was blood or sap, but the wound did not seem to trouble the thing much. This made Rose doubt whether her sword would be any use against it either, but nevertheless she drew the blade and raising her shield dropped into a defensive stance. Lightning too, must have realised that his wand was not enough to stop them, though he fired a second burst at the ten or so lurching tree men. The blast split the bark of a second tree man, but this one did not even take notice, but continued to lurch slowly but inevitably towards them. Lightning however, had another trick up his sleeve or rather, on his hand. Thrusting out his hand before him, he growled a word of power and from the ring's red stone there shot a ray as bright and warm as a ray of sunlight and where it touched burst into fire. Lightning used this fiery beam to draw a line between them and the tree men. The line became a high wall of flickering flames that held the tree men back. It held most of them back, for two of them did not stop in time and they stumbled into the wall of flames. As they lurched through the wall of fire, their bodies now ablaze and as the smell of wet and rotten wood mixed with smoke filled the air so too did low groaning and the tree men collapsed smouldering at their feet.

"How long will it last?" Rose asked, as she watched the tree men through the wall of dancing flames that was holding them back.

"Not long and the ring only has so much power in it."

"So what do we do now?"

The answer that Lightning might have given Rose never found out because, they were both distracted by something that was happening on the other side of the fire wall. Suddenly there was another grown of wood on wood and Rose saw that one of the tree men had burst into flames and then a second thing's block like head was engulfed in flames.

"It's Flint!" Lightning cried, in delight as the red dragon wheeled around the tree men her claws taring splinters from another tremens face.

Rose's glee at the realisation that the dragon was still alive vanished as the fire wall did, allowing the six or so remaining tree men to lurch forwards. Rose hated that Lightning was doing all the work, but she was not sure what she could do other than hack at the tree men, then she remembered that she had been taught one spell that she could fling at the approaching things. Sheaving her sword she gathered her strength and shakily performed the spell of lighting.

"Incendium," she cried allowed and the nearest tree man's outstretched branch like arm was suddenly a flaming torch. That the creature waved about, as if trying to put it out, but all it did was fan the flames. Spreading them up its arm and lighting its body while at the same time flicking sparks at its brothers. The remaining wood creatures lurched to a stop and began to retreat from their flaming brother.

"Excellent Rose!" Lightning cried in delight, as he used his ring to ignite the remaining things, which turned tail and rushed away. Their fiery bodies casting strange leaping shadows on the valley walls.

"Is that it?" Rose asked breathlessly.

"I don't think so," Lightning said, as he took his crossbow from his horse's saddle and loading it, passed it to Rose. "The Homunculus didn't fire that black bolt at Flint."

As if to confirm this thought, Flint landed beside them on a large rock and Rose saw that one of her smoky wings was blackened and charred as if some great heat had melted it and Rose wondered how the little dragon could fly with such a crippling wound. The little dragon hissed angrily at Lightning and for a moment Rose thought that the creature was blaming Lightning for the wound, until Lightning translated.

"Flint thinks that there are several powerful spell casters beyond that bolder line," when he said this, Rose noticed that his Adam's apple bobbed and she realised that for once he was frightened.

"What do we do?"

As he opened his mouth to answer, a bolt of black lightning lashed out at them. Fortunately the bolt shot between them, missing them, but when Rose span round to see where the bolt had struck, she saw her horse lying in a twitching heap on the ground. Its flesh smoking and filling the air with the smell of burnt flesh.

"Rose get behind me," Lightning cried, as he grabbed at his tunic front.

Rose did as he asked without question and when she was hunkered down by his right side, she saw that he was holding out before him a small shield like medallion. He spoke the words of an incantation and as Rose watched a glowing disk appeared before them and as she watched a glowing beam of blue light slammed into the forming disk and she realised that Lightning had used this pendant to form a magical shield before them.

"Will it hold against them?"

"Yes, but for how long..." Lightning said, through gritted teeth, as another blast of magic slammed into the shield. Rose suddenly seized by rage at their unseen attackers, fired the crossbow towards the boulders and growled with frustration as the quarrel bounced harmlessly off the rocks. A shot that earned Rose a black lightning bolt that clipped the edge of the shield and was only just deflected, as its dark discharge was partly absorbed by the shield that turned from red to black momentary before returning to its normal red. While a shard of the black stroke, flashed past. Her hair stood on end, as she felt a freezing blast pass by her. This unseen assault angered Rose, more than she had thought possible. An overwhelming rage seemed to blast up like a fire inside her and before she knew what she was doing, she had dropped the bow and her hands were clawing at the air, as they performed movements that Rose only just perceived. She was only just aware of the words that her tongue was forming. As she completed the last words of the incantation, her hands lit with a red glow, as magic collected at her tingling fingertips and she realised that she was about to unleash the summoned energy, but a the last moment her attackers managed to get an attack past the shield. A blast of magic slammed into Roses side that was exposed and she was spun towards Lightning. As she swung round and fell in Lightning's direction, she released the magic she had been summoning. She screamed in rage and denial. She had not meant to cast this spell at Lightning, but at their attackers, but the blow that span her towards him and also been the last factor to trigger the magic. Against her will, the power shot forth from her hands to engulf Lightning, in a cloud of red magic that slammed into him and hurled him to the ground. As though he had been punched by a giants hand. This was the last thing she saw, as the darkness claimed her, but her mind continued to hear his cry of "Rose no!"

EPILOGUE

"Blood and flames, are the result when dragons play their games."
Lea to Rose, The Wereding Chronicles.

Robin looked about her a the very large clearing that she and Luna were in, to find that it was true, they were not alone. Not ten feet away their lounged, the largest creature Robin had ever seen. The thing glowed scarlet in the half light and its great horned head regarded Robin with eyes of fire that made her feel as if their glance would ignite her. The scarlet scaled beast could only be one thing.

"A dragon!"

"She has the use of her eyes then," the dragon's voice rumbled through the air and growled like thunder.

"Robin may I present Lord Tahane," Luna said, as she drew Robin forwards, to bring her closer to the huge creature.

As Robin neared the thing, she realised two things. The first was that heat radiated from the beast in waves, as if a furnace burned inside it. The second thing she realised, was that she was not afraid of the huge monster. As she approached the beasts coal like eyes they followed her and a long forked tongue flicked out to taste the air.

"You are Luna's new ally?" Robin asked, as she tentatively reached out to touch one of the huge shield like scales that covered the beasts hide.

"I am, but more importantly I am your ally too," rumbled the giant beast.

Robin stood back and gave the monster a long, measuring look.

"You will help me rescue Rose?"

At the mention of her sister, the dragon gave a great snarl and smoke poured from its nostrils.

"Your sister may be beyond saving," the great beast snarled. "It was she that gave me this."

The dragon turned its head and gestured with one of its head horns at the right hand wing. Which when Robin looked more closely saw was not the light Smokey colour of the left wing, but had long dark blisters running from the long hooked thumb to where the bat like wing joined the dragons body.

"Rose did that?" Robin asked, unable to believe it. "Did you attack her first?"

The dragon snarled at that and it sounded like hundreds of stones, grinding together.

"I was minding my own business, when your sister, aided by an Elf and her Werewolf slaves attacked me. I only just escaped, with my life I tell you it was your sister who cast the magic that did this to me."

"Rose performed magic?"

"Yes, didn't I say so," growled Tahane. "Don't you cast magic at that school of yours?"

"Rose wouldn't hurt anyone unless..."

"Unless her heart has been twisted by the Weredings' magic," Luna said, from behind Robin, as she wrapped her arms round the taller girl.

Robin felt tears of fear and rage prick her eyes, but she would not show her weakness before this monster.

"We have to help her! We have to save her?"

"We can," rumbled the giant dragon.

"We?"

"You can only learn so much, from those petty wizards in the Crimson Circle, but I can teach you magics that will bring the Weredings' world crashing down around their ears."

"And that will help me get Rose back, how?"

"If we take the fight to them, we may be able to rescue your sister. If their magic is weakened, we may even be able to break their enchantment over your sister."

Robin considered what Tahane was saying and what he said called to her need for revenge, while it also spoke to her love for Rose and her need to recover her sister.

"Wait a moment," Luna cut in, from beside Robin. "What you are proposing is to go to war with the Wereding nation."

"That is precisely what I am proposing," came back Tahane. "Only by weakening their magic, can we weaken their grip on your sister."

"But we three are not enough to do this," Luna protested.

"Don't the Weredings have enemies?" Robin asked.

"The Darklings! You would join forces with the Darklings?"

"I would descend into hell and do a deal with the Red Dragon! If he could help me get Rose back," said Robin, knowing that her words rang with the power of truth.

"Then I offer my services, as teacher and war mount," Tahane said, lowering his head, as if he were submitting himself to some form of bondage.

"Wait a moment," Luna said and she drew Robin to one side. "Robin please consider what you are doing, accepting Tahane is one thing, but going to war with the Wereding nations is quite another."

"If it will get Rose back I will do it," Robin said determinedly. "Will you help me with this or not Luna?"

A look of pain flared in Luna's eyes and was gone, replaced by a single tear.

"Robin I love you, I would follow you into hell if you went there."

Robin was touched by Luna's tears and she gathered the smaller woman up in her arms and covered her face in kisses.

"I love you too, but I must do this Luna! I must save Rose!"

"Then I will stay by your side, but please Robin, listen to this warning because, I fear that you may lose something if you go down this path."

"If I don't, then I will lose Rose and I couldn't live with myself, if I didn't try to save her."

A rumbling like thunder, behind them reminded Robin of the dragon's presence and she supposed that this was the dragon's way of clearing its throat. The two women turned back to face him.

"Do we have an agreement?"

"We do," Robin said and Luna, who it seemed could not speak, just nodded her head.

"Good, then we shall begin."

The Wraith King allowed the image of the clearing fade, so that the mirror smooth basin of blood only reflected his glowing eyes.

"So Fire Lord your plan advances another step, so far everything has gone according to your plan, but how long can your luck last?"

From the balcony Grast, the Wraith King's servant spoke.

"My Lord the army awaits your review."

"Perhaps, I will answer my own question," the Wraith King muttered to itself, in a voice that chilled the blood and the air.

It swept from the scrying chamber, to join Grast on the balcony and looked down into a huge subterranean cavern. As soon as its crown mounted head appeared on the balcony, the air was filled by a roar of thousands of bestial voices. Below the Shade, a sea of metal rose and fell in waves and thousands of axe, spear and sword blades rose and fell as an army of Darkling Orcs saluted their lord and master. The lips, that might have been behind the Shades armoured mask, might have twitched in pleasure.

"So at last we go to war. White Wolf you don't stand a chance."

THE END

THE AWAKENING OF MAGIC
BOOK ONE
OF THE
WEREDING CHRONICLES

"... *the curtain was swept aside, to reveal a figure almost as startling as the wolfman. However, where the wolfman was scary, this figure was beautiful, if in the way in which a tiger is beautiful. She too had long black hair, but whereas the man's hair was dark, this woman's hair was the darkest black that Rose had ever seen. Looking at it she felt as if you could be lost in it. The hair was swept back and fell to her waist. Her hair was swept back from her long catlike ears that were pointed and which moved as if they had a life of their own, as did a short prehensile tail. The cat woman looked at her with a pair of green eyes, that seemed to glow slightly in the dim shadows of the canopy. This cat woman was very short and she barely came up to the wolfman's elbow, but she seemed to fill the space she took up with a whirlwind like presence and when she grinned at Rose, Rose couldn't help but smile back.*"

Rose is plunged into a world of magic and monsters and must learn to master magic, or be consumed by it. At the same time, she learns that she may have to work with Elves and Werewolves – creatures that she believed evil – to save her sister Robin from dark magic users.

Will she succeed or be transformed by the magic ... into what?

ABOUT THE AUTHOR

Christian Boustead is a blind author who lives in Hanley Staffordshire. *Dragon Games, Book Two of The Wereding Chronicles* is his most recent novel. He has also written: *Awakening of Magic, Book One of The Wereding Chronicles* and *The Voice of Nature*, a collection of poetry.

If you wish to learn more about Christian and his works then you might like to visit his website: **www.christianboustead.com**

Lightning Source UK Ltd.
Milton Keynes UK
UKOW06f1950290416

273246UK00001B/2/P